Before becoming a bartender and crime writer, Karen Kijewski taught English at Brookline High School in Massachusetts. Her first Kat Colorado mystery, *Katwalk*, won her the Shamus and Antony Awards and the American Best First Private Eye Novel of the Year Award. Karen Kijewski lives and works in Sacramento, California.

The Kat Colorado series is available from Headline and has received tremendous critical acclaim:

'The book is lively and entertaining throughout'
Times Literary Supplement

'An intriguing mystery... an engaging heroine'
The Times

'Outstanding among today's female detectives, private eye Kat Colorado exhibits conscience and compassion, muscle and wisecracking savvy in an appealing and believable combination'
Publishers Weekly

'A seamless syncopation of sleuth and setting that will have mystery buffs recalling Grafton and Paretsky'
Booklist

'Kijewski's breakout book, lifting her to the front ranks, right up there with that other smartmouthed private-eye specialist, Sue Grafton . . . a strong contender for the best mystery of the year'
Kirkus Reviews

Kat's Cradle

Karen Kijewski

HEADLINE

First published in Great Britain in 1995 by
HEADLINE BOOK PUBLISHING

10 9 8 7 6 5 4 3 2 1

ISBN 0 7472 4309 3

Typeset by Avon Dataset Ltd., Bidford-on-Avon, B50 4JH

Printed and bound in Great Britain by
Cox & Wyman Ltd, Reading, Berks

HEADLINE BOOK PUBLISHING
A division of Hodder Headline PLC
338 Euston Road,
London NW1 3BH

In memory of my parents

Acknowledgements

Many people helped in many ways. Thanks to John Anderson, Chief, California Highway Patrol, for the spark that became an idea and much more. To Detective Russ Martin, Sacramento County Sheriff's Department, for his expertise and generosity in sharing it. To Wendy Everard for the years of faith when it seemed impossible. And especially to Deborah Schneider, my agent and friend; and to Kate Miciak, my extraordinary editor. Thanks are not enough, words are not enough, but here they are anyway.

One

76% of Americans have eaten apple pie. 34% have eaten artichokes. 82% have eaten fried chicken. What percent have considered murder?

She was not given to small talk. That was immediately apparent.

'Have you ever seen a floater?'

I didn't answer.

'Have you?' Her voice was insistent. 'Have you?'

'Yes.'

'They wash up on the riverbank, get caught in the branches and vegetation there. The worst ones don't look like people anymore. Their bodies are bloated and swollen with gasses or something.'

She glanced at me, then looked away. Her eyes were vacant and brown, almost yellow, and they looked stale and dead like leaves here in the fall. In Sacramento it never gets cold enough for vivid autumn colors.

'The first one I saw I thought it was a sheep, it was round and white, only it had clothes on so it wasn't. And they smell. If you touch them pieces fall

1

off. I watched them, the cops, one time as they pulled one in, but I wish now I hadn't. This one guy, this cop, he kept hitting the body with an oar by mistake and – and the pieces kept falling off. The fish like it, I guess. It was horrible.'

I watched her in silence. Her eyes met mine and flicked away. There was no horror in them.

'If nobody knows what happened to you, you're a floater.'

Outside, tires squealed and protested. I waited for more, hoped there was more and that it would make sense. A boom box walked by blaring rap music to everyone within a hundred yards. Me, unfortunately. I waited, listened – *Wanna get down / wanna get high / gonna pump it up / time to fly* – and I didn't feel like doing either one. 'Miss—'

She started slightly. 'I'm sorry. I'm not doing this very well, I'm not explaining. I've played it out in my mind over and over so many times that I get lost in it now, don't quite know how to put it in words, I guess—' She opened her hands helplessly.

'My name is Paige Morrell. I'm an orphan. I want you to find my parents.'

First a floater, then an orphan with parents: In my business that's what we call a clue. I let it slide, but I shouldn't have. Some investigator. In retrospect I wasn't impressed.

'Find their grave sites, you mean?'

'No. Oh, well, yes, that too.' She thought about it and nodded. 'Yes, but that's not what I mean. I want you to find *them*, the *real* people.' Clouds moved in across her horizon and settled in her eyes. Storm clouds, rain clouds.

'There aren't any real people, Miss Morrell. They're dead. That's what you told me.'

She laughed, the storm clouds gone, and waved my expression away.

'No, oh no, don't worry!' Her eyes lit up and I wondered why I had thought they looked like dead leaves. Impossible. Her cheeks were flushed as she leaned her elbows on my desk and propped her chin in her hands. There was a ruby ring on her middle finger. 'I'm not totally zoned out.' She laughed again at my expression.

'You see, my parents died when I was just a baby. They were younger than I am now.' Her twenty-one-year-old eyes got puzzled at the thought of life working out that way.

'Nobody ever told me anything about them and now I want to know.' She spaced the words out solemnly, seriously, her eyes holding mine. 'About them, their lives, their deaths.' She sighed. 'Maybe you can even find someone who knew them, who could tell me things about them.'

She broke off. I let the silence be, knowing she wasn't through yet. 'Do you know what it's like, not knowing *anything*? Not what they looked like, or who they were or if—' she stammered, '—or if they loved you or, or anything,' she finished lamely. 'I want to know.'

I nodded. It was a tough one. I'd faced it myself. Maybe that's why I was still listening instead of showing her to the door.

'Most of this is a matter of public record, Miss Morrell. You could do it yourself and it wouldn't cost you anything. For me to do it—'

'I don't care. And it's not that, not the money, I've got money.' She said it defiantly. 'I want to hire you to find these things out. I don't know how to, and I don't want to. Will you do it?'

I thought it over. 'I'll consider it.'

'Thank you.'

'I'll need to know more.'

It sounded simple but I knew better. You don't hire a private investigator to do something simple; you do it yourself.

'Oh, yes!' She smiled another dazzlingly bright smile. 'I'll tell you everything. It's just that—' She shrugged and her smile got smaller, shyer, more diffident. '—that's all I know.'

The boom box strolled by again. *Dishing up a bad deal / bad deal / bad deal / dishing up a* . . . The ficus in the corner curled its leaves under the assault. *Bad deal!* A leaf dropped to the ground.

'What were their names?'

'My mother's name was Ruby.' She looked at her ring.

'Ruby Morrell?'

'Yes.'

'What was her maiden name?'

4

'Morrell.' She said it in a low voice. The boom box was on the next block so I heard her whisper.

'Your father's name?'

'I don't know.'

'His first name perhaps?'

'No.'

'Your mother's date and place of birth?'

'I don't know.'

'Nor your father's?'

'No.'

'The date and place of their marriage?'

'No.' Her voice was tight and hard.

'Do you have a copy of your birth certificate?' She shook her head. 'Have you ever seen it?' Another head shake. 'Where were you born?'

'In Sacramento. At least that's what my grandmother said.'

'How about the dates and places of their deaths?'

'Umm—' She knew something. At last. 'It was winter, there was snow and ice on the roads.' She broke off.

'An automobile accident?'

'Yes. Tahoe. It's one of the few things my grandmother told me.'

'Where in Tahoe?'

She shook her head. 'I don't know.'

'North Shore or South Shore?'

'S-south,' she said tentatively. 'On Highway Fifty, I think.'

'Did they die in the accident or survive it briefly?'

She shrugged. 'Are you an only child?'

She looked at me strangely. 'Oh yes. As far as I know—' She broke off. 'Actually, I've wondered if maybe they weren't coming back here after I was born hoping that with the baby, with me, there might be a reconciliation, that everything might be okay. My grandmother was *so* angry about the marriage. Instead,' her voice was bleak, 'instead they were killed.

'And then my grandmother said she changed my name back so that she would not be reminded—' Paige covered her eyes. The ruby ring flashed briefly as she moved her hand. 'She was a bitter, angry, unhappy old woman. I don't think she cared for anyone, not even my mother. Certainly not me.'

'Your grandmother raised you?'

'Yes.' Her voice was dead.

'In this area?'

'Yes.'

'Was your mother raised here as well?'

'I don't know.'

'Surely your grandmother told you—'

'She told me nothing. Nothing! That's why I'm here. At first I asked, but then I learned not to. She would yell at me, or grow cold and hostile.' Briefly Paige looked like a small, frightened child.

'Do you have any pictures, old letters or documents, even mementos?'

'Oh no.'

'Clothing? Anything that might have belonged to

your mother?' She shook her head. 'Is there anything else I should know?' I made the question gentle. 'Something I've forgotten to ask?'

She shook her head again. 'No. I really don't know anything, you see.' I saw. 'It doesn't matter. You'll find out, won't you?' Her mouth was smiling but her eyes were serious: full of trust, innocence, the desire to know and the belief that knowing will help, will make it better. She didn't give me a chance to answer.

'Is Kat Colorado your real name?'

'Kate. Kat is a nickname but it's the name I use now.'

She nodded solemnly. 'Paige isn't my real name, Well, it's real now, I changed it.'

'What was your name?'

'Pearl.' Ruby and Pearl, mother and daughter. 'It's an ugly name, isn't it?'

'No, it isn't.' And I meant it, it wasn't. 'Old-fashioned, perhaps, but nice.'

She stared at me. 'Do you know what pearls are? They're ugliness: dirt or sand gets in an oyster and the oyster coats it over and over so that it won't be irritating.'

'Yet it becomes a thing of great beauty and value.'

'It's not my name anymore.' She shrugged her shoulders as if to shift thoughts and ground. 'Will you know soon?'

'It will take a while.'

She looked disappointed but not surprised. 'It's

all right. I've waited a long time, I can wait a little longer.' The boom box wandered back down the street. The same one or were there a whole lot of kids out there with lousy taste in music?

Got to make it/make it!/do it/do it!

'If nobody knows what happened to you, you're a floater.'

We were back to floaters. It didn't seem like a good sign.

'Like your parents?'

'Like them.' There were tears in her eyes now. 'I can't bear it.'

I could see that. I could see the tears.

'Anything's better than that, than swollen, smelly bodies with pieces that—' She looked at me in despair. 'I get nightmares. Please, I need your help, and can you hurry?'

'I can't promise anything.'

'But you'll try?'

'Yes.'

'And you're good?'

'Yes.'

'You'll find out about my mother and get a death certificate?'

'I'll do my best.'

She nodded and wrote me a check, put it on my desk without words as if, for now, all her words had been used up. Her eyes were dead leaves again as she picked up her purse and headed for the door.

There's more than one kind of floater. I knew it;

she was afraid of it. And with good reason.

I let her get almost to the door before I spoke.

Two

*The heart has reasons the mind can't
understand. The mind has reasons the
heart doesn't care about. Cross purposes.*

'Tell me again, Miss Morrell. Tell me the truth this
time.'

I am not given to small talk either.

She stared at me, wide-eyed, innocent, trembling,
then turned and tumbled helplessly into the still
warm, just vacated chair across from my desk. There
were tears in her eyes again. Delicately she wiped
one away. It was good, very good. I wondered if she
practiced, or if it came naturally.

'Wha-a-t?'

Her voice was a stammer. The hand she raised
slowly and protectively to her mouth was trembling.

'When you first spoke of your parents you wanted
information about them: the kind of people they
were, the lives they led, what happened. You were
emotionally distraught at your lack of knowledge,
the void in your life, the feelings you had about
floaters.'

'Ye-e-es.'

Still stammering, still trembling. Still pathetic.

'Your last statement was very different.' Lashes fluttered at me. 'It was a simple straightforward request for your mother's death certificate.' I leaned on my elbows, rested my chin in my hands, and looked at her steadily, hoping I hadn't called it wrong. 'From parents to mother, from sentiment to death certificate. What's going on, Miss Morrell?'

Her eyes filled up again. This time tears splashed over and ran down her cheeks. Her lower lip trembled. Damn! Had I called it wrong? I waited it out, callously counting to ten while she cried. Nothing. I started over again – 7–8–9 – I was almost down for the count.

'Well, *shit!*' She stood up and pushed the chair back fiercely, glared at me, then stomped around the office for a bit before sitting back down. The tears were gone; there was a healthy flush to her cheeks. She was excited, pretty, and mad. Very mad.

'Shit!' She pounded a hand almost clenched into a fist on my desk, glared at me again.

'It takes experience to lie well,' I explained, consoling her. 'Lying looks easier than it is. Almost anyone can think up a simple everyday lie and get away with it, but once you start getting into complicated ones . . .' I shook my head. 'It's tough to keep it all straight.'

She glared at me, then laughed suddenly, prettier now than ever. 'Okay, can we start over?'

'Sure.'

She nodded. 'My grandmother died just recently. The estate comes to me, I'm the only one, but in order for me to inherit, my mother's death must be clearly established. According to the will that can be done in one of two ways.' She sighed. 'It couldn't be simple, no, of course not, not in my family. Either there is a death certificate or we have to advertise in the papers for six months, then she is presumed dead and it comes to me.'

She stopped and looked at me. 'I don't get it. She *is* dead, isn't she? I mean my grandmother wouldn't have lied about that? So, why all the fuss?' She looked the questions at me but I didn't have the answers. I didn't even have a guess.

'I mean, of course she's dead. Otherwise why didn't she come for me? She would have, surely? Her own daughter! Of course she would.' More questions I couldn't answer. 'So, if she's dead why isn't there a death certificate, and why advertise for six months?'

Reasonable questions, no doubt about it.

'I don't want to wait six months, I need to get on with my life. And I want to get married. Now. Well, soon. But my fiancé doesn't want to until everything is all settled and stuff. We were going to get married before but my grandmother didn't approve.'

'So?' I was puzzled. 'You're of age.'

'But that's my home.' She said it simply. 'I couldn't leave it. Anyway, now we *can* get married. Well, we can as soon as this is settled.'

I was still puzzled. 'Why does it have to be settled?'

13

'Paul, my fiancé, says it would be better that way.'

'What is he marrying, you or the estate?'

Her eyes filled with distress and maybe with tears. *'Don't*, please. You sound like my grandmother. And it's not true. Paul just wants the best for us. Anyway, when it's settled we can have a nice wedding, and a honeymoon, and everything.' She twisted the ruby ring and looked at me pleadingly.

'But it's not just that. I want to *know*; I want it settled. Okay? I don't want to wait forever, first six months and then probate and . . . hey, no way! Find out for me. Okay?'

Apparently the fiancé didn't have money. Was he marrying the estate? Probably. Women without much love in their childhoods often picked the wrong man. I mused on that for a while.

'—so, you will, won't you?' I was paying attention but not in time to hear the whole sentence.

'Why did you lie, Miss Morrell? Wanting to inherit is a legitimate reason. You didn't need to invent a story for me.'

She hesitated. 'My grandmother's lawyer and the executor of her will wanted to handle it the other way, by advertising. He asked me to stay out of it, although he didn't explain why.

'Paul, my fiancé, doesn't want me to pursue it either. Well, he did at first so we could get the money, but now he doesn't. He'll be furious when he finds out.' She wrinkled her brow. 'That's another thing I don't really understand.' She looked the question at

14

me, eyes wide. I shook my head. I couldn't enlighten her, I didn't know enough yet.

'And it's not a story. Really.' She glanced my way to see if I was buying it. I wasn't. Not yet, anyway. 'It does make me sad and lonely that I don't know anything. I wish I did, I want to, and I want you to find that out for me. I have dreams about floaters too.' She shivered. 'The tears weren't fake, they weren't. I really do feel that way, although—' Another sideways look.

'Although you encouraged them. For the effect.'

'Yes.' She dimpled at me. 'And it was effective, wasn't it?'

I smiled, I couldn't help it. It had been, and I liked her. She smiled back.

'I really want a family,' Paige said after a moment, her voice wistful, on the edge of sad. 'I wish I had a live family, but even a dead one would be better than nothing. Much better.' Her eyes were narrow and thoughtful. 'You don't know what it's like not knowing, not having a family.'

'What do you want from me, Miss Morrell?'

'I want you to find out about my mother and about my family like I said, and I need a death certificate so I can inherit. Will you do that? Can you?'

'I think so.'

She jumped up, her eyes sparking again.

'Thank you. Will you call me Paige, please?' I nodded. 'And may I call you Kat?' I nodded again. She smiled and headed for the door, turned around

15

and waved carelessly, then walked out.

Pump it up baby/pump it/pump it . . .

Rap music drifted my way again. I let it drift off.

She was young, eager, and in love. She was an orphan and a liar. I wondered which was lies, which truth, and how long it would take me to sort it out.

She was also wrong. I knew what it was like, not knowing, not having a family. I also knew it was no reason to take a case.

But I had.

I looked at the address on the check: Grand Island. She lived in the Delta on an island bounded by rivers and sloughs. That explained the floaters.

Sort of.

Bodies in the Delta were not an uncommon occurrence; neither were they an everyday one. I found it strange that this vibrant young woman should be obsessed with such a morbid image.

Strange and disquieting.

Three

Every day Americans throw out roughly 4.3 million pens, 5.5 million blades and razors, and 670,000 tires. We don't count the people we discard.

Paige was expecting me. I'd called early that morning. I wanted to check out the poor little rich girl on her own ground.

The calls I'd made had, so far, verified the information she'd given me: the family was an old and respected Delta family, the grandmother had been a dominant figure in local social, charitable, and political circles. I was curious to see the house, to get a sense of the woman who stood at the center of this conundrum, a woman who had brought her granddaughter up in a loveless home and maintained years of silence about her daughter and the past, and who was, even after death, still creating controversy and conflict.

I took 160, the river road, and crossed the drawbridge to Grand Island; it was miles of river banked by levees with spring a wild May riot of green and wildflowers. Spring is good news.

I didn't see any floaters. More good news.

Paige was standing under a palm tree and next to a BMW convertible and a hulk. The house was an old one facing out toward Steamboat Slough. It and the yard were elegant, huge, and immaculate. Someone had recently been over the house with a paintbrush and the yard with trimmers.

I pulled the Bronco II up beside the girl, the hulk, and the car. Paige waved and tried to smile. The hulk had his hand clamped on her left shoulder. A smile and a wince fought it out on her face. As I got out she shrugged her shoulders hard; the hand dropped; her smile won.

'Good morning. Kat, this is Paul, my fiancé.' Paige, Paul, and a BMW under a palm tree; a wave of yuppieness washed over me leaving me unmoved. 'Paul, this is Kat Colorado, the one who—'

'I know.' Paul scowled. I smiled and held out my hand, which he shook with his paw. It was hot and moist. The backs of his hands were furry. Strike one.

'Nice to meet you,' I lied.

He scowled again. 'I can't say the same. Paige knows how I feel.' She stood by his side twisting the ruby ring miserably. 'I'm against raking up the past. Let sleeping dogs lie. Leave the dead alone.' Three clichés in a row. Strike two.

'Oh, Paul, please, I'm doing this for *us*, too.' Paige put her hand on his arm. He shook it off like a moose twitching off a fly. 'Oh, please!' she said again. He climbed into the convertible. No good-byes. The exhaust, the squeal of tires, and loud rock music assaulted our senses simultaneously. Strike three and he was out. Gone, too, fortunately.

'Isn't he overplaying it a bit?' I asked.

She shrugged and blushed, then sighed into the silence broken now by bird calls on the river. 'Men are so difficult.' Perhaps, although personally I didn't think a generic description was called for here. I looked at the house instead of answering.

'Beautiful, isn't it?' There was pride in her voice.

'Yes.' It was. There is nothing more beautiful than the Delta and many of the houses there.

'Six generations of my family have lived here. My great-great-great—' she stumbled over the greats, '—whatever grandfather came by covered wagon to California in 1859. First he lived in Angel's Camp and worked the mines, then he came here, homesteaded a hundred and sixty acres and farmed. Eventually he got married and built this house, or maybe it was the other way around,' she said vaguely. 'The palm tree was brought from San Francisco in a tea canister by a friend as they were finishing the house, a housewarming present that has brought much joy throughout the years.'

Okay, I could buy that. Paige looked largely untouched by the joy, however.

'The spacious sweep of the yard was curtailed in 1917 when the new levees were built. Much of the original landscaping design remains, however – the rose bed, the bed of annuals, the vegetable garden. The house itself, like so many Delta homes, was situated on an artificial mound with a ground-floor basement. Living quarters were placed above because of the flooding that regularly overwhelmed the inadequate levees and spread for miles.

Her voice had a pleasant, rehearsed, singsong quality to it. Her eyes were the color of dead leaves again. 'On the first floor are front and back parlors with original stained glass and flooring, a dining room with the original leaded chandeliers, pantry, kitchen, and bathroom. A beautifully carved original staircase leads upstairs to—'

I laughed, I couldn't help it.

'—four bedrooms, two with baths, and a full attic,' she blurted out. 'What's so funny?' The dead leaves in her eyes crinkled up, crackled, and showed the hurt and vulnerability all crowded in there.

'Nothing, I was rude. You are very interesting and knowledgeable on this subject. It's just that for a moment I felt that I was in Living History Week being firmly shepherded by a docent through the pages of the past.' Damn, I'd mixed my metaphors. Badly. Paige didn't notice.

She was silent for a moment. That was okay. I was getting so I could read into her silences.

'Coffee? Have you had breakfast?'

I shook my head. We started walking toward the house across a lawn the size of a small town.

She grinned at me. 'The southern boundary for

the armed Chinese who patrolled Courtland in the 1930s was not far from here.' She gestured. 'The San Francisco Chinese Tong wars had spread to the Delta by then.' She looked at me and the smile faded from her face. 'Oh dear.'

'I hadn't known that,' I said, quite truthfully. Nor could I remember exactly what the Tong wars were about. Chinese fraternal societies vying for control of gambling, prostitution, opium and other fun stuff, I thought. I was tempted to ask, but just briefly. I got over it.

'My grandmother *was* a docent, a member of the Sacramento Delta Historical Society. Every year she gave tours of old river houses and ours was one of them. What I said ... oh God, those were her *exact* words. I never realized, not until now and you ... oh shit, shit, shit,' she chanted rhythmically, methodically. 'I think of myself as a *totally* different person from her. I didn't, don't, want to be like her in *any* way. I *hate* her! Hate, hate, *hate* her,' she intoned.

It was a lot of hatred, I thought, for someone who was dead.

We walked up the wide, flat steps to the porch that surrounded the house on three sides. It was a porch that was pillared, lovely and spacious, and spoke of iced tea and the homey comforts and graciousness of another era.

I said nothing. Paige's last line was a difficult one to follow.

She stalked through the house and I trailed behind, trying to catch a glimpse of the stained glass and the leaded chandeliers. A carved staircase swept up impressively from the entryway. I saw old and worn but still beautiful Oriental rugs, polished antiques, dusted knickknacks and geegaws.

There were no photographs and no personal touches. It felt like a museum display or a stage set rather than a house that was lived in. People had lived and loved and hated, fought and died and cried here, but those echoes were all old now, faint, empty, and somehow sad.

The kitchen was at the back of the house and fully modern, fully sterile. Paige bounced around making coffee and burning English muffins. I waited.

She banged a bowl of marmalade, a jar of preserves, a plate of muffins, and a pot of coffee down on the old-fashioned drop-leaf pine table. How did that girl live with so much anger inside of her?

'Try this.' She pushed the preserves at me. 'It's pear, from our orchards. My grandmother made it herself using an old family recipe and it's very good. She did everything well.' Paige smiled beatifically at me.

And how did she live with those wild mood swings? I was exhausted being around her.

'*Florence Edna Mae Morrell, born in November nineteen-aught-something-or-other, died April of this year, at the age of eighty-something. She is survived by a granddaughter, Pearl—*' She broke off. 'She never called me Paige though I changed it when I was eighteen. Every time she said Pearl I hated her more.' Her mouth was grim and her eyes challenged me to disapprove. I did, but not out loud. She continued. '—*survived by a granddaughter, Pearl, and a bunch of dead memories*. Can you be survived by dead memories?'

'I wouldn't have thought so.'

'—*and mourned by no one, missed by no one, regretted by no one. Amen. May she toss and turn and fry in all eternity*.' She buttered a muffin, covered it with preserves and ate it with eagerness. I finished my coffee and looked at her thoughtfully. I suppose hatred gives some people a vigorous appetite. It was having the opposite effect on me.

'Your grandmother has been dead less than a month?'

She nodded and stretched luxuriously. 'It seems longer than that. Even the days are longer, nicer.'

'You hated her so much, why did you stay?'

'This is my home! And I love it: the river, walking along the levees, the orchards and this house. Oh, I love this house! It was never *hers*, she married into it, but it is *mine*. Grandfather Morrell's blood runs in me.'

Runs cold, I thought, at the love and hatred in this young woman.

'In the summer the sun beats hot on your head as you walk through the afternoon stillness of the orchards, pick a perfect pear and sink your teeth into the warm, sweet flesh.' She licked her lips. 'The juice runs down your chin and fingers. In the evening you can go down to the river, listen to the birds chatter and settle in, watch the fish feed, and feel the waves splash your toes and calves when the boats go by. There is no place more beautiful!' she said passionately.

'Oh, and the surprises! In back of the house, at the edge of the orchard is a bed of bulbs: The daffs are first and the snowbells, then the tulips and the – Come!' She jumped up and grabbed my hand, heedlessly smashing a coffee cup in the process. 'I'll show you.'

She headed out the kitchen door and clattered down wooden steps. I followed. There was a lush lawn in back, roses greened in new spring foliage and flowering annuals edged in borders around the house. Beyond the expanse of the lawn stretched the pear orchard with acres of trees. We walked that way.

'Some are very old.' She ran her hands lovingly over a thickened, gnarled trunk. 'This one has a few more good fruit-bearing years, then we'll replace it. See,' she pointed, 'over there is a new section. They will bear fruit this year but not significantly. Next year will be a decent crop year, though.'

'You know a lot about it.'

She laughed. 'I've run the ranch for years, since I was about fifteen. We have a foreman, of course, and

I followed Wiley around from the time I could walk. My grandmother admired excellence wherever she found it, even in me.' She said it grudgingly. 'When she saw I did a good job she put me in charge, first with Wiley, then on my own. I went to U. C. Davis and majored in agriculture so I know the new ways, but I've gone back to some of the old.' She laughed at the expression on my face.

'I'm surprised, and impressed.'

She grinned and held out her hands for my inspection, hard, tanned, calloused farmer's hands. 'It's in my blood. It's why I'm still here and what saved me. I'm a Morrell. Look, isn't it lovely?' She jumped subjects again with acrobatic ease. 'It's odd how someone would put a bed of bulbs here, but who cares? It's lovely, isn't it?'

The bulb bed was still a riot of color and contrasts, not planned but passionate. It was lovely. Very.

'No wonder your grandmother left it to you.'

'No. She probably would have but that's not why. My grandfather's will stipulated that it had to be left in the family. There was no choice.'

'May I see a picture of her?'

'If I can find one. She was not fond of having her picture taken. She didn't own a camera or care for photographers. Call her Florence,' she added abruptly. I raised my eyebrows. 'I did. She didn't care for the term "grandmother," at least not spoken by me.'

'I would like to meet her lawyer.'

25

'All right.'

'Is he acting for you?'

'For now, yes. Paul doesn't like him, says he's a country fuddy-duddy. Well, and he is, but sound, I think. Paul wants me to hire a downtown hotshot, at three times the rate, no doubt.' She smiled wryly. 'Paul goes for stuff like that. He's city; I'm country.' She said it simply.

I was having a difficult time reconciling this practical businesswoman with the impassioned child/woman banging jam pots and breaking a coffee cup in the kitchen a half hour earlier, or the young woman speaking of floaters yesterday.

'I'll need to talk to the lawyer as soon as possible.'

'Of course. I'll call him immediately to introduce you.'

'And may I look through your – through Florence's records, both personal and business?'

She laughed. 'There's very little business that she handled. At first I just ran the ranch but gradually she turned everything over to me. There's even less that's personal. You may, but why?' she asked, puzzled.

'There might be something that would take us back to your mother.'

'No,' she said positively. 'I've looked. Many times. If there were anything, I would have found it.'

'You might have overlooked something, or not recognized the significance of—'

'No,' she said with the arrogance of youth.

And she was right. I wasted the rest of the morning checking it out, proving it.

Four

People who watch a lot of television perceive the world as a more violent place than it really is; they see things more readily as black and white (color TV notwithstanding); they have grossly unrealistic expectations of police officers, of our justice system, and of life.

The lawyer was a dried-up raisin of a man with crinkly, smiling eyes set deeply under thick white eyebrows that looked like untrimmed, snowed-over hedges, a large version of a leprechaun dressed in browns and earth tones. The silk tie at his throat was tightly and impeccably knotted and his Adam's apple bobbed frantically above it as though afraid each swallow could be the last. He greeted me personally. There was no secretary in the office.

'Ms Colorado, please come in. Paige just called. I am delighted to be of service; I have a long and valued association with the Morrells.' With his hand on my elbow he escorted me in a fussy, old-gentlemanly way to a chair in front of a large antique desk.

29

Herbert Sanderson was at least seventy-eight. I felt as though I should be escorting him. After seating me he tottered around to his chair and eased himself in as I scrutinized his office.

The room, like its owner, was of a different generation, an older, gentler one. Much of it was antiques, not boughten, as my grandmother would say, but things that had been in the family forever, had been handed down and over. The heavy flowered curtains and upholstery were worn but not shabby.

Photographs of forbidding ancestors stared sternly at me from the walls, an Albrecht Dürer etching was grim and humorless, and a Civil War general in a gilt frame likewise declined to smile. I didn't smile at them either. A black rotary telephone and manual typewriter were the only 'modern' items in the room. In the back of the house somewhere a grandfather clock bonged. Sanderson folded his hands on his desk and, unlike the ancestors, the etching, and the general, smiled at me before he began.

'Where shall we start? The will? Paige mentioned that. It is hardly remarkable but certainly would be of interest. I have a copy here for you.'

I nodded. 'Thank you. There are other things I hope you can help me with as well.'

'Of course.' He inclined his head graciously.

'Mr Sanderson, how long have you known the Morrells?'

'All my life. Letitia – Florence's sister-in-law – was

a schoolmate of mine. Her brother, Joshua, married Florence.' He smiled. 'Letitia and I were married shortly after.'

His eyes twinkled at my surprise. A good investigator, I'm convinced, should cultivate a superior poker face. I'm still working on it.

'The family tie is a strong one,' Sanderson continued, 'as indeed it is amongst many of the old Delta families. We were therefore closely connected, close but not intimate. Florence was not the easiest person to get along with and my wife was also, ummm, a very strong woman. There was a clash there.' His eyes twinkled. 'But that is history, I am the only one left now.'

'I'm sorry.'

He nodded. 'Letitia died last year. It was a great loss to me.' He shuffled a neat stack of papers on the desk. 'I expect to follow shortly. My work here is almost done.' His eyes twinkled again. 'My Letty never could get rid of me.'

'I can't imagine that she tried.'

He smiled and changed the subject. 'Well, Ms Colorado?'

'Can you tell me about Paige's mother, about her death?'

'I know only what Florence told me, that Ruby died in an automobile accident with her husband, though the baby, Pearl, was unharmed. Florence did not require or ask for my assistance in that situation.'

'May I assume that you are advertising, that you do not have a copy of Ruby Morrell's death certificate?'

He nodded. 'That is correct.'

I changed course.

'Mr Sanderson, this is a story about people, not just legal documents. Paige wants to know about her family, her mother and father. Mrs Morrell apparently maintained an absolute silence on the subject, forbade the topic completely.'

'Yes. I was very much against that and I told her so. Florence was a stubborn woman, fixed in her ideas of what was right, what was appropriate. Her estimation, however, was not always accurate; indeed, frankly, it left a great deal to be desired. We disagreed over it many times.'

He spread his hands out helplessly. The chair squeaked as he leaned back. 'I am an attorney. I could and did counsel Florence; I could not make those decisions for her. Since she refused to tell the child directly I urged her to leave a written explanation to be opened on her death.'

'And did she?'

'I don't know. Certainly not with me.'

'Mr Sanderson, you know the story.' It was a statement, not a question. 'Will you tell me?'

He nodded. 'I know a great deal of the story.' It was not the question I wanted answered. 'Not all of it, but perhaps there is no one living now who knows all of it.'

I was intrigued by the perhaps, the possibilities there.

'Though there are a few still who know bits and pieces of the story. Some of us old farts. Us old local farts.' He chuckled, making a sound like dry leaves being walked on. 'The younger ones have long since moved out, moved on. To be honest, I expected Paige to come to me with these questions.'

'And she did not?'

'No. Perhaps the child felt that since I was a contemporary of Florence I was also an ally, a supporter of hers.'

'And?'

'And that was far from it, far indeed.' He sighed. 'Ms Colorado, I have an appointment with Paige tomorrow afternoon. Perhaps you will join us? I am an old man and tire easily.' He didn't look tired. Thoughtful perhaps. 'It will be easier for me if I tell the story but once to all concerned.'

'I should be glad to join you.'

'For it is quite complicated. Some of it, indeed, is not her story, is, no doubt, better left dead and buried. Much better.' He shook his head. 'Difficult.'

Dead and buried. It was the second time today I had heard that expression, this time from a far more credible source. I did not find it reassuring.

'So often poking about in the past does not make one happier. Not at all.' Sanderson sighed again, deeply and from the heart. 'It merely opens a terrible, wretched, smelly can of worms which,

33

like Pandora's box, one cannot close again.'

'That's true, but living with the unknown is a great burden.'

'Yes,' he agreed, 'it is. Most definitely. Still, I am afraid for the child.'

We looked at each other in silence. He walked to the window and gazed out.

'Once,' he said, 'before these new levees—' He chuckled his dry leaf chuckle. 'Well, new to me, anyway, not to you young 'uns – the river flooded almost every year. The silt that builds up now in the waterways and the bays was washed out over our farmlands. We were flooded, chastened, enriched and, I think, cleansed, purged perhaps. Each year, in a way, we started over. That does not happen now. The river no longer floods and enriches our valley but is contained, clogged, even contaminated.' He turned back to me. 'I am glad I will not live to see many more changes.'

'Does silt build up in lives as well?'

Dead leaves crackling. He was laughing again.

'I like you, young lady. I like Paige as well and I think that she has a right to this story. Alas, that it is so complicated, that her story is part of another's that perhaps she has not the right to, one that should not see the light of day. I have thought it over carefully. Most carefully. You understand, I know.'

'Yes.' I did. I even agreed with him: about the sometimes rotten/sweet smell of the past, about worms, about the difficulties in reclosing a Pandora's box.

'The important legacies that are left us are, so often, not property and possessions, not material things.' He turned back to the window and gestured. 'Our waterways are banked and damned, the silt and contamination a problem not just for us but for the next generation and the ones to follow them. So it is in families, contamination damning not just the first unfortunates but, all too often, all those who follow.'

'What is the legacy, the contamination in the Morrell family, Mr Sanderson?'

He stood with his back to me for what seemed like a day and a half before he turned and answered. 'Florence should never have had children.' His voice was sad, his answer oblique. 'She did not want them, agreed only on Joshua's insistence. She disliked children yet hers was the hand that raised Ruby, Opal, and then Pearl.'

'And were they jewels?' I asked.

Still sad. 'You have heard the old saying that one may not make a silk purse out of a sow's ear?' Still oblique.

'Yes.' Who, or what, I wondered, was the sow's ear? 'And?'

'I fear it is true. Tomorrow, then?' I was being gently and kindly dismissed.

'Yes, and thank you.'

'Indeed. Afterward, will you do me the honor of

taking tea and visiting? I should like,' he hesitated, then winked, 'to try out an idea on you.'

'I would be delighted. May I bring something, cookies perhaps?'

'No, no, no,' he chided me, the perfect, fussy gentleman host again.

I smiled. 'Very well.'

'My office, as you see, is in a separate part of the house. Tomorrow, four o'clock, we will meet in the parlor.'

'At four then.'

'After all these years—' He shook his head. 'I had not thought to see these old questions come up again, these old bones be unburied. And now, twice in one week—' His Adam's apple bobbed frantically, almost fretfully. 'How remarkable it is and how little one knows about life after all.'

I felt my interest quicken. 'There was another inquiry?'

'Yes, my dear, that is what I am telling you,' he said fussily.

I thought quickly. 'Because of the mandated advertisements to establish Ruby Morrell's death? Was that it?'

He shook his head to shush me. 'Tomorrow. That, too, is part of the story,' and he walked around his desk. He did not shake hands but instead held out both his old hands and took mine in a surprisingly strong, firm grip. 'Please send my regards to Paige. Tell her I look forward to seeing her tomorrow.'

'Gladly.' I had a sudden impulse to lean over and kiss his dry, wrinkled cheek. I'm sorry, now, that I didn't.

'Tomorrow?'

'Tomorrow,' I agreed.

But tomorrow came only for me.

A young woman met me at the door and introduced herself as Sanderson's grandniece. As I entered, I could smell freshly baked cookies. The front parlor was filled with people, most of them elderly, all of them eating and talking, some of them sniffling. Their voices were clear and quiet in the background. I was early, but surprised still by the party.

'Not a surprise, not really.'

'Well, yes and no.'

'Another tuna-cheese crisp, dear? They are *quite* good.'

'Oh Hilda, *you* made them, didn't you?'

'Why, only last week he said—'

'And you are?' the niece asked me politely.

'Kat Colorado. I have an appointment with Mr Sanderson at four.'

Her face crumpled. 'You didn't know, then? No, of course not.' She looked at the flowers from my garden, the first, the sweetest of the spring roses.

'I thought he would enjoy them.'

'Oh yes,' she said, 'he would have.'

'Would have?' I asked, but I knew. The past tense is final and definite, inarguable and unforgiving.

I smelled gingerbread now, too, and corned beef and cabbage. It seemed an odd combination, but comforting somehow. In a small country town news of a death moves fast and friends would gather immediately with offerings of food, love, and consolation. Death brings out the best, the curious, and the morbid in us.

'He passed away yesterday evening. Shall I take these? They'll still be fresh and beautiful for the service.'

Dumbly, numbly, I held the flowers out. 'How? Oh, please forgive me, how rude that sounds. I'm so sorry about your loss.'

And mine, too, I thought. He was a dear old man whom I had liked. And the story? Was it gone now? I wondered and then briefly hated myself for thinking of business, his body barely cold.

'Yes.' Her eyes filled with tears. 'He said he was ready to go but we, of course, were not ready to lose him. He died in his study, working. Come in, do. I think you'd better sit down and have a cookie.'

She led me to a seat and came back with a small plate of cookies and a glass of punch.

'Is Paige here?' I asked.

She shook her head. 'She spent all morning with me.' Her eyes filled with tears again. 'She'll be back later. Such a dear, *dear* thing!' The tears spilled down her cheeks. 'I'm sorry, I—' She wiped her nose with the back of a finger and walked away abruptly.

Dutifully I ate a cookie I didn't want and couldn't

taste, drank my punch, and waited for my mind to adjust to the shock, to start working again. Three little old ladies, their heads to one side like inquisitive pigeons, stared politely at me.

'Were you a friend?' one asked at last.

'Yes. Well, no. We only met recently on business, still, I liked him very much.' I stopped, not knowing what else to say. All the ladies nodded wisely and in unison.

'Herbie was like that, he had that effect on people,' one of them ventured finally.

'Had he been ill?'

'Oh my, no.'

'He had a heart attack, you're forgetting that.'

'Oh pish, Hilda, that was long ago. He had recovered completely.'

'When was his attack?' I asked.

'Eighty-seven, I do believe.'

'You're wrong, Edith.' Hilda pounced gleefully on her. 'It was eighty-six, the year of the flood. We couldn't find the doctor right away, don't you remember?' Hilda was triumphant, not a gracious winner.

'Oh, yes, that's right,' Edith agreed meekly.

'He'd had no health problems since then?'

'Oh no,' the until now silent one of them said. 'He was up at six, rain or shine, and took a walk every morning before he had breakfast. That's how we knew, you see.'

The other ladies nodded sagely. 'How?' I asked,

lacking their clear evaluation of the situation.

'At nine o'clock his paper was still on the porch,' one said.

'And that would never happen, never,' added another.

'Not unless he was dead,' the third said baldly.

'And he was.' They all shook their heads sadly.

'Who found him?'

'Someone phoned Cora. His grandniece,' she added when I looked unenlightened. 'She came over directly.'

'She had a key?'

'Oh yes, not that it mattered. Herbie always left the door unlocked and everyone in town knew it. Said he didn't want to live in a world where he had to lock his door. Never had, never would, he said.' That was Hilda.

I found that interesting. 'Was his doctor a local person?'

They stared at me.

'Of course, wouldn't go to Mercy, or one of them big hospitals—'

'Never had, never would, he said.' Hilda again, and on a roll.

'—went to see Dr Jonas. Elrod Jonas. He's right over there.' She pointed to the bay window where another old fart, as Sanderson would have said, stood drinking tea and munching cookies. There was a trail of crumbs down his old-fashioned suit coat.

'Always had, always would, that's what he—'

'Oh shush, Hilda,' Edith admonished. Hilda looked a little stricken but she shushed.

I stood up. 'May I get you ladies more punch or tea?'

'No, thank you, dear.'

'Quite stuffed, I'm sure.'

'Only one cup. Always have, always—' Hilda broke off. 'More cookies, please, the ones with the jam in the middle.' I went to fetch them and then I drifted over to Elrod Jonas.

'Dr Jonas?'

He cleared his throat and brushed the crumbs off his chin. 'Yes? Have I had the pleasure—?' he asked, knowing he hadn't, and waited.

'My name is Kat Colorado. I am an acquaintance of Mr Sanderson and the Morrell family. I spoke with Mr Sanderson yesterday on both business and personal matters. He seemed very well. We had an appointment for today. I can't understand—'

Dr Elrod patted my arm. It was like having a bony little bird land on my elbow three times in rapid succession. 'Herb had a strong constitution,' Jonas agreed. 'He was a tough old geezer. Still, he always said he didn't want to outlive his Letty, or just long enough to finish up what was important to him. I've seen it happen many times, the one follows the other. They seem in perfect health but, without the will to live, something takes them just like that. After all those years together they just don't want to be apart.'

'But he wasn't finished. We had an appointment

today to discuss something very important.'

'Who made the appointment?' I looked at him, puzzled. 'Whose business was it?' he added. 'Yours?'

'Yes.'

'Perhaps,' he said gently, 'it wasn't as important to him as it was to you.' The dry bony bird landed on my arm again and he started to walk away.

'Dr Jonas.'

He stopped and turned.

'Is there any question of—' Dear God, now what? I didn't want to say murder and foul play sounded too Hollywood. '—of death by other than natural causes?'

'Murder?' The doctor asked loudly, exhibiting neither my restraint nor reticence. 'How? Who? Why?' A fine spray of spittle misted the air. 'Good grief, you young people watch entirely too much television. Entirely too much.' He stomped off.

I paid my respects once again to Cora and asked if I might call upon her later. She nodded distractedly and readily gave me her phone number.

Then I left. Herb Sanderson's little front yard was flooded with color, with the flowers he and his Letitia had so lovingly planted and tended. How do you say good-bye to a dead person you hardly knew? I had to pull the gate firmly behind me to latch it. Paige damned Florence to toss, turn, and fry. I felt sure that Herb Sanderson would rest in peace, was already at peace with his Letty. I wished him godspeed.

That night I watched part of a made-for-TV movie. A lot of people died, some of them old. They were all murdered. I wondered if maybe Elrod Jonas was right and went to bed early.

Five

89% of women say love is more important than sex; 31% of men agree. Men are 3 to 4 times more likely to be unfaithful to their partners than women. What is love, anyway?

Ranger started barking, that was what woke me up. Then the pounding on the door began and continued in a steady rhythmic pulse. Maybe that plays in a jazz club; it doesn't work in my country part of Orangevale. I pulled on jeans and a T-shirt and headed for the door. Ranger was barking up the dead still but he was wagging his tail and smiling with his one blue, one brown Australian sheepdog eyes. He knew the noise.

Great. I didn't.

'Kat, lemme in.'

Yes, I did.

'Ka-a-a-ty,' Charity wailed.

I opened the door and she stumbled in. 'Charity, you're hammered.'

'No, I'm not. Well, yes, I am.' She thrust a bag of groceries at me and staggered toward the kitchen, turning on every light she passed. 'Why don't you have any lights on?'

'I was asleep.' I looked into the bag: a quart of Bombay, a half gallon of Dreyers double fudge excess something, a can of chocolate syrup, and a spray can of whipping cream. 'You forgot the maraschino cherries.'

'Damn! I did. Do you have any?'

'Charity, I can't stand that kind of junk and you know it.'

Charity, uninvited, was rooting through my cupboards and drawers, producing bowls, spoons, and glasses. If she weren't my best friend I'd never let her get away with this kind of shit, I thought in resignation. But she is, and I do.

She poured the gin first, then she started on the ice cream. 'Do you want a sundae?'

'No, thanks.' Sleep in the near future was clearly not a possibility. I poured myself a glass of wine.

'Ice cubes in your drink?' Charity asked helpfully, sweetly.

'Charity, it's cabernet.'

'So?'

'So, no. Thanks,' I remembered in time to add. It *was* the thought that counted. I repeated it to myself twice so that I would believe it. 'You don't put ice in cabernet.'

'Oh?'

'Charity, it's two-thirty in the morning. What's the matter?' Two-thirty, that was a tip-off. Bars close at two. I'd been a bartender for too many years not to notice the timing.

She was standing at the counter with the half gallon of ice cream open, pouring chocolate syrup, spraying whipped cream, and crying. Right into the carton, tears and all. No bowl. So much for style and manners.

'Oh Katy, Katy,' she wailed between octaves and in between stuffing large spoonfuls of ice cream and gooey junk into her face. 'Oh, oh, oh!'

'Charity.' I put my arm around her. 'Slow down. Talk.'

She ignored me, poured syrup into the cavity in the ice cream carton, sprayed whipping cream over it all and kept her spoon flying. Charity, mind you, is an advice columnist. Daily she tells other people how to handle their problems. And she's big time, syndicated nationally. I think I'm the only one who sees the other side, which is just as well.

'Kat, it's Brandon.'

'Mmmmm.' I made what I hoped, but didn't believe, was a neutral, nonjudgmental noise. Brandon is the class-A jerk she's been going out with. Charity was recently widowed and the common sense in her column was conspicuously lacking in her personal life.

'He's seeing someone else. What shall I do-o-o-o?' She blew her nose into a napkin, paper thank goodness, and poured more chocolate sauce and gin. Charity, under stress, can eat an almost unimaginable amount of sweet junk, more than anyone I've ever known. I poured more wine and cleared my throat.

'*Dear Charity*,' I recited. '*My boyfriend and I have been going out together for six months. We have a committed relationship and now I find out that he's been seeing—*'

'Fucking!' Charity shrieked. 'I went over to his house and found them in *bed*!'

'*—someone else. What should I do?* Signed, *Distraught*.

'*Dear Distraught*,' I continued. Charity moaned. '*Only you can decide what is best. Consider leaving. If you do decide to stay with him, plan to watch your self-respect, peace of mind, and possibly your health go down the toilet.* Signed, *Charity*.'

Charity's head snapped up out of the ice cream carton.

'Kat! I would never say *toilet*, that's crude. Tubes, maybe. Down the tubes.' She pushed the ice cream away from her with revulsion. 'Yeeech.' She sighed. 'That does sound like me, doesn't it?'

'It should. I've been reading you for years.'

She nodded. 'Kat, it's so easy when I'm writing answers, when I'm me, not them, but now I'm *them*. Dammit, I *love* this *bastard*!'

I decided to ditch the sympathy. 'Check out your choice of words, Charity. "Love" and "bastard" are antithetical terms and don't really belong in the same sentence, never mind concept. Anyway, how can you love someone who's in bed with someone else?'

She started to cry.

I felt like a jerk.

The phone rang.

My house was a happening place all right. I answered the phone.

'Kat, Brandon here. Is Charity there by any chance?'

'I'm sorry, you have the wrong number.'

'Don't *fuck* with *me*, Kat.'

'Wrong number,' I repeated firmly and hung up, turning the ringer to off. 'Obscene phone call,' I explained. Which, God knows, was practically true, but Charity was wallowing in tears and ice cream again and didn't care.

'Kat, I've got to get away. Tomorrow let's go off for the weekend. Let's, okay?'

I hate to rain on someone's parade but life is what it is. 'Charity, tomorrow's only Wednesday.' It didn't faze her.

'Is it? Okay. Fine. A long weekend, then. Starting tomorrow.'

'I can't, I'm on a job. I'm leaving town.'

'Where are you going?'

'Tahoe.'

'Great.' She pushed the ice cream away again and covered the remaining ice cubes in her glass with Bombay. 'I'll go with you. Do you want more wine?'

'No,' I said, and then thought better of it. 'Yes.' I held my glass out and she poured, only spilling a little and that not on me. It was going to be difficult getting out of this one. I wasn't even sure if I could.

'Kat,' she said eagerly, 'I'll call him. Now. We'll get this straightened out!'

'No way.'

'Yes, it would be the best thing. He loves me, I know he does.'

'Then why is someone else in his bed?' It was a reasonable question but I knew I couldn't bank on a reasonable answer. I was right.

'He slipped, I guess. It happens even to the best guys.'

Maybe, but I didn't think so. To the not-so-great guys yes, frequently.

'How many times has he slipped?' No answer. 'More than once? Twice? Dozens of times?'

'A lot, I think,' she said in a small voice.

We both knew the answer, and that there was no point in rubbing salt into wounds. 'C'mon, it's nearly three o'clock. The spare bed is made up; you can sleep there. Let's call it a night.'

'And tomorrow?'

'Tomorrow?' I sighed and bit the bullet. 'Tomorrow we go to Tahoe.'

'Thanks, Kat,' Charity said in a tiny, thin voice.

I poured the Bombay and wine into the sink, slamdunked the double fudge excess into the freezer, and we went to bed.

In the warm spring light of day my decision to take

Charity with me to Tahoe didn't look better. It looked worse. So did Charity. She sat limply and lumpily at the kitchen table, drank coffee and moaned.

'Katy, I've got an overhang.'

'Hangover?'

'One of those, too.'

'You need to eat, you'll feel better.' She moaned more loudly. 'Toast, cereal, something.'

'Cereal,' she said feebly. 'No milk. I don't want to watch it move around. Or slosh.' She put her hand to her mouth and burped. 'No sloshing.'

I poured some corn flakes into a bowl and handed it to her. She picked them up one at a time and began eating. And crying.

'Dear Charity, I'm crying in my ice cream at night and my corn flakes in the morning. I can't seem to get over this guy, who is a jerk. What shall I do?' Signed, *Falling Apart.'*

'Kat, you're making fun of me.'

'No, I'm not, I'm trying to snap you back to reality. What's your answer?'

'Oh, shut up,' she said crossly.

So I continued. *'Dear Falling, Jerks aren't worth crying over. Sing a lullaby to an unwanted child, read a book to a forgotten senior citizen, pick up litter in a park—'*

Charity made a largely unprintable and very rude noise. It was most unlike her, and therefore a positive and encouraging life sign.

'Good, you're perking up. Munch up those corn

51

flakes. We're leaving in ten minutes.'

Another rude noise. I stuck a notebook and a microcassette recorder in my purse and dumped the dishes in the dishwasher.

'Should I bring sandwiches and apples along? Or coffee? Will you be hungry later?'

'Bleech!'

That was also very unlike Charity. I ignored it. You've got to cut brokenhearted friends some slack. In the Bronco, she sat limply, one hand over her eyes, the other over her heart. It was a bit overdone and melodramatic but I was still cutting her slack. Bad call.

'Kat, stop!' she shrieked.

I braked sharply, pulling over to the side of the road. So far, not so good. We weren't even out of town yet and she was already clutching her stomach and moaning. I wondered whether I should take her back. I should, I decided. Definitely.

'What's the matter?'

'Over there,' she said, waving wildly and still clutching and moaning. I looked. I couldn't see anything but a 7 Eleven and a gas station.

'Where?'

'There.' She pointed at the 7 Eleven. I looked at her. 'Please?'

I counted to ten. Twice. 'Okay, only next time don't shout. A shout is at least worth a skunk.'

'Sorry.'

We, drove over and she climbed out of the car and

disappeared into the store. In three or four minutes she reappeared with a full-size paper bag. I didn't know that you could get that much stuff at one time at a 7 Eleven. Charity started unpacking immediately.

'Here.' She popped the top on a diet Dr Pepper. 'I got you a six-pack.'

'Thanks.'

She popped open a Coke for herself, took an unhealthy slug, and peered into her bag. 'Want a cupcake, Twinkie, Mars bar, Snickers, or beer nuts?'

'We just had breakfast, Charity,' I said reasonably.

'I'm not eating for sustenance, Kat,' Charity said in her third-grade-teacher-speaking-to-a-slow-child voice. 'I'm eating to repair a broken heart. There's a difference.' Oh, right. Of course, how foolish of me. She ripped open a Mars bar, ate half of it in one bite, and opened the bag of Fritos. 'This is purely,' she waved her Coke and candy bar, 'for medicinal purposes.'

'Oh.' Well, live and learn.

She blotted her lips daintily with a tissue, crunched her Coke can, tossed it in the bag and opened another. 'We can't all be lucky like you, and have Hank.'

My heart skipped a beat. It was true, I *was* lucky, very, although if I didn't get it together I wasn't going to have him much longer. I hate it when we fight. I started to feel sad inside, sad and hungry for junk food. Charity is a bad influence on me.

'Do you think you should be eating all that sugar? Won't it make you even more hyper and—'

'*Phlbt*,' she said with a little crunch in the middle. Fritos. She held out the bag and I shook my head. 'You should talk! With all the diet junk you drink, you're a walking chemical spill.'

It was hard to answer that one so I didn't try. We were on Highway 50 now heading north to South Lake Tahoe. Charity finished her Coke and Fritos, climbed into the back seat, curled up and fell asleep. She didn't wake until I pulled into the parking lot of a California Highway Patrol station.

'Where are we? A casino, I hope.'

'The CHP.'

'Not the same.'

I had to agree. Not the same at all. Not even close actually. I started to get out of the car. 'I'll be right back.'

She yawned and stretched. 'I'll come too. I'm bored.'

'Okay, but I'm working. Remember this is an investigation, not a goof-off.'

'Oh, Kat.' She hit me with wide, hurt eyes in her serene and beautiful Madonna face and flipped her blond hair back. 'You know me, give me a *little* credit.'

I did and I wasn't. That's why I mentioned it. I let it go though: Unfortunately, I was still cutting slack. We walked into a modern office. Two young female clerks were working on computers; a uniformed desk officer on the phone looked up at me and nodded. One of the clerks slid back the glass panel that separated them from us and asked politely if she could help me.

'I'm looking for information about an accident.'

'You do have the report number? Fill out this form, the report number here. That will be six dollars and it takes six to ten days to process—'

'No.' I interrupted her recitation.

'No?'

'No, I don't have the report number and the accident occurred over twenty-one years ago.'

'Oh.' She flapped her hand helplessly. 'I don't think we – I'm new and I – Al?'

Al looked up from his desk. He was pushing forty, graying and nice-looking. Very. Where does the Patrol find so many hunks? I wondered idly. And he wasn't a desk officer; there was hardware on his collar.

'Our records only go back three years, ma'am.'

Ma'am. I hate it when that happens. I'm thirty-three, look twenty-eight, and am too damn young to be called ma'am by anyone, especially someone with gray hair. I tried not to frown.

'Then what? Are they placed in a central file somewhere?'

'No. We don't maintain records after three years.'

'Gone?'

'Gone,' he agreed and seemed pleased I was finally

catching on. Charity snickered in the background and the clerk gasped.

'Wait a minute, I *know* you!'

She did? I didn't know her. I smiled politely anyway. 'Where could I find—?'

'You're somebody famous. TV. It was *Hotline*, wasn't it?' The other clerk and the uniform were paying attention now, too. Not to me, to Charity. Charity modestly studied the ceiling, her best profile to them, I noticed. I tried not to gag.

'You're, you're—' The clerk snapped her fingers again and looked at me.

I gave up on business and let the star take over. 'Charity Collins.' But only because I had no choice. And I wasn't that gracious about it.

'Oh!' the clerk gasped again. 'That's it, *Dear Charity!*' Charity inclined her head demurely. 'Oh, Miss Collins, I read your column *every* day. You're *so* wise and helpful.' Charity didn't even have the grace to blush. 'I don't know what I'd do without you to start my day.' Charity smiled and murmured incoherently. 'May I have your autograph please, Miss Collins?'

'Of course, let me see if I have—' Charity broke off and fished through her purse. I snorted. She carries a stack of five-by-seven glossies without fail. I knew it as well as she. 'To—?' Her pen was poised and ready.

'Suzanne.'

The other gal and the uniform, lieutenant I

thought, were lined up now too. She signed the girls' photos and then lifted wide blue eyes to the uniform.

'Officer?'

'Al,' he said. 'I'm a fan of yours too. Do you come up here often? I'd be honored to show you around, buy you lunch.' He smiled and his eyes crinkled up in wrinkles the way they do after years of squinting into the sun.

She smiled back. 'Why, thank you, Al. I'd *love* that.'

They stood there looking at each other, then traded business cards. Great, at least one of us was getting something accomplished. Business cards. Romance gets less romantic all the time. I cleared my throat.

'Yes, miss?' With an effort Al slid his smile over to me. At least I was a miss now. 'Sorry we can't help you on your accident.'

I nodded. 'Thanks anyway.' I shot him a few more questions. He was friendly and cooperative and then gave me the directions I asked for. I started out with Charity trailing in royal fashion behind me.

'Ugh,' she said as she climbed in the Bronco and looked at the junk food debris, stuffed it all into a bag, and dumped it into a waste receptacle in the parking lot.

'Hey, what about my diet soda?'

'Who cares?'

'Me. I'm thirsty.'

'We'll get more,' she said grandly. 'Oh, Kat . . .'

She paused and fluffed out her hair. Good-bye Brandon, hello Al. 'Isn't life sweet. Isn't it?'

I nodded. It is, but puzzling too.

I made Charity stay in the car when we got to the coroner's office. She'd been enough help for one day.

Six

I'm gonna videotape my life so I can fast-forward it through you. The faster, the better.

From the coroner's office we went to the County Clerk. All births and deaths are registered there. I didn't find what I was looking for. I didn't find it in the microfiche of South Lake Tahoe's only newspaper, the *Tahoe Daily Tribune*, either. There were no deaths in the name Morrell.

There were no deaths of a young male and/or female in an automobile accident in the one-year period after Paige's birth. There was no mention of an automobile accident involving such a couple in the paper, no mention either of one with serious injuries not resulting in immediate death. In the days when an assault/murder made front page news in a small town paper surely that would have rated at least inside coverage?

No mention. Nothing.

Every day a lot of people die. Very few of them die in Lake Tahoe. The fact that I didn't come up with bodies didn't mean that Paige's parents weren't dead. It did expand the possibilities: They weren't dead in Tahoe but they were dead somewhere else; or missing; or alive and well and doing life's business elsewhere. And, after all these years, if they weren't dead and hadn't surfaced, they probably didn't want to be found.

I wondered if Florence had lied to Paige, but it didn't seem in character. As far as I could tell Florence didn't lie, she just refused to talk. It was, however, difficult to say that people were dead and not offer a pretty concrete explanation. The world tended to find that inadequate and confusing at best, criminal at worst.

So maybe she had lied.

I also wondered about the kind of person who could drop a whole chunk of life, a large chunk, as though it had never happened, as though life were a film and each of us the editor. Cut out a chunk here, splice it in/ hey, here's a nice bit, let's use it/ maybe rearrange this stuff too.

Could the past be dropped that completely without a trace, with nothing personal left? And no, it couldn't. Alma. I would have to ask her about that. I filed that thought away under later.

Back in town I'd dropped Charity off and was on my way to my midtown office. It's one of four offices in a moderately fixed-up Victorian on the edge of the fashionable and pricey part of town. Rent is still reasonable and parking readily available. It suits me. I parked the Bronco out front and headed up the steps and in the door.

'Hey, doll face.'

'Hi, Mr A.'

I poked my head into Mr Addison's adding machine repair shop. Thank God he's got retirement because who's got adding machines that need to be repaired? No one that I've ever met. An old-fashioned toaster lay dismantled on the worktable before him.

'Did you know, doll face, that eleven percent of Americans believe in Bigfoot?'

I shook my head and laughed. Not at the question, though he thought so, but at Mr A. Laughed with affection and appreciation because he's a dear, loving man, someone I'm very fond of, a friend, not just an office neighbor. His eyes were earnest, his mouth straight and serious, his white hair tousled, and his shirt missing a button. I laughed again.

He smiled. 'And that thirty-eight percent of people with fish wish their pets were more affectionate and communicative?'

'You're making this up. Who could have high expectations of a fish?'

I had a goldfish once. He wasn't a snuggler. Or she. I couldn't even teach her its name. The toaster was back in one piece. Amazing.

'A man who's spent his life with adding machines, his life!' He sounded shocked. 'And you think I'm making up *statistics*?' He pronounced statistics as though it were a sacred word and holy concept and shook his white head at me.

And yes, that's what I thought. I was pretty sure of it, in fact. I grinned at him.

'Eighteen percent of Americans believe in UFOs and four percent would go for a ride on one if asked.'

'Where do you get this stuff?'

'Stuff?'

'Statistics.'

'Ah.' He motioned vaguely. 'Everywhere.' He snapped the toaster button down and grinned. 'White or wheat, doll face?'

I waved and headed for my office. Boredom is an ugly thing. I popped my head back in. 'Would you?'

'What?'

'Go for a ride on a UFO?'

He sat up straight. 'You got that right. I'm sixty-eight. What a way to go out! Golly, what a heck of a way! Would you?'

I shook my head. 'No,' and left again. But then I have Charity, Mr A., and Alma. Who needs UFO's?

In the office there were messages on the machine and mail on my desk. Both were routine except for the phone message from Hank. He sounded cool and businesslike. Uh-oh. He's a detective in the Las Vegas Metropolitan Police Department. We met last year when I was on a case there and have been together ever since, or as together as two people can be who live miles apart. We're going through a rough patch now. Very. And it would take a lot to smooth it out. I picked up the phone and punched buttons.

'Alma, hi.'

'Katy, dearest, I wish you hadn't called now.'

'What's up?'

'Stella's trying to decide whether to have an abortion. She's been trying for a baby forever and the doctor says this is absolutely her last chance, she can't get pregnant again, but there's a fifty-percent possibility that the baby has something awful only they can't tell for sure, and would be born retarded. Poor girl, oh poor poor thing,' Alma clucked sympathetically. 'What would you do, dear?'

'I—'

'And David is no help at all. He doesn't want the baby and is half in love with Joanne.'

'Who's Joanne?'

'A seventeen-year-old who delivers pizza. David always ate a lot of pizza and now he eats even more. That little slut.'

'Who?'

'Joanne, of course.'

'How old is David?'

'Thirty-five.'

'Seems to me that a thirty-five-year-old man is more to blame than a seventeen-year-old girl. A lot more.'

'Mmmmm. You don't know Joanne. She's seventeen going on forty.'

'Alma, I'm sorry about interrupting the soaps but I need your help.' Alma is my eighty-one-year-old adopted grandmother and the one person I can *always* count on. Years ago she taught me how to love and laugh and to stand up straight and face the

world with pride. Alma's little and frail-looking and
that's deceiving; she's about as fragile as a hand
grenade. If there's a feistier old lady with a bigger
mouth I haven't met her yet. Thank God.

'All right, dear.' She sighed. 'Fire away.'

I filled her in briefly on Paige, Florence, and the
river house. 'There's nothing personal there: no
photographs, letters, scrapbooks, no books with
inscriptions. Nothing. And I can't believe it. There's
got to be something. Where would she hide things?'
There was a long silence. The TV blared in the
background. 'Alma?'

'I'm thinking, Katy,' she said tartly. 'Don't rush
me, dear. Was she short?'

'Yes, your height, just over five foot.'

'Nowhere high. Forget the closet shelves, the tops
of bookcases, and tall cupboards. We can't reach up
there and at our age we don't want to climb. Ditto
real low things and stooping. Try old-fashioned stuff,
something taped to the back of a picture, under a
drawer, or in the paper lining her bureau drawers.
Remember those glass-topped tables? Look under the
top displays, I knew a gentleman who kept dirty
pictures under the family snapshots. My, but was
he red-faced when the grandkids poked around and
found them one Christmas!'

'In the attic?'

'Maybe. Of course if she'd boxed them up years
ago when she was younger, spryer, they could be
anywhere.'

'Yes.' I'd thought of that too. Bummer.

'Uh-oh.'

'What?'

'David and Stella are fighting. He hit her! Suppose she loses the baby now? Oh, that bastard!' I winced. My grandmother can out cuss a punk rocker and I can't get over it. 'I've got to go, dear. Come for dinner soon. Lindy is fussing and wants to talk to you about something.'

'What?' I asked, but the line was dead; soaps are top priority for Alma. I wondered what was on Lindy's mind. She is Alma's foster child, a fifteen-year-old runaway and former hooker I'd pulled off the streets in the course of another job. She's a good kid, and tough, almost a match for Alma. And she's another one I love.

I dialed again. Hank was 'out in the field,' the snippy secretary with the hots for him and the hates for me announced with considerable satisfaction. In a bored voice, she offered to take a message. I left one but we both knew he wouldn't get it; my messages regularly get misplaced. I had to spell my name too. Of course it's a tough one: K-a-t. The taxpayers of Nevada were not getting their money's worth.

I had better luck with Paige.

She sounded breathless and rushed. It had taken her nine or ten rings to reach the phone. 'Kat, you just caught me. I'm on my way out.' Her voice choked. 'I'm going to help Cora . . . Uncle Herb . . .' Her voice dwindled and died.

65

'I know, I'm sorry.'

'Paul says it's better this way, that none of that old stuff should come out, that it's all dead and should be buried and now it will be.' She finished and was silent. 'Will it, Kat?'

'No, not necessarily. Paige, I want to go through the house again.'

'Oh? It seems like a waste of time, doesn't it?' I was silent. 'No, never mind. Of course you may. I'll leave the door open and tell Wiley to expect you. It's all yours. I'll be home this afternoon, whenever, I don't know yet.'

I didn't see anyone as I parked and walked across the property. Even from the outside the house had a museum quality about it, a monument to a bygone era rather than someone's home. I half expected to see a park ranger come around the corner and demand my historic site admission ticket.

As I got to the porch a man who was not a ranger, who I assumed was Wiley, approached me. He was tall, gaunt, and a bit stoop-shouldered, his face brown and lined. He looked to be in his early fifties.

'Miss Colorado?' I acknowledged it. 'Miss Paige said to help you if I could.' He was polite but he made it clear that that was the only reason he offered.

'Thank you.'

He stared at me with eyes that tried to face me down, eyes that dared me to drop mine. I didn't.

'Miss Paige, she went off to college, filled her head

up with book stuff. Some of it's okay, I reckon.' He shrugged, obviously not believing it. 'And a lot of it don't amount to a hill of beans, a lot of it can lead you off track, fuss up your mind if you know what I mean.'

I didn't. I didn't bother to say so.

'You can come back from college thinking you know it all, thinking you can poke around in things that should be left laying. See?'

I was beginning to, yes.

'If they ain't left laying, they could be a bother. To her. To someone. To you even. See?'

I saw. It was a threat, and only thinly veiled.

'Yeah, it could be. Something for you to think on, I reckon.'

He nodded and walked off, and I entered the house. It was cool and dark, austere and unwelcoming. I felt like an intruder. Perhaps I was.

I'd been through the house once and hit the obvious spots, like the window seats next to the fireplace in the elegant living room with the high coved ceilings. And of course Paige had searched everywhere she could think of many times. I started again.

Two hours later I stood at the kitchen sink drinking a glass of water and wondering if I should go through it one more time. I'd followed Alma's suggestions and looked behind pictures, beneath marble bureau tops, and under dried flower arrangements on glass-topped tables. I'd poked into nooks and crannies until I was sick of it, and found nothing remarkable. Nothing except the complete absence of the natural clutter of human lives.

Actually the complete absence of any life. I had seen no spider webs, no flies, no mouse droppings, and this was the country. There were flowers outside but none within. There were no magazines or newspapers, no spine-cracked or dog-eared books, no dirty coffee mugs, no cracker crumbs. There was nothing that said: A human being lives here.

I found it sad at first; then disconcerting; then eerie, almost frightening.

Paige's bedroom, for this house, had been a scene of wanton disarray. There were wrinkles in the blankets underneath the light cotton bedspread that covered the single mattress in a pine frame. A sweater was tossed on a cedar chest; a pair of earrings lay on top of a jewelry box; a scent of soap or cologne hung in the air and reminded me of her. The window was open a crack and a breeze stirred the curtains gaily, brought life and air and sunshine into the room. I looked for pictures, a journal, books, something personal, and found nothing but clothes, some jewelry and basic cosmetics.

Florence's bedroom/sitting room was dead. Yet there was an intangible sense of the woman who had lived, and then perhaps died, there. It was not pleasant, not gentle and kind, not welcoming. I had hurried there.

And I had moved quickly through the several

unused bedrooms. In one had been a calendar, time frozen: the month forever August, the year forever in the 1950s. A faded spaniel flopped its ears and looked coyly at me over the unmarked squares that were the long gone days of the week. I shivered. A ghost of summer past?

In the whole of the house there were only two clocks in operation. One was a small digital alarm clock on Paige's nightstand, the other an analog clock on the kitchen stove. I glanced at it, aware of time passing, aware of my desperate need to be in the sunshine and fresh air, to feel life around me.

I hadn't done the kitchen yet. Why bother? I thought. The sunshine called to me. The kitchen was modern, streamlined and yellow; I saw no hiding places there. A quick sweep through the cupboards and broom closet confirmed that supposition. It didn't look as though anyone used it anyway. The cupboards and refrigerator were stocked with convenience foods, not staples.

There were cookbooks but they, too, were new, except for one ancient one. I pulled it off the shelf. The covers were detached from the binding and held in place by a pale faded blue ribbon knotted around it. The writing on the front cover, dark brown on tan and barely legible, told me it was *The Settler's Cookbook*. It was the kind of thing that would interest Alma. I leafed through it.

Twenty minutes later when Paige walked in I was still looking.

'Do you ever cook, Paige?'

'Never,' she said absently and scrubbed at her cheek like a small child. She had jeans and a pale pink sweatshirt on. The white Peter Pan collar of her blouse peeked out. I didn't know they still made blouses with Peter Pan collars. 'Why?' she asked.

'Did Florence?'

'Oh yes, she was a good cook. But she never used a cookbook, it was all in her head.'

'Page fifteen, Immigrant Stew; page forty-four, Beaten Biscuits; page sixty-eight, Apple Dumplings; page—'

'What the hell are you talking about, Kat?'

I shook the rest of the photographs out of the book and spread them across the table.

'Oh, dear God,' Paige said, breathing out slowly and reaching for the photos.

Seven

Hardly anyone remembers things accurately; the mind and the heart play tricks with memory. When faced with documentary evidence people will deny it and believe the memory.

'Who are they?' Her hands were shaking.

'I was hoping you'd tell me that.'

'It's the house, isn't it, this house?'

'Yes.'

'It looks so different.' There was a note of wonder in her voice.

'The house was painted a lighter color then. Mostly it's the landscaping. The years have made a difference.'

'Oh, of course. How long has it been, do you think? How many years?'

I looked at her in amazement. 'Paige, who are these people? That's the question.'

'How long, Kat?' Her voice was still and quiet, almost dead in tone. She was afraid.

I shrugged. 'How fast do palm trees grow? This one is considerably smaller.' She let her breath out.

'And I'd guess that the clothing styles here go back to a period at least twenty years ago, maybe longer. The people, Paige.'

'I know.'

'The woman is Florence, isn't she?'

'Yes. It must be. She looks so young, though.'

'And the girls?'

'I – I don't know.'

'How old was Florence when your mother was born?'

'I don't know. Wait, she married late, an old maid I heard someone say to her once. They said it like a joke but it was meant to hurt her. And it did,' she said with satisfaction. 'She was almost forty, maybe thirty-eight or nine when she got married. The baby came soon, in a year or two, I think.'

'The baby?'

'Ruby. My mother.'

'There are at least fifteen pictures here, Paige.'

'Yes, I know.'

'Florence isn't in every picture, but the children are. Not one baby, or one child, or one teenager—' I left it unfinished.

'No,' Paige said. I looked at her steadily. 'Two.' Her eyes didn't meet mine at first. 'What does it mean, Kat?' she asked at last. I still didn't answer. She knew as well as I. 'They're twins, aren't they?'

I nodded. 'Identical, I think.'

'One of them is my mother?'

72

'That's a reasonable assumption. Did you know—?'

'No!' There were tears in her eyes. 'I *told* you. I don't know anything. *She* wouldn't tell me.'

'Who would know? Your grandfather—'

She shook her head. 'He died shortly after my mother was born. He was twenty years older than Florence. They were only married two or three years. Smart,' she muttered. 'He was smart.'

'How?'

'Getting away from her.'

Dying was smart? I let it go for the moment.

'People would know, Paige.' I looked at the snapshot of Florence standing behind two sixteen- or seventeen-year-old girls, her left hand on the left shoulder of one, her right on the right shoulder of the other as if to say, 'These are my girls, mine.' The girls were solemn, even demure, but not unhappy looking. Their clothing was plain and simple, looking a little out of fashion even allowing for another generation's style and choice. Florence was grim-faced and proprietary.

'People must know, Paige. It had to have been common knowledge. Herb Sanderson, for instance—'

'Dammit.' She slammed the cookbook on the table. It lost a few more pages, this time to anger, not age. 'Just shut up, okay. *Just – shut – the – fuck – up!*' She put her head down on her arms and burst into tears.

'Paige—'

'Go away!'

73

I'm a private investigator, not a nanny, not a counselor.

I left.

I took several of the pictures with me.

There was no one at Herb Sanderson's house. I hadn't expected it and I wasn't surprised. I sat down on the front steps to wait. It wouldn't take long, it never does in small towns.

'May I help you, miss?'

Her eyes were bright and birdlike, inquisitive and eager. She stood on the walk before me. It had been ten minutes, tops. I recognized her, or thought I did, as one of the elderly ladies I'd met the day after Herb Sanderson died.

'Miss – or Mrs – I'm sorry. I don't remember your name.'

'Lottie Shepler.'

'Kat Colorado.'

'Oh yes, *I* remember.'

I nodded, sure that she did. 'I've come on a rather unusual errand.' I paused and she waited patiently. 'Herb Sanderson and I were going to work together on this but—'

'Yes,' she agreed. That, at least, needed no further explanation.

'I'm trying to track down a family history. Perhaps Mrs, Miss—?'

'Ms,' she said firmly, straightening her back.

'Perhaps, Ms Shepler, you would know of someone

who has lived here much of her or his life, who knows the area, the people, the history?'

'Oh yes.' She nodded vigorously. 'I would indeed. Would you care for a cup of tea, Ms Colorado? I live just across the way.'

I accepted and we walked to her home, a neat, white wooden house. 'Have you lived here very long?'

'All my life.' There was a note of sadness there. I looked at her out of the corner of my eye. 'In my father's day it was more common, you know. People were born and died in the same place, sometimes in the same house. I was born here.'

We walked up the steps. Her house was warm and inviting, not a museum piece, not a stage set.

'And I'll die here. I wouldn't mind if I could have done something else with the in-between. I always wanted to go to the Orient, to walk down crowded, roughly paved streets, smell strange exotic foods and spices, hear foreign tongues and see bright colors and new—. Oh my.' She laughed nervously. 'You didn't come to hear all *that*. May we be informal and drink tea in the kitchen?'

She seated me in her immaculate kitchen and busied herself boiling water and setting out dainty cookies. Tea was served in china cups and the cookies on china plates. I admired them.

'My grandfather had them shipped from China for my grandmother,' Lottie said wistfully. 'From *China*.' There was a note of wonder in her voice. Then a pause. 'Well, my dear,' she said briskly, 'ask away. More tea?'

I nodded and smiled my thanks. 'Perhaps you have guessed?'

'Perhaps,' she agreed.

'The Morrells.'

'Yes.'

'Paige wants to know about her family, her past.'

'Yes, that is natural, understandable.'

'Her grandmother told her nothing, refused to discuss it with her.'

She shook her head. 'How very Victorian Florence was, and an autocratic, harsh, unloving woman to boot.' She *tsk*ed a few times.

'One should not speak ill of the dead but,' she sighed, 'in Florence's case, dead or living, it was God's own truth. There were many who feared or respected her but few who liked her. Nor did she care. About being liked, that is. Florence cared greatly about being feared and respected, about power.'

I spread the photographs out on the kitchen table. 'These were not meant to be found, I think. I searched the house from top to bottom and found nothing else; no pictures, letters, or mementos.'

'Oh my goodness,' she breathed. 'It does bring it back, oh my yes.'

'You know them?'

'Oh my, my, my. This is Florence, of course. And these are her two daughters, Opal and Ruby. Her husband, Joshua, named them. He said they were to be the jewels of his old age. *She* would never have thought of names like that. There wasn't an ounce of romance or sentiment in her body. Not an ounce,' she said firmly.

I believed her.

'I don't know which is which. No one outside the family ever did for certain. Thank goodness for those girls that they had each other. They formed an alliance against their mother and gave each other the love they didn't get from her.

'Alas,' she sighed, 'that Joshua died when they were just nursing babies. He was a good man, a loving man. It would have made all the difference. All the difference.'

'There are pictures of the girls as infants, growing up, and as young women of,' I looked at her, 'sixteen or seventeen? Then they stop.'

'Seventeen, I think. Yes, it all stopped then. Or eighteen perhaps. It all stopped.' She got up and poured hot water into the china pot. 'More tea?' and she poured without waiting for me to answer.

'What stopped, Ms—'

'Call me Lottie, dear.'

'Lottie.'

'What stopped? Everything,' she said dramatically. 'Everything.' She leaned forward, still dramatically. 'She said that Ruby had run off, had eloped. That, of course, was unforgivable to Florence.'

'The elopement?'

'Yes and no. In time Florence would have gotten over that. It was the boy. Very unsuitable. And *that* she never would have gotten over. Never. That compromised the family name, her pride, her dignity. She said publicly that Ruby was no longer a child of hers.'

'How did Opal take all this?'

'No one ever knew. Florence shipped the child off to a school in the East without so much as a fare-thee-well, a we'll-be-seeing-you, or a by-your-leave. No one around here has ever heard tell of her again. She never came back and she didn't write her friends, she didn't write her mama.' Lottie blushed. I carefully didn't ask how she knew. Her small-town network had obviously extended into the post office in those days.

'Where did the information about Opal going to school back east come from, Opal or Florence?'

'Florence, of course.'

'So we don't really know?'

'No,' Lottie agreed, 'but why would she lie?'

'That wasn't the end of the story?'

'No,' she agreed with me again. 'It wasn't, was it, not by a long shot.'

'The baby.'

'Exactly.' I waited. 'It was less than a year after Ruby left town and eloped that word got out one day that there was a child at the Morrell house. Mind you, no one had seen hide nor hair of the girl or her husband all that time, nor heard a peep, not a single peep out of them. Not that, in a way, it was strange. No, Florence hated them, hated them down to the bone for that marriage.'

I thought how often hate is the legacy passed from one generation to another. In this family. In mine. And I thought how sad that was.

'A week later there was a brief announcement in the paper. It was like Florence to do that, to combine a birth and death announcement. She always felt she could make her own rules. And she could, she did. People, well, we, let her get away with it.' She sounded exasperated with herself and everyone else.

'The announcement?' I prompted gently. She slid out of her reverie and back into tea and cookies.

'The announcement, yes. It caused quite a stir, a sensation really. In just a few lines she stated that Ruby and her husband – she never even mentioned the boy's name, can you imagine?! – had been killed in an automobile accident, and that Ruby's child, Pearl, would be raised by Florence and assume the Morrell family name.'

She popped a cookie into her mouth and munched thoughtfully. 'And that was it, absolutely it. She refused ever to discuss the subject. It was just like after the elopement. Did I tell you that part?'

I shook my head. 'No.'

'Florence was, and had been since her marriage, a very powerful figure in our local life. Not too much happened but her finger wasn't in a pie somewhere. After Ruby eloped and Opal was sent away to school, Florence made it clear that she never wanted to hear their names spoken again or hear any reference whatsoever made to them. It was to be as though they never existed.'

I laughed. Florence was a strong woman but not a dictator, not a god. Lottie laughed with me. Nervously. 'And?' I asked.

'And it worked.' I stared at her. 'About a week later Florence walked into a meeting of our local historical society and overheard a woman gossiping about Ruby. Of course she stopped talking, that woman did, and right away. Florence gave no indication that she had even heard. But she dropped the woman off the board, ran her out of other committee meetings, and kept her from joining the garden club. Then her husband was asked to leave his job at the bank.'

'She couldn't have done that single-handedly?'

'I— We—' She dropped her eyes to the hands folded in her lap. No, of course not, I thought; Florence had collaborators. 'She was a very powerful woman,' Lottie repeated sadly. 'It took a lot more courage than most of us had, well, *have*, to stand up to her.'

'Did anyone?'

'After her husband died, only one: Herb Sanderson.'

I thought that one over in silence.

'And after that no one ever mentioned their names again, not even amongst themselves, *ourselves*. Small towns, backbiting and gossip,' Lottie said in explanation. 'There was always someone who might run to Florence. It was easier to drop it. So we did.'

'Lottie, who was the boy?'

'The boy?'

'Ruby's husband – if in fact they were married – Paige's father.'

'I don't know. There was talk, rumor, but nothing real, nothing definite.'

'A name?'

She shook her head. 'Not that I heard of. And I would have, I surely would have.'

'What was the talk?'

'That he was a farmhand, or rather the son of one. Not our kind of people.' She said it simply and as though I would understand, would have to understand. And I guess I did. Things were pretty much the same now, though we liked to think they had changed, *we* had changed.

'Would Herb have known?'

'I don't know, he might have. After Joshua died, Herb was pretty much the only one Florence consulted. *If* and when she consulted *anyone*. She mostly kept to herself.'

'Would he have spoken of it?'

'To her?'

'Yes.'

'I don't know. He had the courage and she couldn't run *him* out of town. Still, whatever he had to say to her would have been said in private.'

She stood and wandered aimlessly about the kitchen. 'I've thought a lot about that, you know.

And is it so wrong? Wanting your privacy, I mean?' She plopped down into her seat.

'It's not wrong.'

She nodded, knowing what I meant. What you want and how you achieve it are two different things.

'Still, there *was* something very wrong there. There was too much mystery, hush-up, and fear for it to be anything else.'

'But you don't know?'

'I don't *know*,' she said, resting a finger on her temple, 'but I *know*.' She placed her hand on her heart. 'We all did. Maybe then, if we'd asked and talked, we could have figured it out. That was what Florence was afraid of, of course. Now it's gone, as dead and buried as she is.'

She looked at me with a question in her eyes. I didn't answer it, but I knew the answer. Things are rarely that gone, that dead, that buried. There are a lot of skeletons in a lot of closets. Instead I answered with another question. 'Pearl?'

'That's something, isn't it? Ruby must have named the child, named her hoping that she would be a jewel in her heart and life. But she was no more a jewel in Florence's life than Ruby and Opal were.

'Do you know— oh—' Lottie shook her head and sighed. 'Here I go, speaking ill of the dead again.' She was silent for a moment, then shrugged it off. 'When Pearl – Paige, that is – was just a child, eight maybe, she had a puppy. And, oh my, she adored that little thing.

'Opal and Ruby had each other to love. Little Paige had nothing until the puppy. It was truly something to see. The child lived and breathed for that animal, and it for her. It was the only thing that Paige ever loved and, God knows, the only love she got in return. One night, to discipline the child, Florence made the puppy stay outside. In the morning it was gone. Two days later they found it in the river.'

A floater. My heart constricted.

'Paige buried the poor little thing and cried for days. Florence, to her credit, hadn't meant *that* to happen and tried to get another dog, but Paige wouldn't let her.

'She said – her Aunt Letitia told me this – how Paige said that now she knew and would never love again, because things you loved could be taken from you leaving you lost and alone, so it was better, much better, not to love. *Eight* years old, for goodness sakes!' Lottie's eyes were misty. 'Oh, how sad that all was. I don't blame the child for changing her name.'

I didn't either. And I wondered if Paige was right after all: that a pearl, however beautiful, is a thing born of dirt and nastiness.

It was beginning to look like it.

I wondered how dirty, how nasty it would get.

Eight

1 out of 3 Americans will be in a serious automobile accident in their lifetime; 79% will be in the hospital at least once; 2% will die at home peacefully in their beds.

It was dusk, close to dark, when I left Lottie's house. It is, at that time of day, especially beautiful and peaceful along the river.

As I drove the winding levee road I let my mind wander. I thought first about love and why people love or don't love, and especially how sad it was that someone would not love a child. Then I thought about Hank. When two people care about each other they should be able to work things out, shouldn't they? Compromise, give-and-take, trade-offs: There were a lot of possibilities. Possibilities but no easy answers, and it was bothering me.

Not as much as the pickups, though, not nearly as much.

I had noticed the first one earlier when it started dogging me somewhere in town but I hadn't paid much attention, not until it was riding my bumper and then my fender. Then I paid attention. Highway

160 is a two-lane levee road there with almost no shoulder and very little forgiveness. A mistake and it's a fifteen- to twenty-five-foot plunge, river on one side, land on the other.

I was on the land side, the pickup was on my left fender. And I was scared. That was before I saw the other one. From the light and placement of the headlights, it was another pickup, first coming toward me, then coming at me head-on in my lane.

Then I was scared shitless.

The Bronco was doing fifty. If I slowed, the pickup behind would be on top of me. I couldn't swerve left; he had me hemmed in. It was a rock-and-a-hard-place choice: Take a dive off the levee to the right at fifty miles per hour and hit something implacable fifteen feet below, or go out in a head-on collision.

And I didn't have a lot of time to debate it.

If this was a bluff they had me going. I took a deep breath, begged for the best, and called their bluff. The lights in front of me got bigger and bigger until they were twin flying saucers, their jets opened full force and coming to take me out. Then the pickup on my left fender dropped off and back. At the last possible moment the flying saucer highlight/ headlight/black angel-of-undeserved-death swerved and blasted past me.

Behind me the blaring of a horn was loud and insistent. I realized it had been going on for some time: hours, days, years, I couldn't remember. The pickup behind me slowed down, spun into a shallow

U driveway, then spun out onto the road again in the opposite direction.

Watching taillights recede was a lot easier on the blood pressure than watching headlights coming to take you out. I drove along feeling like a sponge someone had wrung out twice and then thrown back on the counter. My hands hurt from gripping the steering wheel; my body hurt from the tense adrenaline rush; my mind hurt from contemplating eternity.

The horn kept on playing. Same beat, same tune. I didn't care for it but I liked being alive, liked hearing it instead of an ambulance siren, instead of nothing.

A couple of miles down the road I pulled off at a bait shop. The horn pulled in behind me. A guy in a farmer's tan, a T-shirt, and overalls climbed out of an old Pontiac and walked over to me.

'*Jesus Christ*, did you see what them guys did?'

I took that for a rhetorical question.

'Goddamn, are you all right? *Shit.*' He spat in the road next to us for emphasis. 'That was one goddamn close call. You sure you're all right?'

I nodded, although if my face were as scared as his, we were both in trouble.

'You get the license plates or anything?'

I shook my head. One pickup was an old beat-up Dodge, maybe blue, with mud on the plates. Which was a good start and narrowed it down to a thousand or so vehicles right there. The other I hadn't seen to identify.

'Hey, miss, you okay, you sure?'

I nodded.

'You talk?'

I cleared my throat and croaked, 'Yes.'

'Right. The name's Bud, Bud Waters.' He held out a dirty hand and pumped mine vigorously. 'Hey, you look like you need a drink and I'll buy you one. Hell, I'll buy you as goddamn many as you can handle.'

'No. Thanks, anyway,' I croaked.

'You sure? You don't look too damn sprightly.'

'I'll be okay.'

'Okey-doke, your choice. You need anything or I can help you, you look me up. Everyone around here knows old Bud Waters.'

I nodded and croaked some more, 'Thanks.'

'I'll git along then. You too?'

Yes, me too. I was going to git along and git out of there as fast as my tires could take me. Forty minutes is what it took and then I was home; forty minutes, but it seemed like a long time. On the other hand being dead would undoubtedly have seemed longer.

That was the mood I was in.

My defenses were down. Definitely. Looking into Death's hollow, bony, ivoried eye sockets does that to you. My defenses were way *way* down.

And that's why I walked into Hank's arms. One reason anyway.

He kissed my mouth, eyes, the tip of my nose, even my ear. I held on tightly and kissed him back as he stroked my hair and shoulder, then hooked a thumb in my belt loop and lifted me up a little to kiss my neck. I love him, really love him, as much as he loves me. Then he blew it by speaking.

'Kat, you look like shit, sweetheart.' His eyes smiled at me.

I pulled out of Hank's arms to pat Mars, his black Lab, who was trying to wag himself to death. Ditto my dog, Ranger. The kitten, an eight-week-old ball of fluff mewling at my feet, narrowly escaped death by squashing three times in the next ten seconds. Then he started climbing up Hank's leg. I was tempted to do the same but restrained myself.

'Thanks. Aren't you the silver-tongued devil?'

He grinned.

'At least I'm alive.'

The grin changed to a frown. 'Why wouldn't you be?'

I told him. He started swearing softly under his breath when I was about halfway through. He was holding me again and his hands tightened on my arms, hurt almost. 'A drunk?'

'I don't think so. And I got the impression that it was a team effort, that they knew what they were doing and who I was.'

'Could have been a couple of good old boys out for a good time.'

Yes. God knows there are plenty of them, especially down on the river. 'Could have been, but I don't think so.' I started toward the kitchen and stumbled. Hank caught me around the waist.

'Kat?'

He stood and looked at me, everything written on his face: his love for me, the way he felt about my job and life style.

'Don't start,' I said softly. 'I'm too tired, scared still too. A little.' That was a lie. I was scared a lot.

He pulled the sweater over my head. 'Get in the bathtub. I'll bring you a glass of wine.' He started unbuttoning my blouse. I laughed at the expression in his eyes and the way his hands felt on me and because, dear God, it was good to be alive. He kissed me. 'You're beautiful, Katy.' His voice was husky. He kissed me again.

'Can I have a bath first?' I asked, laughing still.

'Maybe not.'

Afterward I lay in the bathtub drinking wine and making waves with my toes. Hank stood over me, a towel wrapped around his waist. 'Want me to soap your back and those hard-to-reach spots?'

'Okay.' He started soaping. 'Hank, that's not my back.' He grinned at me. 'Hell of a detective you are.' He laughed. 'I thought you were going to start dinner.' I grabbed at my teetering wine glass and caught it just in time.

'That was before I looked through the kitchen. Do you realize what the food situation is?'

'Mmmmm.' He was soaping more parts of me that weren't my back. It felt awfully good.

'Tuna fish, lima beans, stale bread, and ice cream bars.'

About par for my kitchen; no, maybe above par, I didn't usually have ice cream. 'No cheese?'

'I didn't look.'

'I'm sure there's cheese. We can have tuna melts with lima beans and ice cream for dessert.'

'You can.' Hank cares more about food than I do. It sounded fine to me. 'And there's no beer.'

'Drink wine?'

'We're going out, Katy.' He reached over, kissed me and pulled the plug on the bath.

'Hey, my back didn't get scrubbed yet!'

Hank's stomach growled. A big six foot one, he doesn't like to miss meals. 'Later, sweetheart.'

I was drying my hair when he came back into the bathroom. I hadn't heard the doorbell though I'd heard the dogs.

'Honey, there's a guy at the door who wants to see you. Wouldn't give a name.' I frowned. Hank winked.

'Stick him in the front room while I get dressed.' I hurried, dressed quickly – clean Levis and a sweater, pumps even since we were going out – combed my almost dry hair with my fingers, and walked into the front room. In the kitchen Hank had found a beer, probably warm. He was eating tuna fish, cheese, and crackers. So were Mars, Ranger, and Kitty. So much for regular meals, rules, and discipline. We'd deal with it later.

A man with his back to me was fondling my antique crystal paperweight with the air of an appraiser. Or a shoplifter.

'Good evening.'

At the sound of my voice he whirled around and almost dropped the paperweight. 'Hello.'

Well, well. It was Paul, Paige's boyfriend with the BMW and the attitude. And now with my paperweight. He smiled broadly at me and held out his hand. Not the one with the paperweight.

'Miss Colorado, sorry to bother you at this hour.'

'This is business?'

'Of course.' His mind boggled for a moment as he considered anything other than business with me.

'I have a business office and business hours. You've missed both, I'm afraid.'

'Yes, well, I'm sorry but this is very important.' To him presumably, probably not to me. I waited, not very patiently. 'I, uh, look Miss Colorado—'

'Ms'

'Ms. I, uh, we want you to drop this investigation. Paige agrees with me that messing around in the past is not a profitable or suitable—'

I tuned out. How yuppieish that sounded. I remembered Paige with tears in her eyes and trembling hands as she looked at the photographs Florence had gone to such pains to conceal. I was losing interest in Paul. Fast. In the kitchen Hank's stomach was growling. We had things to do: fun things, interesting things. I made myself tune back in.

'So, anyway, you're off the investigation; you're to keep the advance for your trouble, and thanks.

Well,' he dusted off his hands as though he'd done a hard day's work, 'I guess that's it, and I'm glad we've got it settled.' He held out his hand again. I ignored it.

'How many vehicles do you own, Paul?'

'Huh?'

'There's the BMW. What else? Did I see you driving a little blue Honda the other day?' I was baiting him. He bit.

'A little Honda? Blue? Naw, I would never drive one of them. I got a blue pickup but—' He broke off, flushed, and glared at me. 'Why? What is this anyway?'

'Late-model?' He shook his head. 'And you've got friends with pickups, right?'

'Yeah, well everyone does, around here especially.' He flushed again. 'Look, I gotta go, I just wanted to get things settled up, and now we do so—' He started to stick out his hand again.

'We don't actually.'

'What?' he asked stupidly.

'We don't have it settled. You didn't hire me, Paige did. If she wants me off the job she'll have to tell me, not you.'

'Huh. No, hey, wait a minute!' I waited, even though the whole thing seemed straightforward and simple enough to me. His face got red and ugly the way it was the first time I met him; his voice got louder. Then he walked toward me trying to look threatening. I sighed. He was bigger than I am but still no match for me. What a way to work up an appetite.

'If Paige wants me off the job, a phone call from her will do it. Simple.'

'I'll tell you what's simple. I'm her boyfriend and I said so. *That's* simple.'

Oh wow. Macho Neanderthal, one of my favorite combinations. I walked to the front door and opened it.

'Good evening,' I said pleasantly. 'Drive safely. Watch that blood pressure, too. You're young but it looks like it's getting to be a problem.' I shook my head sadly, though, to be honest, I didn't feel sad.

'Look—'

'The lady asked you to leave, Jack.'

Hank stood leaning against the door that led to the kitchen, hands in his pockets. His face was pleasant but his eyes weren't. Paul swallowed hard and backed up a little. Rats. I hate it when things work out this way, when work and life get mixed up.

'I'm just going,' he said with dignity. To Hank, not me. 'Yeah, well.' That was to me. 'You better think over what I said, or else—'

'Or else what?' I was genuinely curious.

'Or else you'll be sorry.' That was original for sure. '*Really* sorry.' More original stuff. He started to shoulder past me.

I held out my hand. 'The paperweight in your pocket is mine.' His face went pink, then scarlet, then purple. Paul looked at Hank, fished it out and dropped it in my hand like a hot rock. And left without saying anything. Of course there aren't many good exit lines in a situation like that.

I closed the door and turned to face Hank. He wasn't saying anything either; I could see the restraint it took. We'd been through this before and neither one of us wanted to do it again. I didn't have the restraint he did.

'Please don't interfere in work things, Hank.'

He looked amazed. 'I wasn't. A man came into your house and started yelling and threatening you. I reacted. That's all.'

'You're not on duty, Hank.'

'Katy, for godssakes, I wasn't being a cop.' He put his hands on my shoulders. 'There is no way a guy is going to act like that to you and I'm not going to react to it. No way. Get it straight.'

I got it. He wasn't being a cop, just a man. 'I was doing fine.'

'You were. I was just there.'

Yes. I turned away. He can't help it, I know. His wife was killed by a guy trying to get to him for a job he was doing. He can't quite get over it or stop worrying about me and what I do. And I can't stop being bothered by it. I sighed inside. Time to move on.

'Dinner?'

'You got it.'

We smiled tentatively at each other.

I love him, I just don't know if I can live with it. There are things in my past I can't get over either: betrayals of love when I was a child, death, loss — and mostly the fear of it all happening again. It was time to get my defenses back up.

Probably past time. And way up. Or way down, but I couldn't do that yet.

Nine

34% of Americans eat cereal for breakfast; 23% eat eggs with or without bacon or sausage; 7% eat pancakes, waffles, or toast; 1½% eat cookies and milk. The rest don't give a damn or weren't up in time to answer the poll.

Something was wrong when I woke up. I knew it but I couldn't figure out what it was, though the sense of it hung over me: heavy, thick, and clouded. I hate it when that happens.

The smell of coffee drifted my way. Hank and the dogs were up and the kitten was a ball of fluff on my pillow. He opened one eye and batted my nose, then draped himself across my neck like a little fur piece and purred. The purr was bigger than he was. I'd have to name him soon. The phone rang twice, then all I could hear was the purring.

I drifted off into sleep, into a dream montage of disheveled, faded, yellowed photographs: the river house; an old-fashioned will with heavy italic printing, seals, and ribbons; Herb, Florence, and the forty-niner who started it all; headlights; money and coffee. No, the coffee was a smell, not a picture. I opened my eyes and Hank smiled at me. There was a large mug of coffee in his hand with a glob of ice cream floating and melting.

'Hank, that is so decadent.'

'But good.' He peeled the kitten off me as I sat up, punching pillows behind me and reaching for the mug. I could deal with decadent. I reached for Hank, too. We didn't get to see each other enough. I leaned on his shoulder and we shared the coffee.

'You've got an ice cream mustache.' Me, not Hank. He's got a real one.

'Mmmm. Lick it off.'

The kitten started climbing.

I started unbuttoning Hank's shirt.

We spilled the coffee.

'That was Lindy on the phone. She's coming over for breakfast and wants waffles.'

I unbuttoned a lot faster and tossed the kitten on the rug. Why do half the people in my life treat my house as a drop-in center and food stop? Why do I let them? The kitten cried but we ignored him. The world would wait but it wouldn't wait long, and Lindy wouldn't wait at all.

Afterward Hank ran his fingers through my hair and kissed the tip of my nose. 'Katy, we have to deal with it.'

I sighed. I knew we did; I didn't want to. 'I want it to go on like this.'

He shrugged. 'It can't. Things change.'

'But marriage?'

'We could live together for a while if you prefer. I'd rather get married.'

'Then we have to decide between Sacramento and Vegas.' He nodded. 'And there's the way you feel about my job.'

'Yes.'

'I suppose you want me to change my name too,' I wailed.

His hands played on my back. I love this man, and I know how much, how deeply, but it's still hard. 'No, do what you want. I don't want you to change, I want you; I want to wake up with you at my side every morning.' The kitten tried to sit on my face. Hank kissed my neck. I put my head on his chest and tried to push the fear away, tried but couldn't. The dogs started barking and whining happily.

A door slammed.

Someone hollered.

'Hey, you guys aren't up yet? What slobs.' Lindy bounced in and plopped herself on the bed. The words 'casual' and 'informal' are inadequate in describing Lindy.

'What happened to knocking, to privacy, to—' I started to ask.

'I lack some communication skills but it's not my fault,' she explained. 'I had a rotten childhood,' she grinned at us, 'so now I can't help it. Naturally I'm constantly rebelling, testing limits, pushing parameters, trying to see if I'm loved.'

I sat there with my mouth open.

Hank snorted. 'You've been reading pop psychology.'

Lindy shrugged modestly. 'So, is breakfast ready yet? I'm starved. I had a doughnut on the way but it wasn't much help. Fluff food.'

And what happened to finishing your sentences? 'Lindy—'

'Are you guys ever getting up?' I frowned at her. She grinned, then leaned over and sort of kissed my cheek. 'Do I really have to knock, Kat? You said I was family. You said—'

'I take it back,' I said grumpily.

'Are you *ever* getting up? Are we *ever* eating breakfast? I'm a growing child.'

'Ha.'

'I *am*, Kat, and I need food,' she said plaintively.

Hank sat up and I pulled the covers up to my chin.

'Scram, kid, so I can get dressed,' Hank said.

'Hey, don't worry about me. I've been there, I've seen it before,' Lindy smarted off. Hank got dangerous looking. 'Okay, I'm going. Don't get hot.' She grinned again.

'Quit acting like a bad-ass, Lindy,' I said, but halfheartedly; my mind was on something else. Hank was glowering, not at Lindy but because we hadn't finished our conversation, hadn't decided. Lindy pointedly slammed the door behind her, rebelling, testing, or pushing, I suppose.

'Kat—'

'I know.' And I did. He nodded, still gloomy, and pulled his jeans on. The phone rang again, three rings this time. The will, it was something about Florence's will that was bothering me.

I unwound the kitten and got up. What? I'd have to look at it again. Soon. Sanderson had given me a photocopy and I'd skimmed it a couple of times. Nothing real obvious. I found clean underwear and put it on. The estate, specifically the ranch, came to Paige as next of kin. An arcane phrase had been used. What? *In direct linear and blood descent.* Something like that. There was a knock on the bedroom door. I looked at Hank who had jeans and a T-shirt on and was tying his Reeboks.

'Come in.'

Lindy did.

'Someone named Paige called. She was all hot and bothered and said she *had* to talk to you. *Right now.* I,' Lindy said piously, 'explained that you were *unavailable* right now.'

I sighed. Why me, Lord? 'Lindy—'

She jumped back in before I could get started. 'But I told her that she could come over, that we were having waffles for breakfast. She said okay, sounded pretty eager, but not very hungry,' she said thoughtfully.

I shook my head. 'Lindy—' Too bad, it wasn't my day to finish sentences.

'Did I do something wrong, Kat? I was just trying

to help.' She looked a little abashed. Very little, not enough – it was probably a fake. Hank looked at me and left the room. Rats.

'Kat?'

'Next time let me handle it, okay?'

'Okay. Are we *ever* going to eat?'

I found jeans and a top and looked for my sneakers. They were under the bed. Of course that was a wrinkle right there, 'direct linear and blood descent.' If her mother wasn't dead – If her aunt showed up – Then we were talking a whole new ball game. Paige might not see the ranch for a long time. Or ever, if either Ruby or Opal had descendants with a prior claim. Whole new ball game. I tied my sneakers.

'I made juice, Kat. Do you want me to boil some water and slice up those grapefruits or something?'

And I didn't think Paige would like that, not at all. I wondered who the first twin was, Ruby or Opal? If Ruby were the eldest, it would come then, I thought, to her firstborn, to Paige, and not to Opal.

'Kat?'

'Hmmm? Boil grapefruit? Why, Lindy?'

She stared at me. 'Boil *water*, Kat.' Oh, okay, that made more sense. '*Slice* grapefruit.'

'Good idea. Thanks.' If, on the other hand, Opal was the eldest and Ruby predeceased her—

'I need to talk to you, Kat. Bad.'

'Badly,' I said automatically.

'Whatever.'

Then Paige was probably shit out of luck.

'I've decided what I want to be when I grow up.'

That was bad enough and that wasn't even it. Dammit. What? It nagged and niggled at the back of my brain. Some brain.

'Kat?'

'Yes, what?'

'A private investigator.'

'A what?' I stared at her.

'Isn't that a great idea?'

To be honest, I'd heard better. I decided not to be honest. Almost anything beat hooker, which was Lindy's last career choice.

'So I'd like to work with you, train with you, get a jump on it. What do you think?'

What I thought broke all the language rules I'd made for Lindy. So I didn't say it, but it was tough on me. In the background Hank was laughing.

'What's so funny?' she asked, all hurt and huffy.

'Not you, kid. It's Kat.' She looked a little mollified. He grinned at me. 'Hoist in your own petard.'

I stuck my tongue out at him. Trusteeship. Was there something like that? Was that it? Damn.

'What's a petard?' Lindy asked.

'Look it up,' Hank said.

'Ha, you don't know. Kat—?'

'I don't know either.' Trustee for who, *whom*, my mind corrected automatically, for what? I headed for the kitchen. 'Isn't breakfast *ever* going to be

103

ready?' It was my Lindy imitation and pretty good, pretty *damn* good.

'Oh, Kat,' Lindy said, but then she laughed. 'So, what do you think? I'd make a great private investigator, wouldn't I? I want a gun. An automatic. Maybe two guns. Maybe three.'

I decided not to tell her what I thought, at least not yet. 'I think we'll talk about it later. After breakfast. After Hank, Paige, and other stuff.'

She scooped up the kitten, suddenly docile. 'Okay. I *really* am hungry, Kat.'

I made waffles. Both she and Hank were fed and placated by the time Paige showed up. Which was just as well – I had a hunch an awkward scene was about to happen.

Lindy answered the door. 'Hi, I'm Lindy, Kat's partner, we spoke on the phone. You must be Paige?'

'Yes.' Paige sounded dubious. I didn't think it was about her identity.

'Lindy,' I said in a dangerous tone.

'Yes?' she inquired sweetly, politely.

'Hi, Paige.' I introduced her to Hank and ladled batter into the waffle iron. Then I gave Hank a meaningful look.

He winked at me. 'Lindy, we got stuff to do.'

'Naw, I'm in training and I—'

I looked at her, a don't-mess-with-me look. She looked back for a long time before she knuckled under.

'Okay,' she said grudgingly. 'Hey, Hank, could we go visit Charity?'

'Call her. See.'

They left the kitchen together. Paige stood in the middle of the room staring stupidly at the door. Her body was tense. She was amped up, maxed out on something.

'Je-*sus*,' she said at last. I checked the waffle iron. 'That's your boyfriend?'

I nodded. Or soon to be ex-boyfriend. Or husband. I swallowed hard. No, I couldn't go that far.

'What a hunk, what a *total* hunk!'

I nodded. It's true. He was, is. Damn. What's with me, anyway? Paige fell silent (thinking about macho-Neanderthal?). Hank came into the kitchen, and Lindy exploded in.

'Back in a couple of hours, babe.' He kissed me.

Lindy punched me on the arm. 'See you, pard.' I glared at her. She shook hands solemnly with Paige. 'Don't worry, ma'am, we've got it all under control.' She sped up a little as I advanced on her, got out of the door just in time. I heard Hank whistle for the dogs and car doors slam.

'Partner, Kat?'

'In her dreams,' I muttered.

'Pardon?'

'No, of course not. She's family, sometimes problem family, but mostly a good kid.'

'Oh.' She digested that and then shook herself back into the present. 'I spoke with Paul this morning.' Speaking of problems, I thought, but for once had the intelligence not to say. Instead I tossed a waffle on a plate and pushed Paige toward a chair. 'He, I, ummm . . . It was, well, it was an odd conversation.'

I bet, I thought, and again had the sense not to say. I was learning, no doubt about it. I basked briefly in the warm glow of achievement.

'Kat, what happened? Paul wouldn't tell me, or just bits and pieces of a strange story. Something happened, didn't it?' She poured syrup generously on the waffle.

'He came over last night.' Her eyes got wide. 'He told me,' I paused and edited briefly, 'that the two of you had decided not to mess around with the past, that I was off the investigation and could keep the advance for my trouble.' I considered telling her about the paperweight.

'He what?'

She looked so upset I relented and decided to skip the paperweight.

'I said that you had hired me, that I was working for you and would continue to do so until I heard otherwise directly from you.' She looked relieved. 'He got upset at that and left.'

I struggled inside. I should tell her the truth: the threats, the tantrums, the paperweight, Hank, everything. (And that everything didn't even include my suspicions about road tag and an old-model blue pickup.) After all, she was planning to *marry* the guy.

'Oh, Kat,' she burst into tears. 'He says he's going

to leave me if I don't stop this.'

'And?'

'And what?'

'Are you?'

'Oh, no.' She was firm, but teary-eyed.

'I don't get it, Paige. I thought Paul wanted it settled so you two could get married.'

'He does, he did, but I don't know now.' She swiped at her tears and looked puzzled. 'At first he was in a hurry, but now he just wants to wait it out, and he doesn't want me digging up stuff. I think he's afraid of what I might find out but I don't know why, and he won't say.' The puzzled look stayed.

I decided to digress briefly. 'What does Paul do, Paige?'

'He's waiting for a job right now, an opening as a stockbroker. His uncle is a partner or something.'

'Is that his field?' She looked blank. 'He has trained as a stockbroker?' Paul didn't seem stock-broker material to me.

'Oh, well, not exactly, but he's naturally very gifted, very quick.'

I nodded. Okay. Odd how I missed it though. Prejudice, I guess; the Neanderthal exterior does it to me every time.

'How does he live, the BMW and all?'

She blushed. 'He gets by.'

'He owns the car outright, maybe?' I said it, but I didn't believe it.

'Well, I think he's borrowing it, leasing it,' she

corrected herself, 'with an option to buy.' Her color was still high. I let it slide; I'd had enough of the digression too.

'Back to business, Paige. What are your plans? Do you want me to continue?'

'Oh, yes!'

'Then call off the dogs.' It was rude, but justified.

She flushed. 'Yes, I'm sorry about that. I will. It's just that he loves me, and he worries and gets overprotective. I wish—'

I nodded. I didn't want to hear anymore and she didn't want to say anymore. Enough is usually more than enough, not just enough.

'I'm still worried, Kat.'

I thought about the will, 'the direct linear descent by blood' etc., etc., and didn't blame her. Then I thought about the possibility of other living heirs, of challenges to her right to inherit, and again didn't blame her, not at all. I tried to think of something bland, noncommittal, and soothing to say. It was taking me a while because I'm not real good at that kind of stuff. Not real good at all.

'Do you think he'll leave me, *really* leave me?'

I stared at her. *That's* what she was worried about? I shook my head. 'No, I don't think so.' And I didn't. Paul might be dumb, but not dumb enough to throw away a meal ticket. She was his ace in the hole, his greenback hand, his— I broke away from that train of thought. 'I thought you said he loved you. Why would he leave you?'

'He's *so* impatient. He wants the ranch to be mine, ours, I mean, so we can plan and do things. And get married.' She flushed. 'Would Hank leave you, Kat?'

'Yes, but not for a reason like that.'

She looked amazed. 'What then?'

It was my turn to be dumb. How did I answer? How could I compare a diamond to a broken chunk of road glass? I couldn't.

'Kat?'

'Hank wants to get married and I don't.'

'You don't want to marry *him*?' For the first time her confidence in me was clearly shaken.

'Another waffle, Paige?' I asked somewhat formally.

'No, thank you,' she replied in kind.

'Who was the first born of the twins, Ruby or Opal?'

'Ruby.'

'Are you sure?'

'Oh, yes, definitely.' She didn't sound sure; she sounded like she was making it up as she went along. She sopped up syrup with her last bite of waffle. 'Definitely. Well, it has to be, doesn't it?' No. It didn't. She finished chewing and put her fork down. 'Kat, shouldn't you be concentrating on the important stuff?'

But it was looking like a whole new ball game, the important stuff. I decided not to tell her, not yet. Not until I knew more.

Ten

98% of people lie at some time in their lives. The other 2% do too, but they're lying about it. 85% think telling 'white' lies is okay. 91% feel guilty some or most of the time that they lie but—
But, we do it anyway.

Paige dumped her dishes in the sink with the rest of the pile. Great. Apparently I'm the only one around here who can figure out how to load a dishwasher.

'Gotta run, Kat. I'd better work things out with Paul, don't you think?'

I thought so, yes. 'Absolutely, it's presumptuous of him to interfere in your life like—'

'Not *that*.' She waved it away. 'Why would he say he'd leave me if I didn't stop this? Would he leave? Would he?'

Hadn't I already answered this question? 'I don't think he'll leave you. Why is he doing it? He's trying to use your emotions to manipulate your behavior.' And it was working, worse luck. 'Doesn't it remind you of something, of someone, Paige?'

'No.' Her tone was hostile. 'Should it?'

111

'Yes.' Definitely. Florence. 'People who love you don't try to manipulate you. They—'

'This is kind of beside the point, isn't it, Kat?' She was very hostile now.

I shrugged. Okay, we could play it that way. 'You asked.'

'Forget it.'

I nodded. She headed for the door.

'You said you were born in Sacramento.'

'Yes.'

'No.'

She sat down again.

'There is no record of it, no birth certificate, not in the name of Morrell. There is also no record of a legal change of your surname to Morrell.' She gaped at me. 'I'm working on other California counties now, and Nevada, too, since Tahoe has come up several times.' I paused. Evidently a cat had got her tongue. 'There must be a birth certificate somewhere in Florence's papers. She would need it to get you into school, to—'

'No.' She shook her head. 'No. Not here, not Florence. What she said went. She didn't follow the rules; she was the rule.' She started to sniffle. 'No birth certificate, no name. No *name*! Do you know what that means?'

I could guess. I didn't want to. 'It means we're still looking; it means we haven't found out yet. We will.'

'No. It means I'm a floater.' She had stopped

sniffling and spoke flatly, matter-of-factly. 'Floaters don't have names, they have tags on their toes.' She held up a sneakered foot for my inspection. 'Paper tags, on wire. Of course the wire doesn't hurt their toes, they're dead. Have you ever seen a dead person, Kat?' I didn't answer. 'Have you?' She was insistent.

'Yes.' And once I killed a man. We all had our nightmares, our floaters.

'You think, until you know, that a dead person will look like a live person, only still, quiet, sleeping maybe, but it's not true.'

No, it isn't. There is no mistaking a dead person.

'Dead people don't look live, they don't look like they're sleeping; they look dead. My grandmother turned gray almost immediately. I watched it happen. Her mouth fell open too. She wasn't very dignified in death and she would have hated that. It would have made her mad. Still,' she stood up and put her coffee cup in the sink, 'she wasn't a floater. See you, Kat.' She started toward the door.

'Paige—'

She shook her head without turning to face me. 'Don't bother, don't fucking bother.'

The door slammed behind her. Through the window I watched her walk to her car. She wasn't a floater but she had a tough boat to row. It's always tough with only one oar in the water.

I sat down with a fresh cup of coffee and the will. The kitten, too. He climbed up my jeans leg. It took

me a while to track it down. I'm college-educated
but, like most everyone else, can't make sense of
legalese.

There was a trust fund providing for the care and
maintenance, daily and medical, of a distant cousin.
The fund had been set up years ago to provide this
care until the cousin's death, at which time the
principal, if any, would revert to Florence, her estate,
or her heirs. There was a considerable amount of
money involved.

The name of the cousin was Garnet Whyte;
gemstones seemed to abound in the Morrell family.
Herb Sanderson was charged with carrying out the
provisions of the trust fund. He or Florence, separ-
ately or jointly, could make decisions or disburse
funds. In the event of their deaths a bank would
take over. I pulled the phone across the table and
punched buttons. The kitten mewed in protest, then
fell back to sleep.

Cora wasn't home. I called the Sanderson
residence. Bingo. Herb's grandniece remembered
who I was but sounded somewhat distracted. I
thought she'd been crying.

'Do you know, I found valentines and love letters
they wrote to each other fifty and sixty years ago.
Aunt Letitia pressed wildflowers from the first
bouquet Uncle Herb gave her. Imagine! It is the most
touching and amazing thing.'

I thought about my own history, which was more
like Paige's, and was amazed too.

'Letters, documents, photos, news clippings, everything is here.'

Everything. That's where I came in. 'Cora, your uncle and I were working together. I'm trying to untangle Paige's family history. Mr Sanderson had documents and information that he thought would help me. We had an appointment the day after he died.'

'Yes, I know. And you saw him the day before. It was in his appointment book.'

'I assume that the information he wished me to have would be out somewhere. If you wouldn't mind looking for it?'

'Oh, well—' She sounded overwhelmed.

'Or—' I took a deep breath. 'I know how very busy you must be. Perhaps I could stop by and look myself?' I held my breath.

'Well, yes, I guess that would be fine. Certainly if Uncle trusted you. Yes, all right. Can you come today? I should be here for a while.'

I let my breath go. And yes, I could come today. I was on my way in fact.

Cora answered the door in a friendly but distracted manner. She had the middle-aged look that married women, especially young married women in small towns often get: a little dumpy, frumpy, and frazzled, a look in their eyes that life is passing them by but they don't know what it is or how to stop the pass. Her eyes were red.

'I'm sorry,' I said, feeling inadequate in the

presence of death and someone else's loss.

She nodded and smiled weakly. 'He was just so special, so dear. I—' The tears welled up.

'I'm sorry,' I said again, still inadequate.

She smiled. 'Where are my manners? Do come in, please. Uncle's study is that way. I haven't really had a chance to go through his papers. I've been concentrating on the personal stuff, you see. I'll get you a cup of coffee, shall I?'

She rushed off blindly. I walked toward the study.

'Milk?' Cora called. 'Sugar?'

'Black would be fine.'

She reappeared with the coffee. 'Please look wherever you want. I know you won't disorder or disturb anything.' She said it tranquilly, a statement, not a question. 'Make yourself at home. Kitchen and coffee there.' She pointed. 'Bathroom there. I'll be upstairs for a while.'

I thanked her as she left. The desk first, I thought. Perhaps the information he had decided to share with me would be there. It wasn't, and it didn't take long to figure it out. Herb Sanderson, not surprisingly, was an ordered, organized, and methodical person. There was a typewriter but no computer, again not surprisingly. I headed for the heavy old-fashioned filing cabinets.

There was one file under Morrell and it contained Florence's will. Nothing else. That was not surprising; it was astonishing. Sanderson had been Florence's lawyer all her adult life. A great deal happens in a long life, much of it legally documented and/or recorded. And lawyers do that in duplicate, if not triplicate. The file folder had a worn, creased look, the bottom wrinkled and bagged out the way they get when overloaded. The will was the one I had a copy of. I looked at it in silence for a while, then put it back.

I found nothing anywhere in the study that related to Florence Morrell, any other Morrell, Garnet Whyte, or Paige. It told me something; it also left me without a clue. I got up to stretch and headed for another cup of coffee.

'Any luck?' Cora asked, coming down the stairs, more cheerful now. She had a bandanna tied around her head and a hot, dusty look about her.

'No. Would your uncle have kept records any-where else?'

'Besides his study, you mean?'

'Yes.'

'Oh no, I don't think so. He kept some original documents in the bank vault but there were copies of everything here. Uncle liked things at his fingertips. And they wouldn't be in the rest of the house. He was very careful, strict even, about keeping his work and his private life apart.'

I nodded. It made sense, it sounded like Herb. I poured another cup of coffee and headed back for the study hoping I'd missed something, although I was pretty sure I hadn't. Hope died quickly. On one corner of his desk was a small pile of personal mail, mostly bills. It was the telephone bill that jogged my memory.

Sanderson had referred to 'another inquiry after all these years,' shaking his head as he spoke. All these years? Probably from someone not in the area. I reached for the bill.

Cora poked her head around the door. 'I'm running home for a bit.'

'May I use the phone? Do you mind?'

'Of course.' She smiled. 'Make yourself at home.'

'I may be gone when you get back. Thank you.'

She smiled again. 'You're welcome. Just set the latch when you leave, will you? Uncle never locked up, but I do.' She blushed as though it were a betrayal.

'I think that's wise,' I said, and I did, I meant it. I didn't have the heart to tell her that the lock wouldn't keep anyone out; it might slow someone down, but only briefly. She waved and disappeared. I looked through the phone bill, especially noting long-distance calls. Nothing leapt out at me. I made a note of the toll calls. The billing period ended two weeks ago; anything more recent would not show up. I reached for the phone book, then the phone.

'Thank you for calling The Phone Company, and how may I direct your call?' a nasal voice inquired.

'Billing inquiries, please.' I pulled the Rolodex toward me.

'May I help you?' a new voice, not nasal but definitely bored, asked.

'Oh, I hope so,' I said helplessly. 'You see we just had houseguests and they had *teenagers*.' I paused. She waited. 'You see?'

'No, ma'am, I don't.'

'Oh. Well, one hates to think such things of one's friends, but teenagers, you know. You know how they are?' I paused again.

'No, ma'am, I don't. Not really.' She didn't sound bored anymore, she sounded irritated. I didn't blame her, I would be too.

I blithered on. 'Teenagers. And they have girlfriends. I'm afraid they may have called long-distance, you see. And I can't afford it. Social Security is nothing. Nothing! So, could you check? Would you mind? My number is—'

'I have your number, ma'am.' In more ways than one, her voice said. I smiled. We all think we have another's number. I wonder how often that's true. Not very, I expect. 'Hold, please.' She snapped me onto hold and into Muzak. I listened to a violinish rendition of the Sousa march that as children we sang: *Be kind to your web-footed friends, for that duck*— We were just down to the last duck when she snapped back in.

'What time period, ma'am?'

'The last month, please.' I hummed a few bars of Sousa under my breath and flipped through the Rolodex.

'I have only one long-distance call and that is to Omaha, Nebraska. Would you like the number?'

'Yes, please.' She gave it to me. 'How long did they talk?' I made my voice quaver.

'Eighteen minutes.'

'Oh mercy, mercy, mercy,' I said to a somewhat Sousa-like beat.

'Will that be all, ma'am?' Her voice was still polite, but getting distant.

'Just the date, please.' She gave me a date a week before Sanderson's death. 'Thank you, miss.'

'You're welcome.' She hung up quickly, the receiver biting off the last syllable.

I hung up thoughtfully, thinking about empty file folders, ducks, and Omaha. With the exception of the ducks it would bear looking into. I wasn't the first one to add it up and figure it out either.

Someone had beat me to the files so part of the answer was there. And someone – Paul playing vehicle tag on 160? – was afraid I would find out. Afraid enough to kill Herb? He was found, Cora had said, slumped on the floor by his desk, as though he had tried to get up and couldn't. Heart failure it was supposed.

That was the simple answer. Still, it wouldn't have taken much to pin the frail old man down and hold a pillow over his face. I doubted that anyone had looked for signs of something like that. Not for a man of his age under a doctor's supervision for a heart condition, and given that there were no apparent signs of violence. Still, I wondered.

And I didn't think it was because I watched too much TV.

I locked the door behind me, headed for my office and the phone, and dialed the Omaha number.

'Harnway Associates.' The woman's voice was clear and efficient.

'Hello.' I made my voice a bit hesitant, diffident. 'A friend of mine gave me your number. She said that you were very good and that I should call, but I don't know. I hate to bother you and I'm not even real sure exactly what it is that you do so—'

That was an understatement – I was playing it by ear and lying through my teeth. I let my voice drift off.

'How big is your company, ma'am?'

'Ummmm . . .'

'Fewer than fifty employees?'

'Oh yes.' I said it in a stronger voice, briefly on solid ground, briefly telling the truth.

'And you are thinking of expanding: in services, markets, or goods?'

'Ummm. Sort of, yes.' My lies, at least, were expanding.

'Harnway Associates does analyses of current trends. We can help you see what is happening in the larger environment as well as in your specific marketplace so that you can make decisions that are economically feasible and viable, so that your service and/or product can be tailored to meet the current or future needs of your target population. Or perhaps you have not exactly defined your target population?'

She paused and I made an ambiguous sound.

'We can help you do that. Or our analysis might indicate that you should consider fazing out a product that will be unnecessary or undesirable in several years and that you should instead consider moving into a new area. And of course we design advertising and marketing techniques to achieve these goals.'

'Exactly how do you do this?' I was curious in spite of myself.

'We have a very broad statistical data base,' she said proudly. 'It's all on computer of course and constantly in the process of research, update, and revision. We devise a program specifically to meet the needs of your company, your geographical area, your goods or services, goals, and—'

'You work only with companies, then?'

'Oh, no. Why, a well-known, *very* well-known writer,' she chuckled, 'is one of our best clients. He wants to know what's going to be hot in two years. It takes that long to write and publish a book, you see, and we give him that edge.

'We saw the California drought coming and now have a very satisfied client in a landscape designer who was one of the first to specialize in xeriscape planning. We work with advertising companies who—'

I interrupted this paean with a bit of common sense. For it's not all statistics and computers. It never is; it can't be. Machines, even computers, are only as smart as their operators and programmers.

And they can't see into the future.

'Who are your trend spotters?'

'Analysts.' She said it stiffly, formally.

'Analysts.'

She named names that meant nothing to me.

'No Harnway?'

'Oh yes, but not for the smaller jobs. Hers is the overall vision.' (Vision? I thought to myself) 'It's all in her book, *FUTUREVISION: Tomorrow's Trends.*'

Something was starting to click. 'Is she on the talk show and lecture circuit now?'

'Oh yes,' the woman said proudly.

And I remembered. I'd heard her on the radio as I was traveling, doing research for an out-of-town case. Anyone could turn on the television, she had said, but very few had developed futurevision. And her insights were good, were interesting, unprovable of course, since the future wasn't here yet, although she did have a track record to stand on. Harnway had stopped way short of claiming divine inspiration but said, laughingly, that she had a seventh sense, the future sense.

We all have it, she had claimed, and with a little practice can use it, just as we turn on the television. Then she discussed trends, what she'd seen coming in the past and what she saw for the future: pale skin, I remember, would be the new symbol of health and environmental awareness; recycling would become commonplace; disposable diapers were out; short skirts, but not minis, would be in; more

123

Americans would eat snails (yeech); the lines between the Republican and Democratic parties were blurring, and voters would cross with greater frequency.

Her past predictions were almost a hundred percent on target. I was less impressed with that than I could have been. Mine are too, that's what hindsight is all about. I was impressed with her though, and interested enough to keep an eye out for her book. It hadn't hit the sale table yet. I tuned back in on Ms Eager who was still doing sales pitch routines.

'That's Julie Harnway?'

'What? Oh, no. Opal. Opal Harnway.'

Bingo. I didn't holler, but it was tough. How many Opals are there? It's not a common name.

'Hmmm. I might have met her once.' *Damn*, but I was lying a lot. 'Small, dark-haired woman in her midtwenties?'

'Oh no, Ms Harnway is tall, with brown hair and about forty.'

Why stop when you're batting a thousand? 'Originally from California, I believe?'

'I wouldn't know. May I set up an appointment with somebody—'

'Is Ms Harnway available?'

'Oh no, Ms Harnway's extremely busy. One of the other—'

'She's in town, in Omaha?'

'Yes, this week, but her schedule is full.'

'Thank you for your help.' I hung up on her scheduling efforts. I made a plane reservation to Omaha and then called home and left a message on the answering machine that I'd be late. Not that Hank would bother checking; he hates answering machines. Then I set out to see Garnet Whyte. Her name had been on the Rolodex. And several numbers.

Whoever had cleaned out Sanderson's files had missed the Rolodex sitting on his desk.

That was sloppy.

And a break for me.

Eleven

Elderly people have one of the highest suicide rates of any age group. They fear the loss of their health, their independence, and their spouse. The elderly, and the infirm, fear placement in a care facility more than anything. More than death.

The address was off Highway 99 in a sprawling suburban part of Sacramento about as far south as you can get and still stay in the city. It was a residential community, pleasant but not fancy. I was looking for a hospital so I drove past it. Twice. The address went with a large, rambling ranch-style house, an older one that had recently been repainted and unimaginatively landscaped. Shabby oleanders, tired azaleas, and yellow-brown grass predominated.

The bell reverberated throughout the house, footsteps advanced and a deadbolt lock turned, then I looked down into the plump smiling face of a midfortyish woman. She looked like a 1950s Betty Crocker housewife. Except for the biceps. Housewives don't have biceps like that. She patted her hands on her apron.

'Yes?'

'Good afternoon. I'm here to visit Ms Whyte, Garnet Whyte.'

Her face got red and flustered. 'Oh, but she never has other visitors. Never. Just—' She broke off and looked at me. I stood there, silent, smiling. *'Never.'*

'Things change.'

'But who are you? Why are you here? Do you have the authority—' Behind her in the house someone started coughing, a horrible, hacking, tortured then wheezing cough. She didn't seem to notice.

'I am here to see Ms Whyte.' I pulled out an official-looking notebook I keep for occasions like this and started flipping pages. 'And you are?' I flipped a few more.

'Gladys Burk,' she said hastily and patted her hair with a fretful gesture.

'Yes.' I stopped at a blank page, looked at it, nodded, looked at her. I kept it up just longer than was polite. 'Do I have the *authority* to visit Ms Whyte?' My voice sounded stern, incredulous, then sarcastic. 'This is a home care facility with medical supervision. Correct?' I didn't give her time to answer. 'Not a prison, or an isolation unit. Correct?'

She flushed deeply, a 1950s Betty Crocker woman who had been baking all day and just taken a tray of hot rolls out of the oven. With biceps. They flexed a bit as she opened the door fully and stood back to let me in.

Someone started crying. I looked around. An old

woman sat on an upholstered chair covered with stiff plastic. Her arms were wrapped around herself and tucked in her sweater sleeves and she cried and rocked back and forth in syncopated rhythm to music I couldn't hear. Gladys didn't notice.

The woman's hand reached out and grabbed my shirtsleeve as we walked by. 'Have you come to take me away from here? Have you? Have you?'

'No,' I said gently.

Tears rolled down her cheeks. 'Please.'

'I can't.'

'Did you bring me a present at least?'

I opened my purse, hoping desperately I had. There was an old-fashioned and beautiful scented lace handkerchief that Alma had tucked there. She hates it when I blow my nose in paper napkins. And a roll of Life Savers. Butterscotch. I took them both out and gave them to her.

She fingered the lace. 'It's very beautiful.'

'Yes.'

'Handmade?'

'Yes.'

'For me?'

'Yes.'

She nodded in satisfaction and began unwrapping the Life Savers. 'Thank you,' she said with her mouth full, her fingers picking delicately, absently at the hanky.

'This way,' Gladys said impatiently and plucked firmly on my elbow. We passed the coughing person, another old lady sitting on a plastic-covered couch. Bright bird eyes watched us and a hand flapped feebly in a wave between coughing spasms. I waved back, feeling sadder and sadder. There was more to come, of course. It would be sad too. Of course.

I followed Gladys to the back of the house. Everything was clean, attractive, and pleasant. Most of it was covered in plastic. I had seen three elderly ladies and all had been neatly, individually, and pleasantly dressed. All had seemed sad. The house was light and airy but it was not enough to penetrate the darkness and gloom that came from within. It was starting to cling and settle on me too.

'Garnet,' Gladys said in a loud voice and knocked perfunctorily on the open bedroom door. 'You have a visitor, dear.'

Dear. That was nice, only it didn't sound like she meant it.

Gladys looked at me. '*She's* the only one who gets to stay in her room during the day.' Her voice made it clear that she, Gladys, disapproved of any monkeying about with policy.

The room was in yellows and pinks, with a twin bed covered in chintz that matched the curtains. There was a comfortable easy chair, no plastic, next to a small round table that held a lamp, a plant, and a virgin-looking copy of *Good Housekeeping*.

The occupant of the chair smiled at me. 'Hello.'

I smiled back, greeted her, and leaned forward to shake her hand. She looked surprised but recovered quickly. Her hand was thin and bony, cool and dry. She dropped mine almost immediately.

'May I?' I asked, indicating the bed. She inclined her head graciously and I sat down after first closing the bedroom door so that we were alone.

'Why are you here? Except for Herb, no one ever comes.'

'Herb died,' I said gently.

'Yes.' She nodded. 'He said it would be soon.' There were tears in her eyes. 'He said that he wanted to go to Letty and that I mustn't miss him, but I will, very much.' She made no effort to wipe away the tears. They rolled out of her eyes, down her cheeks, and sat there or fell off. 'He came to visit me almost every week. He was a good man. I loved him,' she said simply.

The more I heard of Herb Sanderson the more I could understand why so many people had loved him. I was beginning to myself. She shook her head sadly. A tear landed on her nose and rolled down to the tip where it sat poised for a moment before falling off.

'Are you the one who's to visit me now? Herb said there would be someone.'

'No. I don't know who that will be.' I wondered if Paige would, if she even knew about her cousin.

'What is your name?'

'Kat Colorado.'

'Unusual. Mine is too.' She paused and looked secretively at me, waited.

'Garnet? It's a very pretty name.'

She shook her head, looking disappointed somehow.

'Because of Herb they treated me better. If no one comes—' She broke off. 'Before, when I was a long way away from here . . . I don't *know*,' she said peevishly, in answer to a question I hadn't asked, '*they* wouldn't tell me. Before, in those times, they weren't nice to me. They *weren't*. They made me sit in a dark room and didn't give me good food. The water was cold and you couldn't get clean all over without getting so, so cold.' She trembled.

'And sometimes they hit me. Herb didn't know about it, about me, for a long time. When he found out, he was *very* angry. I have never seen anyone so angry.' She said it with satisfaction. 'He took me away immediately and found me this place, a place that was close enough so he could watch over me. And he got the other place shut down.'

I was shaking inside, I couldn't help it. I clenched my hands and tried to act the calm I didn't feel.

'The food is all right and the water is nice and hot. I have a bath, a long one, *every* day.' She nodded and smiled and one hand lovingly stroked the other. 'And I have my own room. Music,' she said and pointed to a CD player and a large collection of neatly arranged CDs. 'Go look,' she said proudly. I did. Classical, show tunes, and opera. 'Music and memories,' Garnet said, 'that's what I have now.'

'Is it enough?' She shrugged. 'How long have you been in care homes, Miss Whyte?'

'Mrs.' She frowned at me.

'Mrs Whyte.'

She held the frown. 'Please call me Garnet.'

'How old are you, Garnet? How long has it been?'

Her face got closed over and furtive-looking, then crafty. I would have guessed her to be early to midsixties but she could have been older. Her face was worn and sad, her once-brown hair mostly gray and pulled into a bun at the nape of her neck. Her eyes were clouded and dim, not clear as they must once have been. Her hands, oddly, looked young and strong still. They lay listlessly in her lap.

'I don't have to tell you.' Her voice was spiteful, defiant. 'Herb said nobody could push me around, hurt me, touch me,' her face got clouded and sad, 'in any way I didn't like. He said,' her voice took on a singsong quality, 'that I didn't have to tell anyone anything either. And that if anyone hurt me or bothered me I should just tell him – I have his number right here,' she patted her pocket – 'and he would take care of it.'

Her face got white and drawn. 'What do I do now? What? Oh my, my, my.' There was panic in her voice. 'Are you the one who's going to look after me?' She waited anxiously. She had already asked that question and I had already answered it, but maybe she had forgotten. Maybe she had been lied to too often to believe me.

'I'm not the one, but I can for a while until we find someone. Would you like that?'

'Yes.' Relief flooded her taut and unhappy, frightened body. 'Give me your number.' She held out her hand imperiously. I took out a business card, one that said consultant, not private investigator. On the back I wrote my home phone number. She took it from me, looked at it, put it in her pocket and patted it.

'Will you tell me about Herb when he was younger? And Florence? And her girls?'

'No.' Her face and voice were hostile. 'Herb says I don't have to talk about anything I don't want to. And I don't want to. Not ever. Well, maybe later when I know you better. Come often,' she said craftily.

I smiled. 'I'll try. Would you like me to bring you anything?'

'The Strauss waltzes.' She hummed a fragment of *The Blue Danube*. Her voice was clear and young. 'I was tired of them for a while but now I want to hear them again; and See's candy, chewy ones; and tulips, I love tulips. Go away now, I'm sad.'

I stood up. She had left already; there was a lost, vacant look in her eyes. The tears started again and she spoke to herself in a soft voice.

'Oh Herbie! Herbie, God bless you. Oh, I wish I could be with you and Letty. I *wish* I could. You should have taken me with you. Please come back and get me, Herbie. Come back for me please. *Please!*'

Blindly I walked out of the room.

Gladys was in the front room watching Jeopardy

and drinking iced tea. She was engrossed in the program. I had to say something before she noticed me.

'Oh, sorry.' She jumped up. 'I just *love* that program. I can't watch it when it's on, so I record it. Everything okay?' she asked brightly, smoothing her apron.

I didn't answer but I gave her a business card, also one that said consultant. 'Mr Sanderson died last week. I'll be filling in until permanent arrangements can be made. Call me if you need something.'

'Oh yes.'

'Take good care of Mrs Whyte.'

'Oh yes.' She said it brightly again, but she was a little on edge.

That was fine, I wanted the power hierarchy clear. 'See you. Soon,' I added and started for the door.

'Wait!' she called out. 'I'll just turn the alarm system off.' She punched buttons. 'Now you can go.'

Behind me I heard a dead bolt slide home. It didn't look like a prison.

Looks aren't everything.

Twelve

What are people most afraid of? (a) Not having their dreams come true. (b) Dying young. (c) Missing dinner. (d) Having their dreams come true. (e) Getting old, fat, and wrinkled. (f) Answering a poll like this. (g) all of the above

I wanted to have a quiet evening with Hank before leaving for Omaha tomorrow. Instead I came home to a bunch of cars stacked up in the driveway and along the street and people wandering through the house and yard. The smell of barbecue was enticing. There was a party at my house. Hank, Lindy, and Charity must have decided to have a cookout.

The door blew open as I came up the front stairs and a hand waving a hot dog came out, closely followed by the rest of Lindy and a teenage boy who looked like a hot dog: long, skinny, and with a mustard-colored T-shirt on. They slid to a stop in front of me.

'Hey, Kat, I want you to meet my friend, Billy.' She blushed. Blushed? Lindy? I looked at her more closely and her color deepened. 'Billy and me, we met at a horse show. We go riding and stuff. Billy, this is Kat, my cousin.'

I smiled. It was the first time she had called me that. Things had come a long way, a good way, since I had pulled her off the streets last year. Nothing about her now suggested the young/old, worldly-wise/terrified, woman/child hooker she had been. Alma had adopted her as, years ago, she had me. If that made us cousins it was fine with me.

And it was better than partners, a whole lot better.

'Hey, Billy.' He ducked his head shyly at me.

'Here, Kat, this is for you.' Lindy shoved the hot dog, dripping with ketchup, mustard, and relish, into my unwilling hand. 'C'mon, Billy.'

Off they went. I stared glumly at the hot dog, holding it at arm's length until Mars and Ranger showed up. It was their seventh sense, their future-vision, and it worked especially well around food. I pulled the hot dog in half and handed it over. Mars gulped his down, Ranger wrinkled his nose at the mustard and relish before he ate it. I held out my hand so Mars could lick the ketchup and mustard off.

'Kat.' Lindy reappeared briefly. 'Hank's looking for you.' I didn't like the way she said it. 'Yeah, right,' she nodded in agreement with my unspoken thought. 'I think he has to go back soon or something.'

Damn! and I had been gone all day. I took a deep breath and headed for the kitchen; the antique round oak table was full, crowded with my family and friends.

Rafe, a good friend from years back, waved a drumstick at me. 'Hey, babe, you're late, party started hours ago.'

Alma said, 'Hi, dear,' in a grandmotherly way and patted my arm before she hollered at Rafe to pass the potato salad. Charity smiled her Hi-I'm-the-princess-who-can't-feel-the-pea-aren't-I-special? look. Huh? I wondered what the occasion was. Then I saw the guy at her elbow, six feet of muscle, dimples, and gallantry. That explained it.

'Kat, you remember Al, don't you?'

I was supposed to, I knew, but didn't. He looked familiar but I couldn't track it down. After a while these gorgeous guys all look alike. Hank created a welcome diversion by hugging me from behind. I leaned back and he kissed my cheek.

'Chicken or hamburger?' He knows how I feel about hot dogs.

'I don't care. Hank, Lindy said—'

'Tomorrow. I have to be on the road by four-thirty.'

'Damn, damn, *damn*. Let's get rid of these people,' I whispered, 'I'll yell fire and you—' He grinned. 'Earthquake?'

'Chicken, sweetheart?'

'Okay,' I sighed. He hugged me and went back to the barbecue.

'Kat!' That was Charity. Oops, my manners had

slipped again. Placerville. That was it, the officer and hunk at the CHP station on the way to Tahoe.

'Al,' I turned back to them with a smile and held out my hand. 'How nice to see you.'

'Where's Tabasco?' Alma asked.

'In the cupboard.' I pointed.

'Madagascar?' Rafe offered. 'New Delhi? South Dakota?'

'Wrong! Mexico. Hah, my turn!'

Oh. They were playing Trivial Pursuit – kamikaze rules: anything goes/no holds barred. I shook hands with Al while Charity held on to his elbow like a mindless birdbrain. It made me want to smack her. Or puke. Maybe both.

'Charity, hey, pay attention,' Rafe chided, which was good coming from him, a ladies' man from way back. 'It's your turn. Who painted the Mona Lisa?'

She looked blank. I mouthed Leonardo da Vinci and got caught.

'Kat!' Rafe and Alma said in unison, their voices dripping with disillusionment and scorn. I laughed. Their version of Trivial Pursuit is a combination of charades, clues, second, third, and fourth chances, and cheating. Rafe will cheat at anything but poker and pool, love especially. Alma will cheat at everything except love.

'Sorry,' I said. They frowned at me.

Alma waved an Oreo and a glass and hollered for more Southern Comfort, straight up this time, goddamn-it! I took her glass, filled it with ice, a little

Southern Comfort, and 7Up. She grumbled but took it. I don't know why I bother, actually. She can drink me under the table. I thought by now, at eighty-one, she would have slowed down. It's another one of the many things I've called wrong.

Hank put a plate of food in my hands, more than I could eat. He worries about me.

'Eat up, it's good for you.'

I smiled. I know what's good for me. Hank smiled back. He knew what I was thinking.

I walked over and said hello to the sweet young thing with Rafe. Rafe is gorgeous, with curly blond hair, blue eyes, and an I-could-care-less attitude around women that, for some reason I can't figure out, they find irresistible. Women swarm all over him; he has to shake them off in supermarkets, pizza parlors, and bars.

Rafe's in the 'family,' too. Alma took me in first and for a long time it was just us, then Charity, Rafe, and now Lindy. Ours is a strange family. I was starting to get maudlin about it when a meatball hit me in the eye.

'Lindy! Dammit!' I lunged for her and missed.

'Nice shot, kid,' Rafe said approvingly.

'*Tsk, tsk*, dearest, language.' That was good, coming as it did from Alma. She can, and does, out-swear me all too often.

'Sorry, Kat!' Lindy was keeping a step ahead of me. 'I didn't mean to hit *you*.'

'Teenage courtship ritual,' Rafe said and nodded

wisely. Lindy blushed; Billy smirked; I laughed, I couldn't help it.

'Did you know,' Mr A. walked in from the patio, 'that seventy-eight percent of hot dogs in this country are made with 'filler' meats and filler meats consist of—'

'Don't even start,' Alma said in a dangerous tone, and popped the last bite of her hot dog into her mouth.

'Chicken lips,' Lindy said, 'hog jowls, Rocky Mountain oysters, and—' Alma choked and Rafe started to laugh. Where *did* she learn this stuff, I wondered.

'See, Kat, see how much I know. That's important for a private investigator, isn't it?'

It was, but I didn't think she was on track of the relevant stuff. The blonde at Rafe's elbow caught my attention and I tried briefly, and vainly, to talk to her. Cancel sweet young thing. Mindless twit, bimbo – that was more like it. I hugged Lindy. Throwing a meatball at your intended beat bimbo any day. She looked pleased.

'So anyway, I have this paper to do in English Comp, "My Aspirations as an Adult," and—' I drifted off into contemplation of the educational system. What was wrong with 'What I Want to Be When I Grow Up'? I drifted back, but not in time, obviously.

'So anyway, I thought I'd do "A Working Day in the Life of a Private Investigator," and I'm glad you agree. Next week, okay?' She squeezed my hand and wandered off. Agree? Had I? No way. I didn't. Rats, I had to pay more attention, had to.

'How many US states border the Pacific Ocean?'

'California, Oregon—' Alma was listing.

'Four,' someone else – the bimbo? – said.

'Washington, Alaska,' Alma continued, then stopped.

'Five,' Al said quietly. 'You forgot Hawaii.'

Charity sighed, smiled, blinked, and just barely got a grip on herself before she looked at him adoringly. I ate a bite of chicken and some potato salad, then put the plate down and poured a glass of wine.

It was spring: Charity was falling in love; Rafe was rutting; Lindy was learning. That left me: What was I doing?

'It's Hank, isn't it, dear?' I looked at Alma, who stood at my elbow. It's uncanny the way she can do this. 'It takes a leap of faith, love always does.'

She was right, I knew, but I was still stumbling over the shambles of the past: a father I never knew; an alcoholic mother who neglected us; a younger sister who died of that neglect. I would have too, died inside at least, but for Alma.

'Leap and don't look before you do.' Alma said it firmly and poured Southern Comfort, no ice cubes, no 7Up into her glass. 'Yahoo!!' She waved her glass and winked at me.

'Katy?'

I looked up into Hank's face. 'Flood. I'll yell

flood, that will clear them out.'

'Not in a drought year.' He laughed.

'Bomb threat? Neighbor with a shotgun?'

'Did you eat?'

'Yes.' I lied and we both knew it.

'Let's go outside where it's quiet.'

'Who was King Arthur's queen and Lancelot's lover?' Alma asked.

'Get real, how should I know?! Give me another one please.' That was Lindy.

'Guinevere.' That was Charity, and then she read another question. 'What sport features snatches and clean jerks?'

'I don't know how *clean* the jerks are,' Alma said thoughtfully, and Lindy began to giggle, 'but—'

Charity's voice interrupted nervously. 'Okay, now *this* is an *easy* one: What's the Boy Scout motto?' Silence. 'Oh *come on*, you guys. Rafe, surely you—?' He shook his head.

'I don't believe I've ever known a Boy Scout.' Alma was pensive.

'Me, either,' said Lindy.

'Be prepared,' Al and Hank said at the same time, but I bet they didn't learn it in the Boy Scouts.

'One more?' Lindy asked.

'One more,' Charity agreed. 'How many years did Sleeping Beauty sleep?'

Hank and I started outside. 'I wonder what that would be like?'

'What?'

'To fall asleep, like Sleeping Beauty or Rip van Winkle, and wake up in a different world.'

'Kat.'

'I can't do it, Hank. I can't get married.' Even the word made me feel tight and afraid.

'Now or ever?'

'Now.'

'When?'

'I don't know.'

'I can't wait forever.'

'No.' I didn't want him to. Yes, I did. I didn't want to be unreasonable. Yet I was. 'How long, Hank?'

'I'm leaving in the morning, Katy.'

'And?'

'And I'll come back when you're ready.'

'If it's not too late,' I said in a small voice.

'Yes.'

I could feel tears in the back of my eyes. I wondered if not having Hank would be worse than the fear, if . . .

'Come on, sweetheart.' He kissed me. 'Let's go to bed. To hell with the party.' He picked me up. 'I love you, Katy.'

And I cried. For the love, the fear, the stupidity, the craziness. For everything.

Thirteen

A significant number of people believe it is permissible to rewrite their personal past. Facts are omitted, revised, or added until satisfaction is achieved. They do not regard this as lying and come to believe in the revised version. Frequently they seem happier for it.

I was in Omaha before one o'clock. It took me twenty minutes to get to the downtown office of Harnway Associates, some of it through green fields, a different color of green than we have in California, and past silos, railroad tracks, and stockyards in the distance. Downtown Omaha was clean and pretty with trees and parks and the Missouri River spitting distance away.

An old brick building, its walls lettered with endorsements of the products of another era – *Enjoy Beechnut Coffee! Smoke Camel Cigarettes, Eat at Buster's Cafe* – historical churches, a high school in yesterday's courthouse, and the Old Market were as much a part of downtown as the new office buildings, condominiums, and the swank hotel where I was staying.

Harnway Associates, downtown in a high-rise office building off Dodge and near the City Mall Park, could have been in Sacramento, New Haven, or Sarasota. The receptionist couldn't have. She looked corn-fed midwestern. And she was refreshingly guileless.

'Good afternoon.' She flashed white teeth, rows and rows of them, at me.

I smiled. 'Hello, I'm Kat Colorado, Ms Harnway's two o'clock appointment.' I looked at the clock on the wall. 'I'm a little early, not much.'

A puzzled expression moved in on the teeth. 'Ms Harnway doesn't have a two o'clock appointment.'

'We made it on the telephone. Perhaps she forgot to mention it to you?'

'Oh. Well, she doesn't usually.' The puzzlement deepened. 'I'll just check with her.' Her hand was stretched out to the intercom as the phone rang. She stared at it helplessly, then at me, then answered it.

'I'll announce myself.'

'Oh, no.' She interrupted her conversation and started to rise. The phone shrilled again on another line. She sank back in her chair and dutifully answered it. I walked past her into Harnway's office. It was modern, trendy, and pastel, the pictures graphics or abstracts. A striking dark-haired woman looked up at me and frowned. She looked thirty but I knew she had to be almost ten years older than that. Obviously she was not used to interruptions.

'What?' The frown deepened. Obviously she didn't want to get used to them. I closed the door behind me.

'Opal Morrell?'

Her tanned face turned pale and took on an unattractive yellow hue. She started to rise.

'Who are you? What do you want? Never mind' – she shook her head – 'just get out of here.'

'You have a niece, did you know that? Pearl Morrell, although she changed her name to Paige. She's almost twenty-one. She would like to meet you.'

'You're crazy.' Her face was pale and sick-looking still. She shuddered, taking several rapid, shallow breaths. 'My name is Harnway, not, not whatever you said.'

'Morrell.'

'Get out.' She punched a button on her desk.

I sat down. 'My name is Kat Colorado. I'm a private investigator and I work for Paige. I have a copy of your marriage certificate, Mrs Harnway. I know your maiden name was Morrell.'

'Ms,' she said weakly and sank back into the chair. 'I'm divorced now.' A door behind her desk opened.

'Opal? What's the matter?' He was big: tall, broad, muscle big, not fatboy big.

She looked at him helplessly.

'Opal?' His hand rested gently on her shoulder.

'I didn't see it; maybe futurevision doesn't work in your own life.' Her voice shook and tumbled the words around. I had to strain to hear. 'Maybe – oh

God, Derek, she *knows*.' Her hand groped for his, found it and leeched on.

'Knows what?' He tossed a brief glance in my direction, an easy bunt. I could see the questions, the quick evaluation in his eyes. I tried to look like a harmless person with a little fun-and-helpful thrown in. I'm pretty good at that.

'About the Morrells.' She spit the words out as though it had nothing to do with her, as though she weren't one of them. 'It doesn't matter,' she stammered, 'but . . .'

'No. It doesn't.' His arm was around the back of her chair, his stance protective and territorial. He looked squarely at me, and he wasn't going to give away a bunt this time.

'Ms—?'

'Kat Colorado.'

He held out a hand. 'Derek Burns. I'm Opal's partner.' We shook.

Opal was taking long, deep breaths. I wondered if they were lovers as well as partners, but thought not. And I suspected he was protective not just of her, but of the business. Why not? Meal tickets are important.

'It doesn't *matter*, but I don't want to talk about it.' Her voice was stronger now.

'You've come from California, Ms Colorado?'

'Yes.'

'And it's important?'

'Yes.'

His forehead was wrinkled so I assumed he was thinking.

'Why don't we sit down, Opal, the three of us, and—'

'No.' She seemed to have recovered. The weakness in her voice, her hands, her eyes was gone. She didn't look right at him as she said it though.

There was a light tap on the door and the receptionist stuck her head in. 'Mr Burns, your two o'clock appointment is getting *very* impatient. He's about to walk, I think.'

Derek glanced at Opal first, then at me.

'It's all right,' Opal reassured him. 'Go on, I'll be fine now.' She pasted on a brave little smile that was moderately convincing.

'All right.' That was to her and sounded reluctant. 'Nice to meet you.' That was to me and sounded somewhat sincere.

He left the room. Opal and I faced each other in silence; I let her break it.

'I don't know how you found out or what you want. I don't know, I don't care. I want you out of here.' She said it fiercely, coldly.

'Did you know about your niece?'

'No. Yes. Herb Sanderson told me. I told him just what I'm telling you: I don't want anything to do with it. Nothing. I walked away from that part of my life a long time ago and I've never looked back. It's dead to me. Dead, over, done. I'll never let it come back, *never*!'

'Your niece is a troubled young woman in a lot of pain. She needs a family, needs you, needs help.'

'She hired you?'

'Yes.'

'To find me?'

'Not in particular. To find out about her parents, her background, her family. She's emotionally desperate. You can help.'

'I can't. If I could, I wouldn't. I told you: I will *never* go back, not in any way. It's too painful.'

She stopped, trembling and afraid, or afraid perhaps that she had gone too far, had said too much. Her color was back. She looked angry, unhappy, bitter almost.

'Florence Morrell is dead.' I expected a reaction and I didn't get one. 'Your mother.'

'My Uncle Herb told me. My mother? In name I guess, not in any other way. Some people should never have children. Florence shouldn't have. I haven't acknowledged her as my mother for years and I'm not going to start now. I hated her for what she did, for . . . I still hate her; it's not past for me, it will never be.'

In my mind her words echoed Paige's. I was beginning to feel the depth of that hatred.

'What happened to Ruby, Opal?'

She looked at me. There was abhorrence in her eyes still: for Florence, or me, maybe even Ruby. I couldn't tell.

'Is there anything you don't know?'

'Yes. What happened? Is she dead? When? Alive? Where?'

'I don't have any answers for you, Ms Colorado.' It was ambiguous, deliberately so, I thought. And there was a flicker of relief in her dark eyes. Damn, I'd gone off the track somewhere. Where?

'Where is Ruby?'

'My sister died. Years ago.' Her eyes changed again, sadness this time.

'Tell me—'

She shook her head. Okay. Next question.

'Have you ever heard of a woman named Garnet Whyte?'

'No. Now leave, just do,' she said tiredly. 'I've said more than I meant to, more than I wanted to.'

'Your mother is dead. Surely you'll fly back? There is a considerable estate, after all.'

She shrugged. 'My mother was dead to me a long time ago. I don't care about the estate or her money. I have a new life, another life, and a good business. I don't need the money and I don't want anything of hers. It's all dead to me, dead long ago and completely.' She sounded very tired. 'Please go.'

'What about Paige, your niece, and her life, her questions, her peace of mind?'

The anger flared up in her, in her face, in her eyes. 'Damn you, *damn* you.' She came out from behind her desk and stood in front of me. Her voice shook. 'How *dare* you walk in here like this, playing God like a clumsy child moving chess pieces about

153

the board, moves he doesn't understand in lives he doesn't know, with consequences he can't fathom?'

Suddenly the anger was gone. In its place was sadness, resignation, maybe fear again.

'She hired you. You found me. Now go back and tell her that I am not her family. I'm sorry, I can't do it. I'm sorry. If I'd known years ago, but . . . but I didn't, and now it's too late. I want nothing to do with her, not now, not ever. She has no claim on me, nor will I allow her to make one.

'I loved Ruby.' Her breath caught. 'But I hated her too. Because of her all this happened. I lost my home, my life up to then.' Her voice caught in bitterness and on the edge of tears I thought, and she was silent for a moment. 'You have your answer. Give it to her and leave me to find again what peace I may.

'People are not chess pieces, you know; lives are not games.' She was almost whispering. 'Now get out. You have no right to play God.'

I got out.

I didn't have that right; I didn't want it.

The conversation had made me feel lower than a snake's belly, and about as likable.

And I'd forgotten to ask which was the firstborn twin. I was one hell of an investigator.

Derek Burns called. There was a message waiting for me at the hotel when I returned. I'd left the hotel name with the receptionist at Harnway Associates.

The please call box was checked and there was a local number. My stomach rumbled. Dinnertime. I picked up the phone and punched buttons.

'Burns,' a male voice growled into the receiver.

'Kat Colorado returning your call, Mr Burns.'

'Ms Colorado, thank you, I hoped you would call. I'm sorry I didn't have a chance to meet longer with you and Opal earlier today. Do you have plans this evening? Would you join me for dinner? I hope Harnway Associates can show you something of our Midwest hospitality.'

'No plans, and yes, dinner sounds fine, thank you.' I was curious as hell, which didn't mean that I bought the Midwest hospitality line. 'I didn't catch your exact position with the company, Mr Burns,' aside from backup, I thought but didn't say.

'Opal and I are partners, Kat. May I call you that?' I agreed and wondered if this were more Midwest hospitality. Burns spoke with an easy male authority that assumed without pressuring. A fine line to walk; he did it well. 'I'll pick you up at seven, will that work?' He paused briefly for my assent. 'In the lobby, then? I'm looking forward to it.'

I had time for a quick shower, then jumped into a green dress. I'm prompt but he beat me and came walking across the lobby to greet me as I stepped out of the elevator. I could read the admiration in his eyes but I didn't have to, he wasn't hiding it.

He couldn't read the admiration in mine, I *was* hiding it, was trying to. He wore a business suit still, his tie loosened, his smile easy.

'How beautiful you are! I didn't notice it before.'

Heady stuff, this midwestern hospitality.

'You were preoccupied, wondering if we could work things out, or if it would take one or two tries to toss me out of the office.'

'One,' he said, 'but let's work it out.'

'Two,' I countered, knowing we would.

He laughed. 'Your dress matches your eyes exactly. I should have brought you flowers.'

'Flowers? For a business evening?'

'Who said anything about business?' His eyes smiled at me, also saying nothing about business, his hand cupped my elbow, and he steered me into the hotel lounge. 'Shall we have a drink here first? You must tell me what kind of food you like.'

I smiled.

'Is that amusing?' His eyebrows went up in a question.

'No, gracious. What is amusing is that I feel sure that you've already made the choice.'

He grinned. 'I should hate to underestimate you.'

'I doubt that you do that often. In any case, it hardly matters. For business, yes; for midwestern hospitality,' I shrugged, 'no.'

We ordered drinks and sat in silence for a moment.

'Do you have futurevision, too?' I asked.

'No, I'm the realist, the pragmatist, the business end of the partnership. Given sufficient data I can spot a tendency, a direction, the beginning of a trend.

There is nothing remarkable about that. Given the training and the data, anyone can do it. Opal spots trends before the data exists. *That* is remarkable. We call it a seventh sense.' He shrugged. 'Whatever it is, very few have it.'

Our drinks arrived. Burns paid with a fifty.

'Have you ever seen a water witch, a diviner?' he asked abruptly.

I shook my head, sipped my expensive wine, and leaned back for the show.

'I saw one as a child. I was about twelve and my grandfather took me. He was just a skinny old geezer – the diviner, not my grandfather. Old,' he laughed. 'Old to me then, he was probably only in his fifties. His rod looked like a Y-shaped stick. When he hit water the power coming through that stick almost doubled him over. You could see it vibrate, feel it. I put my hands on his and it moved through me too. It was something I've never forgotten.' He shook his head.

'And was there water there?' I asked, philistine and doubting Thomas to the end.

He laughed loudly, raucously; people turned to stare. 'I don't know, it never occurred to me to ask. You're something.' He held his glass aloft and clinked it against mine. We finished our drinks on that toast.

'Are you hungry?' He stood and gravely pulled back my chair as I rose. 'Shall we eat at the restaurant I have already chosen?'

A smile danced lightly in his eyes. I let it dance in

mine and agreed. He was something too; I wasn't sure what yet.

'Opal was very upset today.'

'Yes.'

We were halfway through the best prime rib I had ever eaten, sitting in Johnny's Cafe on L Street at the stockyards, before he made the comment.

'The water witch told my grandfather that when he was worried or upset, "het up or stirred up" is what he said, that the power wouldn't work through him. He wouldn't even have sex the night before. He had to be calm, drained – empty, he said.'

It was coming now. I knew it; I knew what it was. And I knew what it wasn't: midwestern hospitality. I waited.

'When Opal is upset she doesn't do her best work.'

'None of us does.'

His eyes flashed with something I couldn't pin down before it was gone. 'What happened?' he asked.

'It's not my story to tell; you'll have to ask her.'

He looked at me for a long time before he reluctantly accepted it. 'Is it over now?'

'I'm leaving town tomorrow, Derek.' It wasn't an answer. We both knew that.

'Don't.' He laughed. 'There's plenty to do here. Stay, I'll take you to the races at Aksarben tomorrow and we'll play the ponies. There's one named Princess Kate.' He smiled at me. 'She's favored, seven-to-one. We'll play her for you, and send you home a winner.'

'Midwestern hospitality?'

'Yes.'

It was more than that. He didn't try to hide it; I didn't pretend I hadn't seen it. What else could I win? Or lose? We went dancing and stayed out too late, drank too much, danced too close. I was skating on the thin ice edge of a rebound but knowing it didn't make things any easier. Memories of Hank danced in and out of my mind to a different tune.

'Stay. It'll be fun.'

'I'm in the middle of something. I can't.'

'To hell with it.'

I shook my head, but I was tempted, I won't deny it.

'Rain check?'

I smiled instead of answering because I didn't know the answer. I was het up, stirred up. Was that it?

He held my hands for a long time as we said good night. 'You haven't seen the last of me.'

I was sure I hadn't, but not sure how I felt about it.

Fourteen

Frogs, toads, and salamanders are vanishing around the world. Amphibians have a highly sensitive biology that makes them 'the canary in the coal mine' – an environmental early warning system.
Are we paying attention?

I didn't go to sleep right away, which was just as well, the phone would have woken me up almost immediately. I found it curious, not that it was a late call, but that few people knew where I was. I'd registered in my name though, no secrets there.

The caller got down and dirty right away: no hello, no friendly stuff. So curious was the wrong word for it.

'You the one trying to get that Harnway lady?' The voice was rough, rural, uneducated.

'I'm not trying to get anyone.'

'You the one is the outa town investigator?'

'Yes.'

'And you saw that Harnway person today?'

'Yes.' Curious was definitely the wrong word for it.

'Well, I've got information that'll help you, because she's not good Godfearing folks, she's the Devil.' He pronounced it divil. And maybe, but I didn't see that information like that would be of much help.

'Futurevision.' He made a sound in the back of his throat. 'Only the Lord Has Vision, only the Lord Can Know the Future. It's Blasphemy, that's what it is. Her Judgment Will Come. She Will Be Brought Down.' He spoke in capitals and in tones of doom. He spoke as one seeing the future – exactly what he condemned in Opal. I was tempted, very, to point that out to him. Instead I asked a question.

'Who are you?'

'A Servant of God.' Great. That narrowed it right down.

'What is your name?'

'I remain Nameless, One of the Lord's Faithful.'

'Oh?' Tattletale was what we called it on my side of town. I was silent then, silent and contemptuous.

'Dare Not Ye Mock Me, Woman.'

'Get To The Point,' I spoke in capitals too, 'or I'm hanging up. You do have a point?'

'I have information for you. If you will meet me—' And he started rattling off place names, directions, times.

I interrupted him. 'I'll meet you in the hotel bar in ten minutes.'

'Bar,' he roared, 'a Den of Iniquity and Corruption, the Haven of the Lost and Faithless, the Hell of the Living Doomed and—'

'In the lobby then.'

I had to say it twice to get through his torrent of verbal abuse. My head started to hurt. Derek had been a lot more fun than this. The races, even at a racetrack that sounded like an Indian name but was really only Nebraska spelled backward, would have been too. And the pony named Princess Katy.

He objected to the lobby and started giving instructions again. I sighed. Leaving the hotel after midnight to meet a crazed religious fanatic in a city I didn't know was not number one on my To-Do List. I told him so.

'In the lobby tonight, or somewhere else, somewhere close and reasonable, in the morning.' He ranted and raved for a minute then abruptly agreed to meet me in the lobby in ten minutes. 'How will I recognize you?'

'*I* Will Know *You*,' he said All-Knowingly and hung up.

I pulled on jeans and a sweatshirt, ran my fingers through my hair, then pulled on a smile, not that I thought I'd need it for this occasion. Just as well; it didn't look convincing. I started out with only my key, then headed back for my purse.

The lobby was deserted. Omaha didn't seem to be full of night owls and party animals. I sat next to a potted plant and waited, studying the pastel carpet, the lamps that were cats with shades worn like parasols and the silent reflections of mirrors. After ten minutes I asked a sleepy-eyed night clerk if someone had dropped off anything or left a message for me. He checked, then shook his head. I went into the bar, ordered a draft beer, and watched. Nothing. I drank the rest of my beer and went back upstairs.

I knew as soon as I walked into the room.

There was a faint indefinable scent in the air: men's cologne, or soap, or after shave, nothing I could identify although it seemed familiar. The bedspread was not thrown back quite as I had left it, my briefcase had been moved slightly.

I'd been set up and I'd fallen for it. The place had been tossed, inexpertly at that.

The balcony curtains belled out in a sudden breeze. I pulled them back. Nothing. No one in the bathroom. I shot the deadbolt and thought about calling hotel security, then discarded the idea. They wouldn't believe me and I'd lose sleep looking like a fool – never an appealing choice. Besides, nothing was missing.

Then I thought about what it meant: Somebody wanted to know who I was, what I knew, what kind of trouble I could make, maybe all of the above. Which meant I was on the right track. Good.

If only I knew which track that was.

And which somebody.

I went back to bed and slept neither easily nor well. That was the only thing that wasn't a surprise.

My plane left early the next morning. It was time to get home, time in more ways than one. The office looked the same, a little dustier maybe, and the plants needed watering.

'Hey, doll face.' Mr A. strolled from his office to mine. 'If you could take one thing with you after death, what would it be?'

'Is this another poll?' He nodded. 'I thought the whole point of it was to shuffle off this mortal coil, not drag it along?'

He grinned and shook his head. 'Guess not. Family members and loved ones, twenty-three percent.'

I shuddered. Did the loved ones get any voice in the matter? Would the dead ask the living first, or just include them? What kind of love was that anyway? Not my kind, for sure.

'Pets, seven percent; jewelry, especially wedding bands and mementos, four percent; a favorite chair, one percent.' I imagined a heaven full of La-Z-Boys. Lounging around on clouds is not for everyone, I guess. 'And one kid said a lifetime of pizza.' I nodded. That sounded like the most sensible response to me. Except of course that he would be dead, and dead people don't have lifetimes.

'Thirty-two percent of people hate answering machines and won't leave messages on them.' Tell me! 'And eleven percent think pink flamingos are an elegant addition to a lawn.'

I laughed and started flipping through the Morrell folder. It took me a minute to find what I wanted: the second name and number on the Rolodex card for Garnet Whyte.

'How about you, doll face, a pink flamingo?'

'Okay,' I agreed, 'but no ceramic Bambis, I draw the line there.'

He nodded in agreement. 'Busy?' His voice was a little sad.

I knew he wanted to talk, to goof around. I thought of Garnet alone in her pristine room in the nursing home, and decided that I would find time, make time, soon.

'What has more fiber, a Nature Valley granola bar or a Snickers bar?' His face lit up with anticipation.

I didn't have the heart to burst his balloon; he takes it too hard. 'A head of cauliflower?' His eyes popped open. 'Did anyone want to take cauliflower along after death?'

'Kat,' he chided me. I wasn't being serious enough.

'It's obvious; the granola bar, of course.'

'No. Ha, you're wrong! It's the *Snickers* bar.'

I shook my head in apparent disbelief, picked up the phone and started punching buttons. He headed out the door waving. I waved back. A soft voice answered after two rings.

I read off the Rolodex card. 'Mary Ellen Webster, please.'

'Speaking.'

I identified myself and said I was calling on behalf of the family of Garnet Whyte. 'Herb Sanderson died suddenly several days ago and many of his records are presently unavailable,' I improvised. 'We find ourselves with, uh, a difficult situation and not a great deal of information. I was hoping you could help us sort a few things out until all the records are located and available?'

'Oh my, my. Dear me.' Mary Ellen Webster paused and sighed. 'Yes, I could do that.' There was a reluctant note in her voice. 'I don't mind helping; it's not that. It's just that she was one of the difficult ones, difficult to think about and to remember; in fact, I've done my best to forget. All right,' she said impatiently, her mind made up. 'Can you get here soon?' She gave me an address in Stockton.

'Forty-five minutes, maybe an hour.'

'Yes. All right.'

We hung up and I wished briefly, futilely, that I'd had a chance to eat, exercise, change my clothes, and wind up my brain, which felt like a child's unwound wind-up toy. No such game plan.

It was an older two-bedroom house, light pink and covered with red climbing roses, on a quiet street in Stockton, and I found it easily. A pretty, plumpish woman of about sixty answered the door. Her smooth face was unlined; she had a pale creamy complexion, calm eyes, and docile permed hair. There was a slight tremble in her hands. Her only jewelry was a wedding band.

'Come in. You're Kat, of course.'

'Yes. Thank you for seeing me, Mrs Webster.'

Her eyes met mine. 'I hope I can help. I can never

quite get that poor, dear woman out of my mind.'

'You knew Garnet Whyte well?'

'Oh yes. She stayed here with me for five years. My health and strength are not now what they once were and I had to stop home health care. Garnet went from me to her present situation. At least I assume it's the same?'

'Perhaps not. She referred to her last situation as dark and horrible, with poor food, cold water, and bad people. It could not have been here.' At least I hoped so.

'Poor dear,' Mrs Webster said. 'That was years ago, but it is still very real to her, very much a nightmare. And understandably so,' she added.

'What is wrong with her? Physical problems?'

'No. Garnet is mentally and emotionally unstable, but even that is not extreme. With care and treatment, possibly drug therapy, she could have been helped, could have become independent, especially at a younger age. I discussed it several times with Mr Sanderson.'

She shook her head. 'I have never seen him so angry, so *very* angry as when I explained it first. He said that he agreed with me absolutely but that her relative did not, and would only make funds available and give permission for custodial and medical care, not for treatment and rehabilitation. It made him very angry. He was a good man.'

'You both felt that a normal, or more normal, life was possible for Garnet?'

'Oh yes, absolutely. In cases like this the life a patient is compelled to lead is a major part of the problem. There was nothing really wrong with her, or no more so than many people who manage to get by, to live quiet, decent, ordinary lives.'

I was shocked and my face must have said so.

'It was very sad. Come,' she said, putting a hand on my elbow, 'sit down. We needn't stand here and talk.' She closed the door and led the way into the front room, a room filled with overstuffed furniture and china figurines. It did not feel crowded but cozy and welcoming. I moved carefully though, I'm not good around breakables, and sank into a sofa.

'She is too old now, I suppose, for a change in her life style to make any difference?'

'Old? My no. Why, Garnet can't be more than forty, a bit less, I think. And it's never too late, dear, never. Why, I've seen—'

'Forty?' I stared at her in disbelief. Were we talking about the same person? 'The woman I met was in her sixties, older than you.'

'Yes, that is what is so tragic. And perhaps, inside, she is older than I. It is a dreadful thing what a life like that will do to you. Dreadful. I do not know how the person who made those decisions about her care could live with herself. I do not know at all.'

'Forty?' I sounded like a demented parrot but I couldn't help myself. 'Forty!'

'Not even,' she said. 'Thirty-eight or nine.'

I remembered the slim unlined hands, the smooth

pretty neck. In my mind I tossed color back into her hair, light into her eyes, life and strength into her body. It could be; it was possible.

And it blew my mind.

'Has she ever borne a child?'

Mary Ellen's face froze over, then again came to life. 'However would you have known that?' I didn't know, yet. I was beginning to, beginning to put it together. 'Yes. We found out with the second pregnancy.'

'Garnet had two children?'

'No. One child, one pregnancy that ended in abortion. It was the cold, dark place.' Her calm eyes met mine and were unreadable. 'She was raped by a male orderly, perhaps two. She would never speak of it.'

I heard Paige's voice in my mind. *I hate her. I hate, hate, hate her.* And Opal's. A different voice, yet the same hate. I no longer thought it extreme. I heard it in my heart now and echoing in my mind. We sat in silence for a while and I listened to the sounds of hatred. They were not pretty.

'We will have some lemonade,' Mrs Webster said firmly.

'All right,' I agreed. 'Thank you.'

'Is Garnet doing well now?' she asked after lemonade and casual conversation.

'I don't know. She is healthy, and she seemed reasonably content. She has music, and flowers, and said the food was good.'

'Mr Sanderson called me a little while ago to ask my advice. He said that he was now Garnet's sole trustee, that her relative had died, and that he wished for changes, for something better for her. He said that he had spoken with her and that she refused, that she was afraid, afraid of life, and change, and anything new.'

'What did you say; what did you advise?'

'I didn't. I told him I was sorry, but I could not, and that he should speak to someone more qualified than I.'

'Did Garnet ever speak of her past, her childhood?'

'Only when—' She broke off. 'No.'

'Did she ever use another name?'

She looked at me steadily for a long time. Outside a car door opened and closed, a child wailed for his mother. 'They drugged her heavily and regularly at the other place, the Bad Place, she called it. I took her off the drugs but it was a long process and a difficult one. Her withdrawal was both physical and emotional and there were many nights when she couldn't sleep. I used to hold her hand for hours, stroke her forehead, try to calm her. Then she would speak of her youth.'

'Tell me.'

'No.'

'Please. I am trying to help.'

'It would be a betrayal. Garnet spoke of it only with the drugs, never the other times when I asked her. Then she always refused. She thanked me for my kindness and told me she loved me and that she was sorry not to answer something I asked but she couldn't, and would I please not ask her again. And so I didn't. I loved her too. She was a kind, gentle person.'

'Herb is dead and there is no one who loves her now. No one but you.' I was hitting hard, hitting beneath the belt. It wasn't fair but I didn't stop. 'She needs that love, that help. Now more than ever.'

She stared at her lemonade. I guess it was easier than looking at me. 'I believe that you are trying to help. I even believe that it would be better if it were spoken, but I will not do it. Garnet has been betrayed many times, by many people, and I will not be one of them.'

'If I say the names?'

Silence.

'Florence.'

Her eyes were deep and unreadable.

'Opal and Ruby. The baby was Pearl. Was there a boy's name? I don't know it and I need to.'

There were haunted pictures in her eyes. 'Have you finished your lemonade? You must go now.'

'All right.'

'Yes,' she whispered. 'Yes, those were the ones.'

I nodded. One was a dim reflection of the other: a garnet and a ruby.

It had taken me too long to figure it out.

Fifteen

Women overwhelmingly believe that a violent reaction to a threatening situation is acceptable but initiating violence is not. Men find both acceptable. Men often do not define verbal, emotional, or psychological attack as violence.

Garnet was standing with her back to me looking out the window when I knocked on her door. She didn't turn, she didn't say anything. Her back seemed to tense.

'Good morning.'

'Hello.' She turned, then smiled. 'It's you again.'

Nothing was changed. The magazine still hadn't been opened, the bed was neatly made, the curtains pulled. I handed her a box of chocolates and a CD of Strauss waltzes. 'It's too late for tulips, unless you want silk ones.'

'Oh no, I like real ones.' She smiled, then laughed. She looked younger now, but not thirty-eight, not even forty-eight.

'Ruby.'

The smile faded, her eyes went blank. She turned

173

and looked out the window again.

'I can see roses from here. I like them, but not as much as tulips.'

'Ruby, Florence is dead. Didn't Herb tell you? Your mother can't hurt you now, or tell you what to do. She's dead.'

'The yellow ones are my favorites. The different colors mean something, you know, in the language of flowers. I used to know but I can't remember now.'

I reached out and touched her arm. 'Florence can't hurt you now, or make you feel sad.'

'Yes.' She whispered it.

'No. She's dead.'

'All my life, she said. I was so bad that I would be punished for ever and ever. She said so that night, and she would, she has.'

'She's dead, Ruby. Things will be different now. Herb told you that.'

'No. Forever. So bad, she said, evil.' Her voice was dead.

'What was?'

She reached for the candy I'd brought. 'Chocolates are good, and music. It makes me forget.'

'Forget what, Ruby?'

'The pictures. Later I wanted to lie under the flowered blanket with him. That was as it should be.' Her face got secretive and sly. 'The baby. There was the baby. She didn't get everything. She thought she did, but she didn't. I was too smart. I hid it. She made me watch it burn, but it wasn't everything.

Someday maybe I'll have it again.'

I was silent. I didn't know where, or how, to try to start untangling this. And I knew that there are some things that can never be untangled, no matter where, no matter how.

'Chocolates are good. They make you forget.' She pulled the wrapper off the CD and put it in the player, turned the music on, ate another chocolate.

'Ruby.'

'Can't you get my name right?' She said it crossly and reached for another chocolate.

'It's Ruby Morrell, isn't it, not Garnet Whyte?'

'Chocolates make you forget.' She ate another chocolate, amped up the volume on the music, and turned her chair so that her back was to me.

'Ruby, let's talk about this.'

She turned up the volume again.

'Ruby.'

And again.

Who are you to play God? her sister Opal had shouted at me, and who was I indeed?

I left.

I stood in the nondescript front yard gulping in air for a moment, then climbed in the Bronco and drove fast. Speeding clears my mind, sort of. I should have called ahead, but to hell with it. I slowed down on the levee road, then stopped and got out where I could watch the river eddying and flowing, throw stones and watch them sink. And wonder why life wasn't fair.

I was walking on eggs now and I knew it. One of them, at least, was already cracked.

Paul was in the driveway at the front of the river house buffing out his BMW and his tan. Both looked pretty good, although the scowl didn't improve Paul's looks any. I guess I'd have to go with the BMW

'What do you want?'

He was a class act, no getting around it.

'Good morning. Is Paige around?' I didn't see her car, so I assumed she wasn't.

'She's out in the orchards, her and Wiley. Won't be back until after lunch. I'm in charge,' he said aggressively.

'That's nice.' I started for the house.

'Hey!'

'I've got a few things to check out. Paige knows.'

'Fuck you do.'

'You giving orders now, Paul?' I asked pleasantly. He flushed a deep red. 'Thought so. I'm going to use the phone too.' Added insult. His hands and jaw clenched up and he gritted his teeth slightly. Macho buttons are pathetically easy to push.

Inside it was still and cool. I stood in the entryway and let the feeling of the house settle around me, wondering if the hatefulness of Florence and the abhorrence she generated had settled into the wainscoting, the Oriental rugs, and the heavy mahogany furniture. I couldn't tell. There was nothing in the air but the faint scent of potpourri and furniture wax. The door opened and something breathing heavily and smelling like sweaty male stood behind me. I sighed and turned around.

'Look,' he said, 'I know you're just trying to do your job.'

'You got it.'

'But I'm worried. About Paige,' he added. I believed him. He looked worried. He also looked mad.

'She's not thinking straight. Look,' he said, waving his hand. 'Here all this comes to her. No problems, no questions. And she keeps digging up shit. You dig up shit and what do you find?' His voice had a despairing quality.

More shit presumably. I shook my head and let him answer his own question.

'You *don't know*,' he wailed. 'Look.' He made his voice sound reasonable. 'It's like those pictures, right? Well, there are two girls there. So who are they? Florence's daughters, right? And one's Paige's mother. And who's the other and where is she, and suppose she wants a piece of the action, a chunk of all this? Or maybe she gets it all? How about that?'

'How about it?'

'Well, I think this had better be stopped right now. What we don't know can't hurt us.' Us. It wasn't just Paige he was concerned about, the cash register bell was ringing for Paul too. 'What we find out could hurt, and hurt bad.'

'You're thinking of money and property?'

'Yes.' He looked at me, stony-faced. 'What else is there?'

'Paige wants to find out about her family, her history. She needs to settle questions in her mind and heart.'

He scratched his head and thought about it. The odor from his armpit wafted in my direction. I stepped back slightly.

'That's bullshit.'

'To you maybe, not to Paige.'

'Money, property, this—' he gestured again '—is what counts. Look, do you have any idea what a fuckin' mess this could be?'

'Yes.'

Far better than he, since I had met Opal and Ruby. I knew what we were facing; he was just guessing. I knew, too, that it would be Paige's decision, not mine or Paul's. Maybe it wasn't even hers anymore. Maybe it had gone too far. I didn't waste my breath on Paul; he wouldn't understand, and if he did, he wouldn't care. Number one was what, who, he cared about; number one was Paul.

'Look, for Paige's sake I think we ought to drop this. I'm thinking about *her*, dammit, *her* interest, *her*—' his inspiration faded briefly, 'her *happiness*. Sometimes when people don't do the right stuff, make the right choices, you have to choose for them. Sometimes.' He muttered something I couldn't catch, wasn't supposed to hear. 'Sometimes, and this is one of those times.'

I shook my head. 'That only works for kids.' And then Ruby crossed my mind, filled it, and made it stumble. 'Not for adults,' I finished finally.

He heard the stumble, eyed me, and calculated. 'Not for *most* adults, but she's emotionally unstable now. We've got to protect her.'

I wondered if someone had said that about Ruby once. I thought of her bare, tidy room, the spill of sunlight on the linoleum floor, the muted sounds of Strauss on the CD player, the light gone out in her eyes.

'Hey, look, I'm sorry. We started off wrong and I haven't handled this well, I know. I'm not really a jerk.'

He shrugged and smiled and flashed sex appeal my way. I saw it then, what it was that caught Paige and held her love and attention. I thought of Hank.

'And I really do care about her and want the best for her. This scares me for her, Kat, scares me a lot. We've got to protect her. It's our *duty*.'

'Not our.' I didn't like the fact that we were suddenly on a first-name basis.

'Mine.'

I shrugged his emotional appeal off. 'Do what you have to do, Paul. I will too. I was hired to do a job. Why don't you get out of my way so I can do it?'

He put his hand on my arm. I could smell car wax now, too, as well as unwashed male. The car wax smelled better. I shook his hand off.

'We could cut a deal.'

'No. We couldn't.' We were back to dollars; my sympathy faded.

'Wait, slow down, at least hear me out.'

He smiled a smile that twisted his lips around into a grimace, put his hand back on my arm. Slow learner. I shook the hand off again.

'No.'

'Hey! Wait, you're doing a job, right?' He waited for an assent I didn't bother to give. 'Well, of course you are, right? And a job is for money, that's why we all work, money. So if a better job comes along, you know, more money, why we drop the first job and go for the second job, the one with more money. Of course.' He shrugged his muscle-boy shoulders. 'Naturally. It's human nature. Money talks, right?'

'There's more to that saying.'

'Huh?'

'Bullshit walks.'

'You turning me down?' His voice got ugly.

'You figured it out. What a guy, what a mind.'

'Just like that: no discussion, no how much, no nothing?'

'Just like that.'

'You want to know what else I got to say?'

'No.'

'You're going to hear it, lady. Listen up.'

I listened, I smelled. Under stress his armpits were really stepping up production. 'First I asked you nicely because I'm a nice guy.'

I laughed.

He got more dangerous-looking.

'Nice guys don't play road tag with their pickups on the wrong side of a levee road, Paul.'

He flushed hotly. '*No way* you can pin that on me. I never—'

It was an admission; we both knew it. He shook his head like a slow-witted and maddened bear.

'Hey, first I made you a good offer, lady, now I'm just telling you: Lay off; take a vacation; get out of town. And fast if you know what's good for you.'

He pulled his face into a sneer, leaned forward and blasted me with body odor. I stepped back and he laughed gleefully.

'That's better; that's more like it.'

'Paul.'

'Huh?'

'Your deodorant's letting you down. Badly. You might want to try another brand.'

He glared at me, his eyes narrow nasty slits. 'Fuck you, lady, I'll get you. One way or the other, I'll get you.' He pivoted on his heel and walked out, slamming the door shut behind him. The old house absorbed the noise, let it die. Me too.

Then I looked around and wondered where a teenage girl would hide something. When I was a kid, I'd never had anything worth hiding. In her bedroom? There were four of them. I picked up the phone and dialed. I had to fight with the receptionist but she finally put me through.

'What do you want?' Today the fear was gone; Opal

181

sounded angry. 'I told you not to call!'

'If Ruby had hidden something, where would it be?'

'What?'

'Where was your sister's hiding place for things as a kid?'

'What are you talking about?'

'Which word don't you understand, Opal?'

Silence.

'Opal?'

'God, I never should have started this. I never should have talked with Herb. Never. It went against my better judgment but I couldn't help myself. I shouldn't be talking to you now.' Her words came in spurts, her breath in gasps. 'Death does that to you, I guess.'

'Does what?'

'Screws up your better judgment. When Herb called, it all came back. After all these years I was stunned that it could be so strong. He said Florence was dead and tried to get me to come back, to believe it could be different. But it's not, it can't be. He said he had things he wanted to talk to me about, but it's too late. I shouldn't have let the past grab me again.'

'You can't help it; it's still there.'

'No.' But she whispered it.

'What happened to Ruby, Opal?'

'I told you. Ruby died a long time ago, and that was the last time I spoke with Florence. After that I didn't want anything more to do with her. Not ever. And I haven't. Why should her death change my mind?'

'Not her death, your niece.' She didn't say anything. 'Who was the oldest twin?'

'My sister,' she said at last, 'Ruby.' But her voice shook.

'Have you seen the will? The estate—'

'I don't care.' Her voice was despairing now. 'I don't care about any of it, the house, the money, the estate. I don't want it, I don't ever want it or anything back there again. Ever. If I lived to be a hundred I wouldn't want it. I'd rather eat shit and die than— Oh, God, I wish I could burn yesterday's memories like today's trash. I wish I could. I wish, I wish. That's why I deal with the future, you know; I hate the past . . .'

'Which was Ruby's room?'

'Room? Her bedroom?' Her voice trembled.

'Yes.'

'Top floor, southwest corner. It was a small one but light. She loved the light.'

I thought of the cold, dark place, the Bad Place.

'Where would she have hidden things?'

'I don't know.'

'You were twins; you know.'

'No, I don't. I—' She was silent. I wondered if I'd gone too far. 'Leave me alone now. Please.'

'What about your niece?'

'I don't have any family, not anymore, Ms

183

Colorado. That was all dead to me long ago; it died with Ruby.' She hung up.

The bedroom on the southwest corner was flooded with light, the windows overlooking the backyard, the orchard, and the flowers. It took me a while but I found the hiding place. I went through the furniture quickly though I didn't think it was there; someone would have found it long before this. The walls were papered in pale old-fashioned paper with lath and plaster underneath. Nothing there. The floor was knotty pine, worn and solid. Except in the closet.

There I found a loose floorboard.

And nails that could be pried out.

And the cache.

Sixteen

43% of Americans believe in love at first sight; 65% believe that love is one of the most important things in life; 8% believe that love lasts.

Charity was sitting on my front steps drinking Cokes and eating Oreos. It was not a good sign. There were two crumpled Coke cans tossed on the lawn in front of her.

'Hi.'

She grinned at me. 'Am I in time for dinner?'

'Will you have room for it?' I looked at the pop cans, the candy wrappers, the half-empty bag of cookies. 'Is everything okay, Charity?'

'Mmrmph.' Her mouth was full.

'What's this all about?' I looked at her and the junk food debris.

'I love to litter; it makes me feel wild and reckless.'

'Not that.' I started picking up trash. 'Sweets. Are you okay?'

'Sure. I was just having a snack until you got here and we could have dinner. I brought Chinese food, all right?'

'Wonderful. I'm starving and glad you're here.' I hugged her. 'I need your help.'

She scooped up her Coke and followed me inside. 'Okay. Kat, do you think I should get married?'

'Not unless you've learned a lot since I last saw you. Your choice in men is terrible.' I thought about Brandon, the class-A jerk who was her last boyfriend. 'Worse than terrible even.'

She looked shocked. 'You can't mean Al?'

'No, I don't know him well enough.' I put the things I was carrying on the kitchen table, washed my hands, and got plates and utensils out. 'Wine?'

'Sure.'

'You don't either.'

'I don't what?'

'Know him well enough.'

'It's very intense. I think it's meant to be.'

'Get real. Next you'll tell me your initials are written together in the concrete of a celestial sidewalk somewhere.'

'What a sweet way to put it!' She sighed happily. 'Yes, that's just what I mean. Shall I warm up the food?'

'I was being sarcastic, Charity.'

She stuck her finger in the take-out box: 'Maybe a little,' loaded up the microwave and pushed buttons. 'Sixty seconds?'

Forget the food, I thought she should warm up her brain. I cleared my throat. *'Dear Charity, I just met this wonderful guy. It was shooting stars, firecrackers, and bells ringing. I think it's love at first sight and we should get married. What do you think?* Signed, *Madly in Love.'*

The microwave beeped and Charity unloaded the food. I continued. *'Dear Madly, It sounds like the Fourth of July, which is very different from love. Slow down. If it's the real thing it will be there next week, next month, and next year.* Signed, *Charity.'*

'I suppose you think you're clever?'

I grinned. I did actually. That was pretty much word-for-word a Dear Charity letter in this morning's paper. Charity dumped the food out of the cartons and banged it down on the table, looking annoyed.

'You guys just met.'

'We had lunch and dinner and stayed up all night talking.' She blushed. 'And stuff. Want some of this, Kat?'

'Sure. You've only been widowed a year or so, Charity. Take your time; enjoy getting to know a lot of people.' We ate in silence for a while.

She broke it. 'I called Hank today. I needed to ask him about something.'

'What?'

'Police procedure on runaways. I told him you looked run-down and unhappy.'

'I wish you'd mind your own business.'

'Okay.'

She helped herself to the rest of the almond chicken. I sat and stared stupidly at a green pepper congealing in sauce.

'What did he say?' I asked finally.

'Hmmm? Oh, Hank.' She started in greedily on the rest of the fried rice. 'That it has been real hot in Vegas, that he was working a lot of overtime, and—'

'Charity.' I said it in a dangerous tone of voice.

'He told me to mind my own business too, only he was nicer about it.' She speared a water chestnut and grinned. 'Want my advice, Kat? You don't even have to write in for it.'

'No.' I started clearing the table.

'Read your fortune.' She handed me a cookie.

I broke it open, eating as I read, 'An out-of-town visitor will arrive soon.'

'Ha,' said Charity. 'I rest my case. Mine says: "Expect a proposal." Well, well,' she said smugly.

'Charity, it's only a fortune cookie.' She smiled in a maddeningly knowing way. 'Has Al proposed?'

'No.' She shook her head, still smug. 'Not yet.' Even smugger.

'Good. At least one of you has some sense.'

I finished clearing off the table, emptied things out of the brown paper grocery bag, wished that thoughts of Hank would go away and that—

'Kat, what is this? And is it old, or just dirty?'

'Old. Well, both.' It looked fragile and crumbly.

'What is it?'

'A yearbook, a diary, and—'

'I see that. I mean, what *is* it?'

'A case: the partial record of people's lives before they got tangled and messed up.'

'You sound like an enigmatic, run-on fortune cookie.'

She opened the diary at random. No, not at random; there was a flower pressed there, dull, brown, and dried now.

'Dear Diary, Today I met a boy. He was kind and sweet and said that he liked me, that he had for a long time but he didn't know how to meet me. He gave me a flower and asked if he could walk with me. I said he could. I know I must not and cannot tell Mother of this. It's not just that she would be angry with me but she would make trouble for the boy and his family. His name is Jose and he is not our kind. She would never forgive me.'

Charity looked at me. 'It's not right, somehow, reading this. It was not meant for our eyes, for anyone's but the writer's.'

'No.' I agreed with her; it wasn't right.

I would read it though, all of it. I had to. But later, after Charity had gone.

He said he loved me today. We held hands down by the river and he said it. Nobody's ever said it to me before. Opal loves me and I love her but we just know it in our hearts and everything and don't have to say it. Uncle Herb and Aunt Letitia love us, I know, because of the way they are and the nice things they do for us. Uncle Herb said our daddy loved us but I don't remember him. I used to wish Mother would say it, but now I don't. I know she won't.

Outside I heard the sirens of fire engines and then a dog started howling. Ranger shifted uneasily at my feet, then laid his chin on my foot. The nameless kitten sat on my lap and pounced on my fingers as I turned pages. Everything in me wanted to stop reading this, not just because of Ruby's pain, but because of mine.

We went walking today, down by the river again. I let him kiss and touch me. Opal knows of course. She says it's wrong and I must stop but she will never tell on me. I tell her it's not wrong, it's good, but in my heart I know she's right. I can't stop. Love is nice.

I stood up, the kitten mewling fretfully, and walked to the kitchen. The young Ruby was alive and real to me – I almost expected to see her at the kitchen table. I drank a glass of water. It wasn't enough. I poured a glass of wine. But that Ruby was gone years ago, gone leaving only this trace. I gulped the wine down faster than I meant to and filled the glass again.

Today I think I have done wrong, very wrong. I didn't mean to, do wrong, I mean. I meant to do right, I meant just to please him. He said if I loved him I should prove it. But I have, I do. He said no, that wasn't enough, it had to be more, he had to really know. Is that right? Should you have to prove it always? And over again? Should you? Shouldn't love just be enough? But I guess it isn't. I let him take the pictures.

Pictures. There was only one and it was stuck into

the back of the diary. The girl was one of the twins, Ruby, I thought; the boy, I assumed was Jose. He was a good-looking boy, tall, slim, with lots of dark hair and a big smile. He had his arm loosely but protectively draped around the girl's shoulder. She was pretty, with a full figure, long hair that was tossed back, and a sleeveless dress that showed shapely arms. Her eyes were large and beautiful. They were both smiling happily into the camera. It was a good picture, sharp and clear.

The phone rang and startled me, jumped me across years and lives in a heartbeat. I almost didn't answer it but Ruby, Ruby was on my mind.

'Kat, it's Paige.'

Damn, damn, *damn*. I wasn't ready yet, hadn't figured it out yet.

'It's late, I know. I hope it's okay to call. I just couldn't wait any longer, though I'm trying to be patient. What have you found out?'

How to answer that? I found your aunt who doesn't want anything to do with you or the family. I found the woman I believe is your mother who should look like your aunt but doesn't; she looks like Herbert Hoover's aunt. I found parts of the past that maybe nobody wants to see in the light and might come, may inevitably come out if we keep digging up stuff. I found relatives who could come in between you and what you think is your ranch, your inheritance. I've found things that could give you nightmares for years to come, that could trip you up

191

not just in the dark but in the sunshine and daylight.

'Kat?'

'Sorry, Paige, I was distracted.' The kitten had followed me to the phone and was climbing up my leg. That was okay, I was still wearing jeans. We were going to have to change his MO before summer and shorts, though. 'Have you ever had a kitten? I'd forgotten—'

'You haven't found anything out yet, is that what you're telling me?'

That wasn't it, no, not exactly.

'I have, Paige, but it's in bits and pieces, it's not together yet.'

'Tell me.' Her voice was eager, excited. She sounded young and vulnerable. The kitten reached my thigh and dug in. I winced, picked him off and stuck him on my shoulder. Then I poured another glass of wine. It was that kind of night: Pour 'em, pound 'em.

'Not yet, Paige, I don't have a clear picture. Give me a few more days.'

'No!' she wailed into the phone. 'Tell me now. *Now!*'

The kitten jumped from my shoulder to the counter and started exploring. I put him on the floor and he started up my jeans again.

'Kat—'

'In a few days, Paige. As soon as I can, I will. As soon as I put it together.'

We talked for a long time, long enough for me to

convince her, but I didn't, I just held her off and hung up. Then I poured another glass of wine. I have a hard time playing God. I didn't want to do it, and I certainly didn't want to do it sober. I was back to walking on eggs. Ruby's was cracked, badly. Opal's? I thought about the competent businesswoman. No, not yet. Could it be cracked? Maybe. I didn't know, I couldn't tell. Ditto Paige. Then there was Paul, hard-boiled but potentially violent and easily provoked.

I remembered Herb Sanderson's comments about secrets and the past and Pandora's box; I understood them far better now. And I wished dearly for his compassionate, levelheaded advice.

Sometimes, when you open the window into what went before, things crumble in the light and air like ancient Egyptian artifacts, become harmless dust in your hands, easily, readily blown away. Or the memories, sweet, even bittersweet, jump out and entertain you, thrill you, tease you with their illusive, dancing quality. And sometimes there are skeletons, threads of flesh, sinew, and hair clinging still. It's worse if the maggots are there and the rotten sweet smell of decay fills your nostrils and brain.

I was pretty sure I spotted maggots.

And smelled something funny.

Seventeen

16% of people see heredity as the deter-mining factor in behavior; 12% believe it is environment and 67% believe it is a combination of both; the rest believe it is God, the Devil, or Chance.

I started early and was back in Herb's river town by eight-thirty. I was betting that his next-door neighbor Lottie Shepler was up and at it with the early birds. I won. She opened the door as I walked up the path, her eyes bright and inquisitive.

'You've come back for more tea?' She smiled at me.

'Really for more information.'

'Oh.' But she knew that. 'Of course. Come in, dear, I'll put the kettle on.'

'Please don't bother. If I could just ask you a few questions?'

'It's no bother. Come in.' Her hands plucked eagerly at me; a lonely little note in her voice like a far-away bird cry. 'It's no bother at all.'

I followed her into the kitchen and watched her fuss around, a fidgety little bird, hunting and pecking. It seemed impolite to bring up business before she finished arranging the delicate, floral teacups and pouring the tea. She offered me coffee cake, too, but I declined.

'Well, dear?' she asked finally, after we got caught up on the neighborhood news, the weather, and her health.

'I have another photograph.'

'Yes?' Her eyes lit up. 'Oh.' She expelled a breath hard and fast as I handed it to her. 'That's Opal, or Ruby.'

'Ruby, I think.'

'And that's the boy?'

'I was hoping you could tell me.'

'No.' She shook her head regretfully. 'I never saw him, you see. I heard the talk, but there wasn't even much of that, not before, anyway. And afterwards,' she shrugged, 'well, you know, I told you.'

'Can you think of anybody who might recognize the boy, might know his name? Perhaps classmates of hers?'

'Perhaps.' She sounded doubtful. 'Ruby and Opal kept pretty much to themselves, although that was probably Florence's doing. Heaven knows what they would have been like on their own. Of course I wouldn't have known their friends anyway. The yearbook? The school keeps all the old yearbooks, you know. Maybe that would help?'

It was a reasonable suggestion. I'd thought of it too and gone through it the night before. Jose, if the boy in the photo was Jose, wasn't in it and there were no inscriptions that sounded personal and close. Just teenage clichés: *Ruby, you're a jewel!* and *Roses are red / violets are blue / you're a great pal / and that's really true.* Eat your heart out, Wordsworth. *Hope you have a great life and all your dreams come true!* That one hit me hard. It was a simple wish but a formidable achievement, and one out of Ruby's reach. I'd put the yearbook away. I might go back to it but it wasn't the most promising lead I had. Mentally I looked up and down a few dead ends. Next most promising, perhaps.

'Where could I find Bud Waters?'

Curiosity lit up her eyes. 'Why would you want Bud?'

'Does he live around here?' I followed her lead and answered a question with a question.

'Yes, but it's right difficult to find the Waters' place. You'd be better off catching him at the shop, he's there most of the time anyway. That's just down the road a piece.' She answered my unspoken question. 'He fixes heavy equipment, farm equipment. He's the best around,' she added.

I thanked her, finished my tea, and started to get up. 'You'll come back?' she asked wistfully. 'For tea? You don't have to have a reason.' She pulled at my heart. The lonely ones do.

'I'll come hack,' I assured her.

I found Bud Waters' shop easily though I thought at first there was no one there. The shop was large, dusty, and dirty. Bud, when I located him under a tractor, was too.

'Bud?'

'Yup. What can I do you for?' I heard the sounds of metal against metal, saw one of his legs move, then there was silence. I looked at the dirt and grease on the floor beside him. Not too bad. I looked at my jeans. Not too good. Down I went.

'Hey.' Bud looked up. My head was under the tractor and I was propped up on my elbows. 'My name's Kat Colorado. I'm the one who almost got run off the road by the pickups the other evening.'

He looked at me more closely. 'Yeah, so you are. How you doing?'

'I'm talking again.'

He grinned. 'Yeah, you are. Hell of a deal. You ever figure it out?'

I had, yes: Paul and a buddy and their idea of persuasion, of sweet talk. That was a lot of beans to spill, too many, so I didn't answer. I asked a question instead. 'You said to look you up if I ever needed anything?'

'You bet, what can I do you for?' He put down a crescent wrench and picked up a can of Liquid Wrench.

'It's a long shot, for sure, but I've got a photograph and I'm hoping you can help me figure out who's in it.'

He grunted, whacked something, grunted again. 'Lemme get outa here. I'm about ready to take a break anyway.' He went through the whacking and grunting routine again, then slid out. Me too, without the whacks and grunts.

There was a Coke machine in one corner of the shop and he headed for it, wiping his hands on his pants and his forehead on his sleeve. 'Coke?'

'Yeah, diet. Thanks.' I started searching for quarters.

'Diet.' He said it with disgust. 'You modern girls. Ain't nothing wrong with a bit of plump.' He squinted at me. 'And you ain't even close. Naw.' He shook his head at my proferred quarters and handed me a diet Coke. 'You modern girls. It ain't much of a drink, but I'm buying. Pull up a chair' – he sat on a forklift and waved at the flatbed of a truck – 'and lemme see your picture.' He stuck out a hand, looked at it, wiped it on his pants, stuck it out again. I handed the photograph over.

He looked at it for a long time, then grunted. 'Old one?'

'Yes.'

'How old?'

'Twenty years and maybe then some.'

Another grunt. 'Thought so.' He took a slug of Coke, burped, wiped his mouth on the back of his hand. "Scuse. I'd say it's one of them Morrell girls. Pretty damn for sure I'd say. It don't quite do her justice, it don't. They was pretty ones, all right.'

'Which one, can you tell?'

He laughed at me. 'You know anything at all about

it, you know I can't. You know anything at all about
it, you know hardly no one could.' He handed me
back the picture but I made no move to take it.

'What about the boy, Bud?'

'Huh? Don't know. Looks like a Mex, don't he?' I
shrugged. 'My boy might know. He went to school
with the twins, maybe a year, maybe two ahead. He's
out getting parts, should be back any minute. You
want to wait?'

I nodded. I did, for sure. He finished his Coke,
crumpled the can, tossed it into a trash barrel
twenty-five feet away. A long shot, but he made it.
Of course he'd had practice. I did the same and I
hadn't been practicing.

'Hey, skinny lady, want another one?' He grinned
at me.

'Why not?' I said. 'What the hell, you're buying.'

He laughed. 'You got that right. Hey, you a
married lady?' I shook my head. 'Spoken for?' I
nodded. I saw it coming and it was easier to lie. It's
the long shots; they do it every time.

'Too damn bad. Junior could use a class lady like
you.'

On cue a buffed-out red Ford pickup, vintage
about 1958, pulled into the shop. Junior climbed out.
He was a younger, cleaner, not-quite-as-cute version
of his dad.

'Hey, Pop.' Junior eyed me.

'Hey, Junior, you git it?'

'I got it.'

'Good. Junior, this here is Kat. She's doing a history project and wants a speck of help. I'm going back to work.'

Junior had the same winning grin, the same wide smile. 'Yeah? What can I do you for, miss?' The same vocabulary and turn of phrase, too.

I handed him the picture. He stared at it, then whistled. 'Well, I'll be damned. I'll be goddamned. It's one of the Morrell girls, ain't it?'

I nodded. 'Which one?'

'Don't know. Couldn't nobody keep them apart.'

'And the boy?'

'Don't know for sure. There was talk, though. Talk that Ruby was stepping out with a Mex. He was a farmhand, or his daddy was. In those days it was something, more than it is today. Hell, today I spose anything goes.' He looked at me. 'So that would make it Ruby, right?'

'Yes, I think so. What was the boy's name?'

His face darkened into a scowl. 'Mendez. Jose Mendez, I think it was.'

'Can you tell me about him, Junior?'

'Why?' His face was closed now, emotionless. 'It's a long time ago, it ain't worth dragging up.'

'Maybe it is. Ruby's daughter has a stake in it, in knowing.'

'Maybe, maybe not. Some things you're better off not asking, not knowing.'

Yes. It could have been the theme song of this investigation, but I was in it too far to back down now.

201

'Some things you have to ask and, when you're grown, you have a right to know.'

He ducked his head; it stuck in his craw. 'Okay,' he said at last, reluctantly. I waited. 'There was talk. You see he was a good-looking boy and the girls fell for him, girls who shoulda known better.'

'Mexican girls?'

'Yeah, some. Some others, too. There was talk of Ruby as well. I never believed it of her. I never did. She was a real nice girl. They both were, those twins, everyone liked 'em. They took after their pa, the saying was, not after Mrs Morrell. Those girls were just good-hearted down-home folks.' He looked at the photo again, then handed it back to me.

'And Jose, what was he?'

'He was no good. I ain't prejudiced,' he said hastily. 'I ain't. His family still lives around here and they're well spoke of. Real well. But not him. Nobody had a good word for him then, I don't imagine they do now.'

'Is he still around?'

He shook his head. 'He left town around the same time the girls did. After, maybe. I ain't never heard of him since.'

'What kind of boy was he?'

'No good, I said.'

'What's no good?'

'He was always chasing after the girls. Dropped out of school, wouldn't hold a steady job. Oh, he'd work all right, work hard, make some good money, then he'd quit. He was a drinker, too, and there was

202

talk he gambled. I don't know about that.'

'Did you ever see him and Ruby together?'

'I wouldn't know about that. Nothing.' His face closed over. If he did know, I wasn't going to hear it; Ruby was a local girl and I was an outsider.

'Do you know where I could find the Mendezes, Junior?'

'I can figure it out, I reckon. Hey, Pop.'

They hollered back and forth across the shop, Bud under the tractor again. Junior got it figured out and gave me directions. I thanked him and hollered in Bud's direction myself

'Good luck, girl. You come back and have a real drink with me someday, hear.' I agreed to it. Junior pointed me in the right direction. 'That way. It ain't far.'

And it wasn't.

I parked in a wide driveway behind two cars and a pickup. The house was an unassuming three-bedroom ranch that was neatly kept up and carefully tended. So was the woman who answered the door.

'Mrs Mendez?'

'Yes?'

I identified myself and handed her a card. 'I need some information and I'm hoping you can help me.'

'Yes?'

'May I have a few minutes of your time, please?'

She frowned slightly. She was about sixty with a clear complexion, large beautiful eyes, and streaks of gray running through her once-black hair. It was easy to see where Jose had gotten his looks. I stood on the porch, the sun on my back, and waited.

'A few minutes?'

'Yes.'

'All right.' She opened the door wider and let me come in, let me sit down. 'I'm a little busy today. This weekend is the youngest grandchild's birthday.' She smiled. 'He is our treasure. He'll be six.'

'How nice for you to have your children and grandchildren close. Do all your children live in this area?'

Her face clouded over. 'Not all.'

'Mrs Mendez, do you recognize anyone in this picture?' I handed her the photograph.

She took it with a sharp intake of breath. 'Holy Mother of God,' she said on a soft, almost sobbing note, then crossed herself

'No.' She looked at me and handed the picture back, crossed herself again. She made herself smile and lean back carelessly in her chair. It wouldn't have fooled a four-year-old or a newborn kitten. 'Should I?'

'Most mothers do.' That same sharp intake of breath. 'It's Jose, isn't it?'

'Yes,' she whispered, then crossed herself.

'I need to talk to him, Mrs Mendez. How can I find him?'

'No.'

'Where is he?'

'I don't know. I haven't known for years. It is true,

as you say, that there are things a mother should know, but I don't, I don't know these things about Jose. I never did. Mostly he would not tell me, and what he did tell, you could not know if it was the truth. He was not a good boy.' She crossed herself. 'Of all my children, he was the only one, the only bad one.'

'Bad, how?'

'He took things.'

'Stole?'

'He took things that did not belong to him.' *Steal* was too emotionally loaded a word for her. 'It was always so. Even as a child he would take other children's toys. It was worse when he stopped going to school. Then I think, I heard tell, one of his brothers said he was gambling. His father beat him, but he was too big by then. We could not make him do anything, not then, not ever. I don't know what it was.' She looked up at a picture on the wall of Jesus blessing small children, then back at me.

'Do you have children, miss?' I shook my head. 'We raised them all the same; we loved them, took them to school and church. And one turns out bad. It should not be—' she crossed herself '—but it is. Only God knows.' She crossed herself again, her gestures reinforcing her words. 'Only He can understand.'

'Stealing, gambling, was there more?'

'Girls and drinking. He was wild, that one was. Now, God forgive me, I do not think of him anymore.

I do not think of him as my son. We do not talk of him.'

'How long has it been since you've seen your son?'

'Not since he was nineteen.'

'Over twenty-one years?'

'Yes. His birthday is almost the same as the littlest grandchild.' Her eyes cleared. 'I must go back to my baking. It is a very special cake, very fancy.'

'Have you ever heard from him, Mrs Mendez?'

'Since he left, you mean?'

'Yes.'

'No.'

'He never wrote or called?'

'No.'

'Not to his father or brothers or sisters?'

'No.'

'To a friend?'

'We did not know his friends.' She shrugged her shoulders. 'They were not good boys and did not come around here. My husband would not have allowed it.'

She looked at me for a long, steady moment. 'It is not true what I said, that I do not think of him. I do now what I did then: I pray for him every day. Every day. For a while he spoke of going into the service, of making something of himself. I pray that he did that, that he is a good man now. Somewhere,' she said doubtfully, 'somehow. But it is in God's hands, not ours.' She crossed herself. 'Unlike the cake.' She smiled at me. '*That* is in *my* hands.'

'What about the girl, Mrs Mendez?'

Slowly she shook her head. 'I do not know her. I heard that there were many of them but I did not meet them. They did not come here.' She stood. 'I hope very much you find out what it is you need to know.' I stood too and thanked her.

'God bless you, child.' She waved once from the door and then shut it firmly behind her.

The cake was more important than Jose.

I could see why.

Eighteen

92% of people, when asked, say they want to know the truth: 35% accept it when they hear it; 31% deny it; 19% react violently; 5% eat, drink, or use drugs to excess; 2% go to sleep. A lot of people must not know their own minds.

'Hey, doll face, what's America's favorite vegetable?'

Vegetable? I wasn't in the mood for this, not at all.

'Can't get it, eh?'

I took a stab at it. It was an effort. 'Peas.'

'Nope.'

'Corn.'

'Nope.'

'Tomatoes.' I was running out of steam, if not out of vegetables, and definitely out of patience. Especially out of patience.

'Potato.' I thought about it. 'It's the french fry industry, that's what kicked it over the top, bound to be.'

Okay, it made sense, if french fries could be said to make sense. They made more sense than what I was dealing with, that's for sure.

'How about the favorite ice cream flavor?'

'Vanilla.'

'Hey, how'd you know?' He was disappointed.

'I went for the obvious. You just showed me in vegetables.'

'Oh. Yeah. Favorite color?'

'Mr A., I'm working. Later, okay?' He looked at the doodles on the paper in front of me. 'I'm trying to work, trying to think.' He didn't believe me; I wasn't sure I believed me either. The phone rang so I was off that hook and onto another one. Mr A. waved and scampered off. I picked it up.

'Kat Colorado.' I pulled the phone away from my ear a bit. 'On what? Slow down.'

'Kat,' Lindy's voice didn't slow down much, 'Kat, I have to write this paper for English.'

'Okay.'

'On "What I Would Change in My Life if I Could." '

'Okay.'

'I can't,' she wailed. 'There isn't anything in my life I'd change, not now, not really. It's not like before.'

'Say that and tell what it was like before and how you changed it.'

'I didn't, *you* did.'

'No, I helped out, but you did it.'

'Tell how I was a hooker and everything?'

'Or just how you ran away from a crummy home situation and—'

'Tell *everything*?' The words sounded lost and afraid.

'Whatever you feel comfortable with.' I thought about that statement and decided to revise it. Lindy's comfort level was different from most of ours. 'Well, don't get too specific.'

'You mean like how blow jobs cost less than a fuck?'

She was over lost and afraid and into shock tactics and, yes, that was exactly what I meant. She knew my answer so I didn't bother to give it. She giggled. When did teenagers stop testing and pushing? I wondered. I hoped it was soon.

'And how blow jobs in a car are less than in a room?'

I sighed. 'I'm busy, Lindy. Anything else?' There was a tap on my office door and Paige walked in.

Rats, I was surrounded. No easy exit, no way out. Damn.

'Kat—' Lindy sounded helpless and confused and I understood then what she was asking, although I still didn't understand how teenagers could go from bravado to vulnerability in a nanosecond.

'It's okay, honey, it doesn't matter anymore. What you are is different from what you did, or were. Why don't you write about how you changed from a family who didn't love you to one who does. Okay?'

'Okay. Do you, Kat?'

'Love you? You betcha. Only about ninety-seven percent of the time, though, the other three percent—'

She giggled. 'The truth? I should tell the truth?'

'The truth is all you have, Lindy,' I said solemnly, thinking of Socrates, Abraham Lincoln, and Doonesbury.

She pondered that in silence, then thanked me and hung up. I looked at Paige but only because there wasn't any other choice, anything else to look at. I even wished the phone would ring again, but it didn't. Naturally.

'Hi,' I said at last. 'Would you like a Pepsi?' She shook her head. 'Coffee? A glass of water?'

'No. Fuck that shit.' Okay, we were skipping the social amenities. I sat and waited in silence.

'I hired you. I paid you. It's my right to know. I want answers and I want them now. You said—'

I interrupted. 'That I would do my best. You want a guarantee, Paige, buy a toaster, a Japanese car, or a dress from Nordstrom's.'

There was a long pause. 'I'm sorry, I didn't mean to be rude. Please tell me what you know, Kat. The truth is all you have, I just heard you say that.' Great. Snagged in my own words again. I hate it when that happens.

'I don't know the truth. I've got bits and pieces, that's all. I'd like you to wait until I know more, until I can piece it together.'

'No.'

'All right.'

'I'm an adult, Kat.'

'Yes.' I pulled my thoughts into some semblance

of order. 'In Florence's will there is a reference to a distant cousin, Garnet Whyte. There is a trust fund set up to cover her medical and living expenses.'

'*I know* all this,' Paige said impatiently, 'and I don't care. She can have the damn money, or whatever. That's *not* what I'm paying you for, Kat. I'm paying you to find out what I don't know, not what I do.'

I ignored the interruption. 'I don't think she's a distant cousin.'

'Not a relative? I still don't care about the money, if that's what you mean.'

'It's not what I mean. I think she's a relative, yes, but not a distant one.'

'What then?' Her face was curious, open, unafraid – unafraid because she didn't know, hadn't a clue as to what was coming.

'Do you know anything about gemstones, Paige?'

She shook her head impatiently at me. 'Kat, for godssakes, get on with it!'

'Opals come in many shades and colors. Rubies are red, garnets are . . .' I paused and waited, waited a long time.

'Red, too,' she whispered. 'What are you saying?'

'Garnet Whyte may be Ruby Morrell.'

'My mother?' She came out of her chair like a bottle rocket. 'Where is she? I want to see her. Have you? What is she like? Now! Let's go, let's go, let's *go!*'

'I said maybe, Paige, I'm not sure yet.'

It took a minute but she slowed down enough to take it in. 'Maybe, what do you mean maybe? All you have to do is *ask* her.' It sunk in a little further. 'You *can't* ask her? Why not? Trust fund for medical care? Is she in a coma or something?' There was horror in her voice.

'Not a physical coma, no.'

'Mental? It's *mental*?' The horror deepened.

'Or psychological.'

'*Jesus Christ.*' She sat stunned. Jesus didn't help out. Me either. I piled some more on.

'I found a woman in Omaha whose maiden name was Opal Morrell. She presently goes by the name of Opal Harnway.'

'Is she . . .' She stopped, searching for a word. 'Is she all right?'

'Yes. Opal is a successful businesswoman, beautiful and very talented.'

Paige sagged in relief, then straightened. 'Okay, I want to meet her. I want—' She stopped when she saw me shake my head.

'No.'

'What do you mean, no? You can't stop me. Try, just *try!*' Her hands were clenched into fists.

'I can't, Paige, but she can. Opal doesn't want anything to do with you, with the family.'

Not yet, I thought, but didn't say. Ruby, of course was the ace, the high card, the wild card I hadn't played yet. I thought Opal would come for Ruby. I was sure of it, but I didn't say it.

Paige glared at me and twisted her ring. 'If I went to see this, this Garnet person, would she talk to me?'

'I don't know.'

'Would she understand who I am if I, if, if . . .'

'I don't know.'

'What the fuck *do* you know?'

'I told you from the beginning how it was.'

She wasn't listening, that was clear.

'This Garnet person, you're saying she might be my, my . . . well, she's not, do you hear? Not, not, *not*! Garnet's a, a – a floater. She can't be my mother, she *can't* be. My mother's not a floater, a mental floater. She's dead. Even dead is better than floater. Fuck you. Fuck you, Kat! And an aunt who won't have anything to do with me? Jesus Christ, whose side are you on, anyway?'

I looked at her steadily. 'You haven't gotten it yet.'

'What?'

'It's worse than that, much worse.'

'How could it be? No, it can't be, it *can't*.' There was a desperate note in her voice. She looked at me and begged me not to say anything. 'No, please.'

It was too late. The fuck you's rang in my mind, and 'The truth is all I have,' 'I can take it,' 'I'm an adult.' Those too. I was too mad to pull punches. I let her have it.

'If Garnet and Ruby are the same person and she is the firstborn twin, which Opal says she is, you don't inherit, she does. That's the direct linear descent.'

Her hand went to her mouth, covered it tightly, as though she were trying not to throw up.

'No.' She said it on a sob. 'No!'

'Yes.' I was still being heartless, implacable. I remembered the floaters and stood up, eased up. 'Paige, none of this is definite, none of this is proven yet. And, whatever happens, it's not the end. Things can be worked out. I'll help you. I—'

'No. Stay away.' She backed off. If she had been Mrs Mendez, she would have crossed herself. 'No!'

'Sit down,' I said gently.

'Paul.' She stumbled blindly toward the door. 'I've got to talk to Paul. *He*'ll know what to do.'

I let her go. Paul wouldn't know what to do, but then neither did I. I wished again for Herb.

The door slammed.

Mr A. opened it and stuck his head inside. He keeps pretty close tabs on me. 'Hey, doll face, it's about that time. Want to knock off and grab a cold one?'

I shook my head. I was too down. I wanted to be left alone. 'What percent of people really want to know the truth?' I asked him.

He shook his head sympathetically. 'Bad day?'

'Even when they *beg* you to find out, assure you they can handle it, promise you it's what they want. What percent?'

'Thirty-five?'

'No way. Three, maybe.'

'Real bad day, eh?'

'Two, maybe.'

'C'mon, doll face, I'll buy the first round.'

I locked up and we walked a couple of blocks to our neighborhood bar, Toll House, it's called, which beats me. There isn't a tollbooth or a cookie anywhere nearby.

The beer didn't cheer me up and two wasn't enough to make me forget. I decided that the percentage of people who really wanted to hear the truth, no matter what they said, was one, maybe less; probably less.

'Too cynical, doll face,' Mr A. said halfway through our conversation, and ordered another beer.

'Too *cynical*?' I looked at him and he smiled back, to all appearances an elderly model of good judgment and decorum. 'You believe in Bigfoot, UFOs, and statistics, and you think *I'm* too cynical?'

'There you go again, doll face.' He patted my knee. 'There might be some doubt about Bigfoot and UFOs, but statistics?' He shook his head in amazement. 'No doubt there: Statistics don't lie.'

'Who said, "There are lies, damn lies, and statistics"? Ha! Do you realize who comes up with statistics? Scientists, for one. Those are the guys who told us the earth was flat and the theory of relativity impossible. And politicians.' Words momentarily failed me. 'Politicians who wouldn't know the truth if it dropped in their laps with a label on it.'

He patted my knee again. 'It's your job, doll face; it's time for a vacation, it's getting to you.'

And he was right. I thought about it as I drove home. I needed a vacation. Definitely.

There was something on my front porch but it didn't look like a vacation.

Not at all.

It looked good though.

Nineteen

Most people think that life is neither predictable nor fair. More people can handle the unpredictable than the unfair. But, if they had their druthers, they'd go for guarantees and free lunches. Hands down.

He had to stand up before I recognized him and then I wondered why I hadn't immediately. He opened the door of the Bronco as I pulled up and parked.

'Hey, Kat.'

'Hey, Derek. You were over on my side of town and just thought you'd drop by?'

He grinned. 'That's it exactly.' He caught me by the elbows, pulled me into a hug and then kissed me lightly. It was a surprise, but not an unpleasant one.

'Dinner?'

'More midwestern hospitality?'

'That's it.' He laughed. 'Exactly.'

'What are you doing here, Derek?'

'Could we talk about it over dinner, drinks, whatever you say?'

'All right. Come in, let me wash up.' I was going

to say change but since we were both wearing jeans, why bother? 'Make yourself at home.' I headed for the back door, let Ranger in, fed him and the kitten both. 'There's wine and beer in the fridge. I think,' I added. 'I hope.' I pulled open the refrigerator door. There was. 'What sounds good?'

'Molson.' He leaned past me to take one, his arm, his body brushing against me. It was neither accidental, nor quite deliberate. I tried to figure it out and couldn't, so I decided to let it go. I had a glass of wine and cleaned up instead.

'What kind of food?' I asked later. He raised an eyebrow at me and laughed. 'And no, I haven't already made the choice.' His other eyebrow went up. We laughed together. It was the second time we'd been together and already we had the easy jokes and references of people who'd known each other for a while. 'Steak, seafood, Chinese, Italian, Mexican?'

'Mexican. We don't get much of that in the Midwest. Not good, anyway.'

I took him to Mama Mia's in Folsom where the *chimichangas* and *flautas* are merely outstanding and the *chile rellenos* are superb. We drank Mexican beer and ate chips, salsa, and guacamole as we waited for our food.

'What brings you to Sacramento?'

'You.'

I thought about it for a while. It was sweet but hard to believe. I said as much in my usual tactful way. 'Oh, sure.'

He laughed. 'Underestimating your allure, Kat?'

'No.'

'Then why the doubt?'

I let him wait while I loaded a chip up with guacamole and ate it. 'You didn't strike me as the romantic, impetuous type. Plan-ahead, businesslike, and levelheaded, yes; wild and romantic, no.'

He smiled. 'We all get carried away by our emotions on occasions.'

'Oh yes, but you probably don't, or at least not often and not like this. Am I mistaken?'

'Partly. I have several long-standing customers in San Francisco. I finished business early, had a car, an afternoon, and less than a hundred-mile drive to get here.' He covered my hand, the one that wasn't shoveling in chips, with his. 'What do you think, would you buy that?'

I would, I did: hook, line, and sinker.

After dinner we went dancing. I should have known better; I do know better. Dancing is dangerous, is romantic. I tried not to think of Hank. It was a warm evening for May, so when we got back to my house we sat out on the patio, had another drink, and talked about our lives and interests the way people do when they're just getting to know each other.

'Is there someone in your life, Kat?'

'No,' I said. Thoughts of Hank filled my mind and heart and then the realization of what was spilled it out again, leaving me empty and lonely. We talked for a long time. Derek filled me up with bits of fun and humor, stories, parts of his life and work, and futurevision stuff. It made me feel less empty overall, which was nice. It got too cold finally so we came in. I didn't ask him to sit down or if he wanted another beer, so he didn't do either. We stood and talked.

'It's almost a two-hour drive back to the City. I'd better get started.' I nodded. We kissed good night. 'I had a wonderful evening, Kat, thank you.'

'Yes, me too.'

And suddenly I was like the tin man: hollow, empty, and without a heart, crying inside and rusting out. All the fun and stories drained out of me and loss and loneliness filled me up. I was sad, desperately so: for Paige; for Ruby and Opal; for the unloved, neglected little girl I had been; for the love we had none of us gotten; for Hank's love that I was too afraid to hold on to. It was bad. Very. It was help-me-make-it-through-the-night time, grabbing-onto-straws time.

Derek was the straw I grabbed. 'Stay,' I said.

He kissed me. His fingers ran gently up and down my back. His lips danced across my eyes and nose and mouth, dropping light little kisses like snowflakes. I came alive again, alive and wired up like a neon sign. And it made me forget: Hank, Ruby, Paige, Opal, tomorrow . . .

Afterward we talked, held each other, quiet at last, and played with words and ideas.

'How far is Omaha from Sacramento?' I'd never thought of it before.

'I don't know, sixteen hundred miles maybe. I'm in California on business often, Kat. At least once a month.' His fingers traced the bumps of my spine, making me shiver. 'I'll come up here, or on occasion you could come meet me in the City for the weekend. Could you?'

'Yes.'

'Would you?'

'Yes.'

'I can't stay long. I've got an early plane out of San Francisco and still have to pick up my things at the hotel. I'm sorry.' He touched my cheek, then got up and dressed quickly. 'Don't get up. I'll call you when I get back and we'll make plans. Next time I'll take a few days off. Does Tahoe sound like fun? Or Reno?'

'Yes.' Tahoe's always fun. I sat up, the covers slipping down to my waist. We kissed again, his cheek rough on my cheek, his sweater smooth under my fingers.

'Soon,' he said and was gone. I heard the door close and latch behind him and went to sleep, heavily, dreamlessly.

The phone woke me up at two. I had no idea how long I'd been asleep; it felt like a minute, two, tops. My voice sounded heavy, groggy, unfamiliar.

'Kat, is that Kat?'

'Yes.'

'Come, please come.' There was a desperate note in her voice. 'You said you would, you promised.'

I tried to shake the oatmeal out of my mind, to fire up my sleep-deadened thoughts, and sated senses, to figure out what was going on. The woman's voice was familiar.

'If I needed you, you promised. And I need you. I'm afraid. Something's gone wrong, something could happen.'

A cog slipped into place. 'Garnet?'

'You'll come, won't you?'

'What's wrong, what's the matter?'

'I don't know, not for sure, but something is. Something!' Her voice had a hysterical edge.

'Go back to bed, Garnet. I'll come in the morning, early.'

'It'll be too late.' The hysteria was gone; despair instead, large, heavy, black. I thought of the Bad Place and the bad people and shivered. 'You promised. No!' Her voice was sharp and then faded out. There were scuffling noises in the background. The phone dropped. I waited.

'Hello,' a breathless voice said. 'Hello, hello?'

'Yes. I'm here. What's going on?'

'Who is this?'

'Kat Colorado.'

'Oh, Miss Colorado, I'm so sorry you were disturbed. That's so unlike her, I can't tell you, but it's all right, everything's all right now. The doctor left us with sedatives for her.'

'No, oh no, no,' Garnet cried out in the background. I remembered her big and beautiful eyes and thought suddenly of those pictures of baby seals, helpless, caught as they looked up at their predators. I shivered again. It was stupid, I knew it, or maybe it wasn't. I don't think clearly, or well, on a hour or so of sleep.

'It's all right.' Gladys's voice rang out in a commandingly soothing tone. It didn't do anything for me. I don't imagine it did for Garnet either. 'Everything will be fine,' she said to us both. 'Now, miss,' – she was back to me – 'you just go on back to sleep. We'll be fine here.' Someone was crying in the background. Someone? Garnet. 'You can call me in the morning to find out how we are.'

Everything in me from the cellular level on up cried: Yes, yes, excellent idea. Go to sleep, take care of things in the morning.

Almost everything. I sighed and swung my feet out of bed. 'Tell Ms Whyte I'm on my way, Gladys. No sedatives, not until I get there.'

'But the doctor says—'

'No. Thirty minutes, I'll be there.' I hung up and reached for my clothes. They were on the floor, the chair, and the dresser. A hot rush went through me as my body remembered Derek. I half stumbled, half staggered with fatigue and didn't dare to sit down to tie my sneakers. Too tired, too dangerous, too easy.

I was there in thirty minutes; less, I was speeding. Garnet's voice rang in my ears, urgent, wild, despairing. And I was all she had. *Very unlike her to do this,* Gladys had said.

The drab ranch-style house was lit up, mostly in the back, with a single light in the front, the kitchen I thought. I rang and knocked. I was getting ready to pound when the door opened and Gladys Burk stood there. Her Betty Crocker look had slipped, her biceps hadn't. She stepped aside to let me in, no 'Hello, how are you?' no 'What's up?' Me either. I pushed past her and headed for Garnet's room.

'Garnet.' I made my voice soft, gentle.

She smiled at me from the bed, her face mushy from fatigue, or drugs, or both. 'I knew you would come.' Her eyes thanked me. There were ribbons on her pink bed jacket. 'They gave me a shot.' Her voice wavered, her eyes too. 'I didn't want it, they made me.' There were tears in her eyes. 'Everyone always makes me do things. Help me sit up, please.' I did and piled the pillows behind her.

'What were you afraid of, Garnet?'

'There, out there.' She waved vaguely at the window. 'Someone was coming, the bad man, like at the Bad Place.'

Was it drugs, memories, or her mind wandering? I couldn't tell. She couldn't tell me. I sat on her bed, she held out her hand and I took it. It was warm, heavy, and solid.

'You believe me?'

'Yes.' I did. Whether it was in her mind or in the room, it was real to her and that was enough for me. 'What do you want me to do?'

'Stay with me please, for now, for a while.'

'All right.'

'Will you open the window, Kat? I want to feel the breezes off the river, like I did as a child. And the crickets, the trees, I want to hear them. Please.' I opened the window. The breeze billowed in, fresh and free. She sighed. 'Thank you.' Her fingers gripped mine, then relaxed. Her eyes started to close.

'It's Ruby, isn't it, Garnet?'

Her eyes fluttered open. It was unfair of me to hit her that way. Drugs and fear: Her defenses were down. It was unfair; I did it; I despised what I did. What a job.

'Not Garnet, no, not Garnet. Florence did that after Opal left. Opal wouldn't have let her.' Her eyes fluttered again. 'I *hated* her.'

'You hated Opal?'

'Oh no!' Her eyes were open and wide. 'I *love* Opal. Florence. I hated her. That is awful, isn't it, to hate your mother? She wouldn't let us call her Mother, can you imagine? I hated her.' Her fingers, slack now with the drugs, reached for mine, 'I loved the baby. Tell her.' Her fingers gripped my wrist, hard. '*Tell* her. I loved the baby, pretty, pretty baby,' she crooned. 'Pretty, a pearl for a ruby. So sad. Life has been so sad. And too long.' Her fingers relaxed and lay in mine, heavy and listless.

'Tell Herb ...'

227

'Go to sleep now, Ruby. We'll speak in the morning.'

'Tell Herb . . . it's coming, coming soon. I want to sleep in the flowered bed. Not mine, but only right. Tell Herb. Tell the baby I love her, Opal too. Not Florence, hate her, hate her. I can't see your face anymore, Kat.' Her voice was thin and whispery, far away. 'You've been kind. Thank you. I love you, too. I want to sleep in the flowered bed. Tell Herb . . .'

The whisper became a long sighing breath; her hand was still and quiet in mine. I pulled the pillows out from behind her and laid her quietly down. I sat there for a time, watched over her, listened to her smooth deep breathing, and waited for the tears to stop, to dry. Mine, not hers. Her face was clear and beautiful and she looked younger than I had ever seen her. She looked like Opal, not her twin, but an older sister perhaps. I started to get up.

'Tell Herb,' she whispered again. I had to lean over to hear it.

'Tell him what?'

'Tell him.'

'Good night.' I kissed her.

She smiled, in a dream somewhere already. I turned out the light and left. Gladys sat, tired and sullen, at the dining room table.

'I'll be back tomorrow, to see Garnet, to talk to you. I said there were to be no sedatives, no shots, until I got here.' She opened her mouth and I shook my head. 'Tomorrow. We'll talk then.' I was too tired to really let her have it tonight. And I wanted to, I planned to. I left then, forgetting about the alarm, but it was off.

On my way home I stopped at a Winchell's doughnut shop and got a cup of coffee and some kind of a chocolate sugar puff thing. I hate doughnuts, hate them with a passion, but I was barely moving now, desperate for unconsciousness. The caffeine, carbo boost, and sugar rush would get me home, I hoped, where I could drop in my tracks.

It did and I did. I didn't even take my clothes off, just pulled the sheet up and climbed in under the comforter. It was almost four. The sun would be up soon but I wouldn't.

Famous last words.

Twenty

6% of American murders are committed without a weapon; 13% of violent crime occurs in or around the victim's home; 17% of homicides are committed by a relative of the victim. Home sweet home.

The phone rang at seven-thirty. I thought it was a dream, a nightmare really. I ignored it because in nightmares you can ignore that kind of stuff and it goes away. Eventually. But it didn't go. Somehow, after a dozen or so rings, I struggled out of sleep, nightmare, and comforter, and picked it up.

'Kat, get your ass over here.'

'What?' And what was it with all these people who called me at inconvenient times? Was it a conspiracy? And couldn't they, any of them, say 'Hello, hi, how are you?' and 'Sorry to disturb you but—'

'Henley, homicide. I want your butt downtown, I want it now, and I want to know what your business card is doing on a dead woman.'

My heart turned to lead and sank. It couldn't be; it mustn't be. 'What?'

'What are you, a goddamned parrot with a one-word vocabulary?'

'Bill, what are you talking about?'

'Homicide, Kat. You're on your way, right?'

'Who was it?' And please God it wasn't—

'Garnet Whyte.'

It was. I was on my way.

I had a bath first, and a cup of tea so black and bitter I could hardly drink it. It fit my mood perfectly, so I had another. I made a piece of toast but I couldn't swallow it. There was going to be a lot about this I couldn't swallow, I knew it already.

Downtown I fought with late-arriving state workers for limited parking places and finally beat a surly, three-piece-suited fat boy out of one. He snarled at me. I snarled right back. Life was not looking sweet this morning.

Henley had left word downstairs that I was expected so the girl at the desk waved me through after checking my ID. What the hell kind of job did I have that I was 'expected' at the Homicide Division of the Sacramento Sheriff's Department?

'Yeah?' I leaned a shoulder against the door frame of Henley's office. I had found it easily; I'd been there before.

He looked up. 'Well, aren't we little Miss Merry Sunshine?' Caustic, graying, balding, and paunchy, with a sprinkle of dandruff on his shoulders. It was Henley, all right.

I sighed. 'I got maybe four hours of sleep last night,

maybe; was woken up twice, the second time with the news of the death of someone I knew and liked, and now I have to listen to your sarcastic cracks?'

He nodded. 'Yeah, that's it exactly. Sit down, Kat, tell me about it.' He said it in a more or less friendly tone. 'What was the first phone call?'

'Garnet Whyte.'

'And make it good.' That sounded considerably less friendly, ominous even.

I made it as good as I could considering how much I left out. I was walking a fine line and I knew it. Bill was a friend and would cut me slack but not here, not now, not ever on a homicide case. And why was it a homicide case? I didn't bother asking yet; he wasn't in the mood to answer, to give me information yet.

'My client is a woman named Paige Morrell. Miss Morrell was raised by her grandmother who told her nothing about her parents or her history. She hired me to find out what I could. Mrs Whyte was referred to as a distant cousin and provided for in the grandmother's will. I went to visit her, to see what I could find out.'

'And?'

'And she was difficult to talk to. I gather she had a history of being mentally and/or emotionally unstable.'

'Yeah. You didn't answer the question.' That's the kind of attention to detail that sometimes, frequently actually, makes me dislike talking to cops.

'Not much. She seemed to mix up the past and the present and to get confused about people. I had a hard time making sense out of it.'

'Why did she call and when, last night or early this morning?'

'This morning at two. She was upset, said that something was wrong, that something could happen, but she didn't know what or why. I went over there, talked and sat with her for about forty-five minutes. After she went to sleep I went home and to sleep as well. That's all I knew until you called.'

He grunted and scratched his head. A flake of dandruff joined the polka-dot parade on his shoulders.

'How did she die?' That was the question my mind had shied away from all along. Not just how, why? And maybe there was a who, too. I didn't know how, I had some ideas about who and why, ideas I didn't like at all, ideas I hoped I wouldn't have to consider.

'Dunno. We're waiting on the autopsy.'

'No obvious signs of violence?'

'Yes and no. There were signs of an injection but the woman who runs the place says she is a nurse and claims she is authorized by the doctor in charge to administer sedatives on necessary occasions.'

'So it could have been a natural death?'

'Could of.'

'What are you guys doing on it?'

'The caretaker left a young woman assistant in charge and went home. The woman panicked and dialed nine-one-one screaming about a dead person. The patrol cop who responded saw the injection mark and a number of bruises on her arms as if she had struggled. It was enough for him to call us. We went out.' He said it laconically. 'That's what we do, Kat, go out for bodies.'

'You're treating it as a homicide?'

'We're considering it. Any reason we shouldn't?'

None that I knew of. All the reasons I could think of were on the other side: Paige, Paul. Maybe Opal. Those kind of reasons. Shit.

'What's Garnet's past medical history?' I'd have to be careful. I almost slipped and said Ruby. 'Anything to indicate sudden heart failure, a stroke, whatever?' I ran out of ideas. What did an apparently healthy woman of forty die of? My mind checked in again. 'Asthma, diabetes, epilepsy, anything like that?'

'Not that I know of. I've only talked to the Burk woman, though. We'll get to the doctor later on in the day. Far as I can tell, she was physically healthy.'

I thought of the fear in her eyes, in her voice on the phone. I remembered her hand holding on, desperately, to mine. *Thank you, Kat, for coming*, her voice said in my mind. *Tell Herb* ... Tell him what, I wondered, and now would never know. *I want to feel the breeze, like the river breezes when I was a child, to hear the crickets ... I want to sleep, to sleep in the flowered bed ... Tell Herb ...*

'Damn. Damn, damn, damn!' It was hitting me. I

didn't want it to, but it was.

'What's eating you?' Henley looked at me. I didn't answer. 'Want a cup of coffee, Kat?'

I shook my head, then I nodded it. 'Okay, black please.' It would be awful, I was sure, acrid, bitter, dark, and ugly, like the stuff in my mind. Good. Penance. I sipped at the cup he handed me. It was fine, not great, but okay. Bummer.

'Well?'

'I shouldn't have left there, Bill. If something happened to her, and if I'd stayed, well then, it might not have if I'd been there and—'

'Get any more ifs into that sentence, Kat?'

I stared at him. Unsympathetic bastard.

'You're an investigator, not a nurse, and this woman isn't even your client. It sounds like you were there as a favor. You did your best, which was a lot more than you had to. Quit being so hard on yourself. Quit playing God.'

Playing God. That again.

'Drink your coffee.' Dandruff floated down and settled on his shoulders in a familiar way. Some things never change. 'Eat this.' He pushed a greasy doughnut with shiny sparkled sugar in my direction.

I felt my stomach rise and a bitter taste in my mouth. I shook my head.

He shrugged. 'Suit yourself, but don't go playing some melodrama with you as the tragic heroine. That's not how life works. You did your best for this lady. You had no way of knowing she was in danger. If she was,' he added.

No way? Was that true? I drank some more coffee, absently broke off a piece of doughnut and ate it before I came to my senses. Damn, I was doing that a lot lately. With doughnuts it didn't matter. The rest of the stuff? It might, it might a lot.

'Will you let me know, Bill?'

'Yeah. Give me a call later. Tomorrow, maybe.'

'Thanks.' I stood up.

He did too, loomed over me, gave me a cop glare. Big deal. I'd seen them before.

'And Kat—'

I sighed. 'Now what?'

'It's a two-way street, don't forget it.' I opened my mouth to answer but he ignored it. 'I know you're not telling me everything, because I know you. I don't know it's a homicide yet. If and when I do, this all changes. Got it?'

I got it. It was even more than that, only Henley was too nice a guy to use it. He'd pulled my bacon out of the fire more than once. We were friends.

'See you, Bill.'

'Yeah. See you, Kat.' He sat down and went back to his paperwork before I was out the door.

I didn't want a job dealing with bodies. So why was I? Why did I?

I didn't have the question answered by the time I reached my office. Mr A. met me with a huge bouquet, a medium-size floral shop. I was stunned.

He shoved it into my reluctant arms. Who knows what it had cost? A fortune. And Mr A. didn't have that kind of money. What was going on in this helter-skelter world? My head began to hurt and spin at the same time.

'Did you know, doll face, that forty-two percent of American households have indoor plants and that twenty-nine percent of the US is forest land?' he asked cheerfully.

I staggered back, clutching the bouquet, and shook my head. 'No, I didn't. Mr A., you shouldn't have, I mean it.'

'What?' I peered at him, what I could see of him through blossoms and fragrance. 'Oh, that. No, I didn't. And forty-four percent of adult Americans like to grow flowers. How about that?'

How about it, indeed? I gave him back the flowers, dug out my keys, and opened the office door. I turned to thank him at the door so I could scoot quickly inside, sort out my thoughts, get moving, get figuring.

'Uh-oh, doll face.' He shoved the flowers back at me. 'This is not good.' I didn't like the sound of it. Not at all. That's the kind of comment that Mr A. makes when he opens the morning paper and sees that fifteen thousand people have been killed in an earthquake somewhere.

'Uh-oh, uh-oh, uh-oh.' I peered through the floral hedge that I was holding again but couldn't see anything, tottered in, and set it down with a thud on my filing cabinet.

The first thing I noticed was the breeze. Not right. The window should have been closed. It was. And latched. It was. Mr A. was leaning through it and muttering.

'Did a nice job,' he said as he pulled his head back in the window. 'Taped it up good, then cut it out. Almost made it in one piece. Nice, for an amateur job, anyway.'

I let him rattle on in the background while I looked around to see if anything was missing or out of place. I couldn't see it if it was.

'I'll just call Freddy and get him to fix that shall I, doll face? We'll have you back in business in a jiffy.'

'Hmmm?'

'The window, doll face, the window. I'll get it fixed, shall I?'

I nodded gratefully and sat down at the desk. The breeze felt good on my back. The flowers bloomed at me. I felt the violation and the fear that comes from having someone intrude on your space. Mr A. scampered back in with a tape measure and started measuring, muttering, and scribbling. The phone rang. I wanted desperately to go back to bed, to sleep. I answered the phone instead.

'Kat.' I didn't recognize his voice at first. 'Kat, how are you? What's up?'

I thought about answering him, but the answer was too long, too complicated. 'Just tired, I guess.' He laughed. 'How was your trip?' The flowers. I stretched the phone cord out and reached for the card: *With love, Derek.*

'Fine. Just checking in. Wanted you to know I'm thinking of you.'

'The flowers already told me. Thank you.'

'Talk to you soon, baby.'

Baby? I thought about it as I hung up. Baby? What kind of name was that for a thirty-three-year-old PI? Dumb, that's what. I shivered, misgivings rampant. I should have gotten a bottle of wine to help me make it through the night. As usual my hindsight was 20/20. Mr A. scuttled off again.

I started looking through my things in a straightforward, methodical manner: A, B, C, D . . . I found it in the Rolodex. Rolodexes were hot for me on this investigation. I had left it flipped shut, I always do, and it was open now. To the W's, to a penciled note on Garnet Whyte.

I sat down and put my head in my hands. If Ruby was killed I knew now how the killer had found her, knew what the killer had come here looking for. I kept searching, in case I was wrong, in case it was a coincidence, but I found nothing else out of place or missing. It didn't surprise me.

I wished again for levelheaded, sensible, compassionate Herb. I wondered again what Ruby had wanted him to know.

Ruby and Herb. Two deaths in the night with no clear signs of physical violence. Neither one, as far as I knew, was ill or had a serious history of life-threatening disease. I put aside for a moment Dr Jonas's theory that Herb Sanderson was through with life. I didn't think so. Almost, he had said to me. Almost, but there were Ruby and Paige to see to first.

Both were in good health, but Herb was old and frail; Ruby was drugged. They were easy prey, easily overpowered and finished. Like Ophelia. And no reason for them to die. Not really. Not unless they knew too much or stood in the way.

I sat and thought of all the things the two of them knew: Ruby's knowledge was scrambled and incoherent, but there; Sanderson's, lucid, cogent, and powerful. I thought of money, property, direct linear descent, and dirty secrets in the past.

I thought of a lot of reasons someone could have for them to die. And wondered who had the most to gain, or to lose.

And who had what it took to kill. Twice so far, I thought.

I thought some more, thought of calling Henley, but I didn't. What percentage of people don't call the cops when they should? I thought about that one and I didn't know the answer to it either, but I admitted that I was part of the percentage. It went against my better judgment: admitting it, and being there both.

Twenty-One

Crimes are frequently built on stupidities. People cover up the first one with a greater one, thinking to end it there. Instead they get in deeper; it gets messier and more complicated. And, finally, more desperate.

I looked at the list in front of me:

sourdough bread	milk
eggs	cereal
salad stuff	wine
apples	tampons
bread	paper towels

My shopping list indicated that I suffered from a boring diet and, probably, the same kind of life. That was pretty bad, but it wasn't what worried me. What worried me was the heading of the list: *Possible Suspects.* That and the fact that any connection between the heading and the list was nonexistent.

I was running on minimal sleep, true, but it didn't seem reason enough, good enough. I decided to start again.

tortillas
cheese
red onions

Well, maybe it wasn't just fatigue; hunger, too. And burritos sounded good. I added:

salsa (hot)
tomatoes

I sighed. It was everything, but mostly it was me. I didn't want to face it: Ruby was dead; murder was a possibility. More than a possibility. That's why Henley was on the case. I started my list again, mentally this time. Obviously I couldn't be trusted with a pencil.

Number one. I gave it some thought. Paige had the most to lose: the ranch, which was both her livelihood and the place that she loved. That was one level but it was more than that; the ranch was what kept her from being/becoming a floater. Without it Paige, as far as I could tell, was dead in the water. Even with the ranch she sometimes had trouble treading water, keeping her head up.

I didn't like it, in fact I didn't like it at all, but there it was. With Ruby dead, Paige was next in line with no complications. If you can murder your mother without suffering from complications.

Paul I liked a whole lot more. And as long as he identified his future with Paige's he had a lot to lose too. Paige's words echoed in my mind: *Paul, I've got to find Paul. He'll know what to do.* Would he? Did he? He talked tough. Okay. Talk is cheap.

Murder? Murder is something else. How tough, how desperate was he? I thought of his threats and bluster and body odor. Nasty, but it didn't make him a killer. Could he? Maybe. He could play road tag for high stakes. I could see him killing little things, defenseless creatures, not ones that could fight back. Like Ruby, drugged and sleeping. So he was in the running. Looking good, smelling bad.

Opal. Was I stretching it now? She had a career and a reputation. She wouldn't kill for the money, the ranch, the inheritance. She said she didn't care about that and I believed her. What then? Her privacy, her life now, a life that was far removed from the past, a past she viewed with anger, fear, sadness, and what else? Something, I was sure of it.

Was that enough to kill for? It didn't seem so, but I didn't know it all. Nor did I know her heart, her fears. Maybe, maybe it was. I hoped not. I liked her. And she, too, had been a victim, not as much as Ruby but a victim nonetheless. Damn. I was one hell of an investigator. I wrote the word IMPARTIAL in block letters on the shopping list under *tomatoes*.

IMPARTIAL

And then three more times: impartial impartial impartial. It didn't help. I still didn't want it to be her, or Paige, so I still wasn't impartial; I still wasn't much of an investigator.

Derek? Impartiality *demanded* that I include him. No, my heart said. My body agreed. My mind was a little slow at falling into line but I could whip it into place, I was sure. Still, if I could make a case for Paul as a killer since he identified his future with Paige and had a lot to lose, then I could make the same case for Derek. He was in partnership with Opal. Without her the business was nothing; without her futurevision had no vision and, by extension, no future. It made sense. I didn't like it, but I didn't have to. I dismissed it for now.

Time to think of more suspects. Past time. And a lot more. My mind wasn't cooperating. A long shot? Okay. Wiley, Paige's foreman, was a long shot, all right, maybe too long. Why would he murder? There was a 'retirement' fund that came to him on Florence's death but that was his regardless and independent of who inherited. Would he kill to protect his position as ranch foreman? I gave him, anyone, more credit than that. My brain wasn't that dead, that tired.

Gladys Burk? *Come on!* I was grabbing at straws now, straws tossed in the wind and blowing away. Pathetic. Ridiculous. Ruby was worth something to Gladys alive, quite something no doubt. Dead, she was nothing, a liability, a black mark on Gladys's home care record. Was she covering up abuse, mistreatment? No, that was absurd. Herb was Ruby's watchdog; he would not have allowed it, nor did I seriously consider it. Ruby had seemed well looked after physically, if not emotionally or psychologically. In terms of their contract that was enough.

My mind faded in, faded out; my body longed for rest. Sleep is sweet. Then I dialed back in and punched out a number now almost familiar. Is certainty sweeter than sleep? Sometimes.

Even if Opal had a handful of aces, I had jokers. And jokers are wild. I turned the pages of Ruby's diary. It was time to drop a dime on Opal.

The receptionist refused to put me through, on Ms Harnway's instructions, she said. She sounded firm about it, and bored. The bored note was the offensive one. I left a message: *I know about Jose.* Then I left my office number and said I'd be there for another ten minutes.

It took her nine. She sounded spun out.

'What do you know?'

'There's a plane out of Omaha early tomorrow morning connecting through Denver and arriving in Sacramento at eleven-thirty. I'll pick you up at the airport.'

'What do you know?'

'I found Ruby's diary, Opal.' She was silent. 'Under the loose board in her closet.' She let out a long breath, half sigh, half sob. 'Have you read it?'

'No.' She whispered the word.

I read from the pages before me. '*Friday, the twenty-third of April. Florence said she'd kill me too,*

*if I told anyone about Jose. I can't bear it. I can't
bear what happened or what she'll do to me if I tell.
She says it's all my fault and that I'm bad, evil. Oh
God, why does it have to be like this, I don't want to
be bad, just loved, just loved. Help me please.'* I
stopped there. It was enough, and it was too painful
to continue.

'You know then.' It was a statement. Her voice
was flat, dead, emotionless.

'Yes. Tomorrow. Eleven-thirty. I'll pick you up at
the airport.'

She was silent for a long time. I could have filed
my nails and slapped on a quick coat of polish. 'All
right,' she said finally, and in the same dead voice.
Then: 'Could we handle this some other way?' Her
voice snagged on the last word, hovered, airborne
and expectant, waiting for my answer, hope alive
again.

'No.'

There was more dead airspace, enough for a
second coat of polish, then she hung up without
saying good-bye.

I cleared off my desk, finished the work piled there
and my shopping list, and was on the way out the
door when the phone rang. I let the answering
machine pick up the call.

'Kat, it's Paige. I'm . . .' She paused and I started
for the phone. 'I wanted to be in touch, but I'm glad
I got the machine and not you. It's easier this way.'

I stopped.

'I owe you an apology. I'm sorry. You did what I hired you to do. I guess you did a good job, I mean you did, you found out things, things I guess I wasn't ready to hear. By now you maybe, probably, know more. But I'm not ready, not yet. I'm going up to Tahoe for a day or two to think about all of this. I'll call you when I get back. Thanks.'

She stuttered the last word out – it was difficult for her to say it – and hung up. I listened to the silence, then erased the message and listened to the sound of the tape rewinding. I tried not to listen to the words in my mind. Paige needed to know that Ruby was dead. I'd planned to call her this evening. I'd hoped to have more information. While I tried to figure it out the phone rang again.

Wasn't I the popular one.

'Kat, Henley here. We're following up the Whyte death as a homicide. I want to talk to you ASAP.'

I didn't pick up Henley's call. I wondered still about calling Paige, wondered if she knew already. I didn't like that thought and I didn't call her back. Henley either.

Opal wore black: black slacks, black wool jacket, black pumps, and a white blouse. She carried a black purse and a brown briefcase and marched off the plane looking neither to the left nor the right. I guess she figured I'd find her. Which I did. She answered my hello with a nod, hardly looking at me.

'Luggage?' I asked.

'No.'

I looked at the briefcase. 'You're a light packer.'

'I'm not staying. Once we finish our business I'm flying out of here. Today.'

'There aren't any late flights to Omaha.'

'There are flights to somewhere: Denver, Salt Lake City, Chicago, Timbuktu. I'll be on one of them.'

She dropped the conversational ball. I didn't pick it up. We walked in silence to my car, then drove in silence. She stared distantly out the window showing no interest in anything, not until we took the freeway south.

'Where's your office?'

'Midtown.'

'We're not going into town.'

'No.'

Her hands were gripped together on her lap, white-knuckled. 'Where?' I didn't answer. We were headed for the Delta, for the river house. She knew it as well as I. 'No,' she breathed out, an imploring note in her voice. 'Not there, please.' I didn't answer. She stared at me for a while, then was silent.

I had chosen the river house on purpose. I didn't want a neutral business setting and the house would be a charged, an emotional experience for her. Good. I wanted her off guard, off balance. Was I playing God again? I shivered and pushed that thought away. Would I ever learn? I pushed the question away too. I couldn't push the shivers away.

Opal and I didn't speak. She sat, rigid and

immobile in her seat, with hostility radiating out in waves, catching me, hurting me. I was exhausted by the time we reached the house.

I parked in the shade, left the keys in the car, and got out. Opal hesitated but then followed me, carrying her purse and leaving her briefcase behind. I breathed more easily. A breeze caught me in the face and felt good. My jeans felt tight, the .380 I'd stuck in my waistband digging into the small of my back and taking up the slack.

It was a precaution, and I almost felt foolish. Almost, not quite. I had learned that my precautions were more sensible than I. I wasn't afraid of Opal, nor did I seriously think that she was involved in what had happened here, not recently at least. Her part had been played years ago.

Spring smells assailed us – flowers I couldn't identify, the river, the scent of newness in the air.

'My God, I'd forgotten how beautiful it is.' There was a note of awe in her voice. She walked up to the palm tree and put her hand on its rough surface, touching it, caressing it, resting her forehead against it. Her breath sounded ragged and harsh.

Wiley came around the corner of the house. 'Paige didn't say you were coming, didn't say it was all right.' He looked at me. 'And this ain't no tourist stop.' His glance shifted pointedly to Opal.

She straightened and looked at him. Their gaze held for a long time, both faces expressionless. He spoke first. 'Miss Opal, you're home now. At last.'

He walked toward her, calm and accepting as though he'd seen her a month before, a week before.

'Hello, Wiley.' She held out a hand, then dropped it before he could respond.

'I'm sorry. I didn't know that would be you. Thought it was just somebody with the other one, with her.' He spoke of me in the third person and as though I didn't count, which was probably true. She nodded. 'You'll stay, won't you, miss? Paige, the little one, she needs you. The other's gone, you heard?' She nodded again. 'Paige, she ain't here, but you go right on in and make yourself at home.'

'Thank you.' It was faint and weak but it was an acceptance.

He led the way and we followed, like docile, well-trained schoolchildren. The house was cool and dark, silent and unapproachable. Opal stood mutely in the front hall, hands clenched at her sides.

Wiley broke the heavy silence. 'I don't know the ways of the house, miss, but if I can do something, anything, to make you comfortable . . .' His voice trailed off and he looked inquiringly at her.

'No, oh no, thank you, Wiley. I'll manage just fine.'

'I was on my way to Stockton to pick up equipment and supplies. Be a matter of hours, that be all right with you, miss?'

'Oh yes, of course,' she said, her breath and voice still raggedy. He nodded at her gently, kindly, then left without looking at me.

'*Anything* to make me comfortable.' She was

crying now, her voice dancing lightly on the sharp edge of hysteria. 'Comfortable? I feel like I'm dying in here, suffocating on memories, on hatred, on lives not lived or loved.' Tears ran unchecked down her cheeks as they had on Ruby's.

I touched her arm. 'Let's go into the kitchen. I'll make coffee.' Her eyes widened, froze, stared at me through the tears for a moment, then the moment was gone. She allowed me to lead her to the kitchen.

'It's different, modern. Everything else is the same, the same things in the same places. Just this has changed, is different.'

I found tea bags before I found coffee so I made tea. She prowled restlessly around the kitchen, touching things, looking out the window.

'The future lies in the past. One can never escape from the past. Or the blood. Especially the blood.' She looked at me and I nodded.

Especially the blood.

Twenty-Two

It is difficult to wash, scrub, bleach, scrape, or sand away blood. Even minute traces can be detected.
And are.

'They say that bloodstains are among the most difficult to remove. Even after years have gone by, even then the blood remains. Even then.' Opal spoke more to herself than to me.

'Tell me.'

'No, I don't think so.' She spoke in quiet, even tones, calm now. 'I don't think I'll tell you anything. It's your play, not mine.'

'I know the story in outline, not the details, of course. Ruby—' I stopped. I'd almost spoken of her in the present tense, forgetting that to Opal her sister had died years ago. And it wasn't time for that. Not yet.

Her hands cradled her teacup. 'I was wrong about you. I liked you at first. Oh, I didn't like what you were doing, but I liked you. Really though, you are despicable.' Her voice was harsh and ugly. 'Dragging up the past, reading a dead woman's diary, violating her secrets, her heart and soul.'

Her voice broke. Then she continued. 'Mine, too. And for what? Blackmail? It has to be that. I won't pay, you know. This time I won't run from the past. I know now what I didn't know then, you can't outrun the past.'

'No, it's not blackmail. Two people have died. The past has reached the present.'

'Two people have died?' Her eyes were wide and frightened, her voice incredulous.

'At least two.'

'Who?'

'That's the end of the story. We are still at the beginning.'

'More blood.'

'Yes.'

'Dear God, will it never end?'

'The story, Opal, how did it go?'

'Once upon a time . . .' She sat motionless for a long time, lost somewhere I couldn't see or imagine. 'Once upon a time there were two little girls. Their daddy died and their mommy didn't love them. They only had each other. They were twins and loved each other very much. One day something awful happened . . . and then, then they didn't have each other either.' Her voice was bleak.

'Now you tell it, Kat.' It was, I thought, the first time she'd used my name. 'You're part of the story, too.'

'Yes.'

She tasted her tea, no longer hot, and got up to boil more water, looking blindly out the window as she waited. Her back was to me, stiff and ungiving.

'You and Ruby had each other to love. Fortunately. But of course a child needs more; there is no substitute for a parent's love, tenderness, understanding, though we learn to substitute. A teenager, a young woman, often and naturally turns to a boy, a young man, for affection, for love. If you haven't learned about love at home, it's easy to make the wrong choice. Ruby found Jose.'

The teakettle whistled. Opal turned it off. 'I was the strong one, always. I didn't mind; it's part of loving someone. And then, after Jose, she wouldn't listen to me. She thought I was jealous, but that wasn't it. I would have been so happy if...' Her hands moved helplessly at her sides.

'If she had found someone worthy of her love.'

'Yes.'

'He used her.'

'It wasn't love. He was only after the money. There was a lot of money. She was so young, so vulnerable, so desperate for love and attention.' She turned and finally looked at me. 'How could it have been otherwise with our background? We were two lonely children in a loveless home. He was a hawk and she a sparrow. She couldn't tell the difference between love and what he offered, and she wouldn't listen to me.'

257

'The photographs, she did them out of love, out of a desire to please?'

'You saw them?'

'No. Only one of the two of them. He had his arm around her and they were smiling into the camera, an attractive young couple. I read about the rest of it in the diary.'

'Today the photographs would be nothing. A little risqué perhaps, no more. But then, in a small town and with a boy who was not one of us, it was something.' There was bitterness in her voice, like the taste of small green apples and unripe grapes.

'They were sexual?'

'Yes, in a naive way. They were explicit, revealing. Of Ruby, not of him.' She was silent; I fought back my impatience. 'Now I know that it could have, should have, been handled differently. Even then it would have worked.' She shook her head. 'But not, of course, with my mother. Jose chose well. She was the intended victim, though we were the ones who suffered.'

'Blackmail?'

'Yes. He came to the house one evening. He was very arrogant, unsufferably so. He knocked at the front door and said he would sit in the front parlor. Florence, naturally, could not bear that; he was, after all, the son of one of her laborers. And,' she shrugged apologetically, 'Mexican. It mattered then.' She fell silent again; I struggled with impatience again.

'And?' I queried, unable to be patient any longer.

She started. 'We were all there. When he said that he must speak to Florence alone she refused. He took out the pictures then. Ruby,' Opal's voice trembled, 'screamed and almost fainted. We dragged her into the kitchen, splashed water on her, sat her down at the kitchen table. I will never forget those moments: Ruby white and trembling, seated at the kitchen table; Jose arrogantly leaning against the kitchen counter, grinning, smirking; Florence, grim-faced, going through the photographs.

'Florence finished looking at the pictures and looked, finally, at him. He grinned at her, a slow, easy, assured grin. She stared at him. You could feel her hatred fill the room. "Five thousand dollars," he said, drawling it out. Ruby cried at that, not at the money part, but because she finally understood that she was a transaction, not a love. I remember looking at him in awe, at his easy assurance, his arrogance and grin. Five thousand dollars was a lot of money then.'

'And Florence?'

'She said nothing and it made him nervous. "Well," he asked, moving a step closer to her. "Well, well?" Each step, each "well" brought him closer. Her face was frozen, vile, hateful, but he didn't seem to care, to notice even. It didn't frighten him.' All these years later, she could not hide her astonishment.

'And then she slapped him. The expression on his face was almost comical. He couldn't believe it had happened. "Dirt, filth," she said and slapped him

259

again. Still he didn't respond. He must have been well brought up,' Opal said ironically, 'it was difficult for him to raise his hand to a woman, an older woman. He would have, though, he was getting ready to.'

I said nothing, afraid to break into her thoughts, into the flow of the past.

'And then Ruby screamed. Foolish, foolish girl, she still cared about her faithless greedy lover. Even Jose wondered at her. I won't forget the contempt in his eyes. Florence saw it too. She hit him hard, very hard. He didn't see it coming; he was looking at Ruby still. The blow caught him off balance, jerked his head back and slammed it into the cupboard. He folded up, collapsed, slid onto the floor.'

A dog howled and another answered it. The sunshine was bright in today's kitchen even as yesterday's words and the past were dark. And red, blood red. A car door slammed somewhere.

'I thought it was just a lucky blow, that she had only knocked him out. Still, I was glad. I hated him. Ruby was screaming. So Florence slapped Ruby too, her angry face grim and ugly. I remember thinking how much she relished the action, the violence.

'Ruby was crouched over Jose, moaning, sobbing. The boy was dead, or dying, and nobody moved to help him. Not Ruby, who didn't know what to do, or Florence. Or me.' Her eyes met mine, then dropped. 'He had struck his head on the corner of the cupboard. There was blood there. She couldn't wash it all off.'

Her voice broke. She turned from looking at the past to look at me. I wondered if she were talking about blood on Jose, or on the cupboard, or both.

'That was why she remodeled the kitchen, why she burned all the old cupboards. She never would have otherwise, she would never take out something old for something new. But that was a little later. Later.' She drew her hand wearily across her eyes. 'I was in an automobile accident once, in college.' She looked at me, pleading with me to follow, to understand.

'One minute we were laughing and talking, the next we were tumbled out into the road like rag dolls, except that rag dolls don't bleed: one girl dead, a boy paralyzed for life, another smashed up inside. I was hurt and broken too, but not forever.

'Not like death, death is forever.' Impossible to argue with that, so I didn't. 'Murder is too. That night, in a heartbeat, everything changed. The dream became a nightmare and there was no changing back, only going deeper and deeper into it, into the nightmare.'

'It wasn't murder, Opal.'

'Yes, I know that now.'

'Given the situation and your grandmother's standing in the community it is possible that it would have been ruled an accident. Case closed.'

'Yes.'

'Sympathy would have been almost entirely with your family. Apparently the boy was not well thought of, even his mother said he was a bad boy. Blackmail is a felony, and no one likes a blackmailer.'

'No, but it didn't, couldn't go that way.' She spoke with finality.

'Because of the pictures?'

'Yes. They would have come out. They had to. Otherwise why was he there? And what else did he have that was worth five thousand dollars to Florence? Nothing. Without the pictures it didn't make sense.'

'And Florence would not have allowed the pictures to come out?' It was a question but it needn't have been. I knew the answer already.

'Never. She burned them in the sink. Right then, right there. She had to step over his body to do it.' There was horror in her voice. 'There was ice water in that woman's veins.

'And all the time Ruby was crooning, petting, and fussing over him. I don't think she knew he was dead, or didn't let her mind accept it. Does that happen? Can it happen?'

I nodded.

'She had a little pocket comb and she kept combing his hair and kissing him. "There, there," she'd say, "all better now, all better." And he was *dead*!'

'He's buried here, isn't he?'

'Yes, out back.'

'The three of you?'

'Wiley and Florence. They tried to make me help. She could make me do almost anything,' Opal said bitterly, 'but not that, not *that*. Wiley was a different story, he would always do anything for her, for the family. They had to half drag, half carry Ruby up to her room before they could do it though. She was wild and hysterical; she wouldn't leave Jose. Something snapped that night, I think.'

'Snapped?'

'In her mind. She wasn't the same afterward. I don't forgive myself for leaving, for letting Florence send me away to school, but I wasn't strong enough to stand up to her. We none of us were. I should have taken care of Ruby then, but I couldn't, I just couldn't.' Her voice caught and died.

'And Ruby?' I prompted gently.

'Ruby?'

'That night.'

'She watched them bury him. She stood at her bedroom window, screaming, crying, pounding on the window glass. She broke it, cracked it; Wiley fixed it the next day. If she hadn't snapped before, that did it; but nobody fixed her.' Her eyes were still blank, dead.

'And you?'

'I ran away, slept outside that night. They called, looked for me, but it was easy enough to stay ahead of them, away from them. I came back in the morning, I didn't know what else to do, and Florence was making breakfast. Fried eggs, sausage, and corn bread. She acted as though nothing had happened. I tried to speak of it, only that once did I ever bring it up. She slapped me so hard the red mark stayed on my face for hours, a day maybe.'

'And Ruby?'

'She went inside. She was changed. Even I had a difficult time reaching her at first, and then I couldn't either. She drowned herself, you know? But that was after I left.'

I shook my head. 'I didn't know.'

'She always said that it would be a good way to die. She was an excellent swimmer, we both were, and we knew the river, knew where the dangerous spots were. The only way she could die swimming was if she chose it. It was less than a month after the boy died. And I was gone by then.'

'Did you come back for the funeral?'

Wildness flared in her eyes. 'Florence didn't tell me until afterward.' The bitterness had changed to hatred and her words ate at the memory like acid. 'She was terrified, I think, that I would talk. And I would have. With Ruby gone there was no one I was afraid of hurting.'

'Where did they bury Jose?'

'I don't know. Not far, else that night Ruby couldn't have seen. I never asked or tried to find out. Somewhere in the orchard, I suppose. Or the river, but no, I don't think so, he would have been found. Floaters usually are, out in our part of the river.'

She shivered. I did too. *Floaters*.

'She made us eat all of our breakfast.'

'That morning?'

'Yes. Eggs, sausage, bread. She made us wipe up the egg with the bread and eat it. I threw it up almost right away. It was then I knew that I hated her. I hadn't known, until that moment, how much, how very much. When she wrote to say that Ruby was dead and buried I knew I would never come back. I never answered her letter, never wrote. Florence was dead to me then.'

'Was there a flowered blanket or a quilt that Ruby cared about?'

Her forehead furrowed up. 'No. Why?'

I shrugged. 'Something she put in her diary.' And spoke about, but I didn't say that.

'May I have her diary?'

'Yes, of course.'

'Florence sent me away to school, you know?' I nodded. 'Paid for it and everything. There, far away, I made it seem as though it had happened to someone else, to some other girl. Some other girl saw the murder, not me. She should have reported it and helped her sister. Not me. I couldn't, so that was how I coped. And I became a different person. A different person, I thought. A successful businesswoman, with her own business. With a future but no past.

'Still, I couldn't forget it. It was like breakfast that morning: I swallowed it, but I couldn't keep it down.'

We sat in silence, thoughtful sad silence, calm if not peaceful silence.

'I wish I could have been a better, stronger person, done something about it. But I wasn't, I couldn't. I'm glad it's out now. I'm glad it's over. Finally.'

There was a long, shuddering sigh. Hers, I thought, but maybe not, maybe mine too. Tentatively she tried out a smile, looked reassured when it didn't fall off.

'No.'

It was a man's voice and it startled us both.

'It's not over.'

Twenty-Three

Many people put business before pleasure, and concede that personal sacrifices have to be made for business success. Many are also willing to sacrifice the happiness of others, especially a spouse, a partner, or a child, to achieve that success.

He stood in the doorway, the light behind him almost a halo around his body. It didn't make him look divine.

Opal gasped. 'Derek, what are you doing here? How did you find me? What's going on?'

'I was behind you, Opal.'

She frowned, puzzled. I was less puzzled: the pieces, at last, were starting to fall into place.

'I was on the same plane and had a rental car waiting; I didn't want you to face this alone. I thought you should have someone with you even though you didn't want me to come.'

'But you didn't tell me? You were on the same plane and I didn't know? I don't get it.' She looked like she didn't get it. She stood up, pushing her chair back. I did too.

'I didn't want to hassle over it and I knew you would. I thought it needed to be done, so I did it.'

She still looked puzzled. He put his hand briefly, affectionately, on her shoulder, then turned to me.

'Hello, Kat. Long time, no see.' His dark eyes smiled and danced at me. He reached out for my hands and held them tightly. 'Good to see you.' His hands were warm and strong.

Opal looked first at Derek, then at me. 'There seems to be a lot I don't know about.'

'Yes.'

I was in agreement with that. Big-time agreement. In fact I didn't think 'a lot' covered it, not even close.

'Tell me,' she said softly. Her eyes, her voice were no longer as warm, as friendly as they had been. 'Tell me now, and tell me everything.'

Derek shook his head. 'This is not the way to handle it, Opal.'

His voice was gentle, caring; his words caressed her, meant, I thought, to soothe and appease, or maybe something else, something that was more difficult to comprehend. I considered him with a new idea in mind.

'Let me take you to a hotel. I'll handle things here. This is my end of it, the practical end, the business end.'

She was puzzled. I could read it in her face. 'This isn't a business deal, Derek, this is family. This is—' She turned abruptly to me. 'I don't know what it is, but I think I have to hear it?' Her voice rose in a question as she looked steadily at me.

I nodded. I thought so too. And some of it was long overdue. Years, decades overdue.

'Derek, let me talk to Kat, please. Alone.'

He hesitated, shrugged, then left the room.

'Tell me, Kat.'

Damn! Why hadn't I seen this in my mind, seen how very difficult this would be, must be?

'Kat?'

'I don't know where to start, how to—'

'At the beginning, that's what you told me.'

'All right.'

That would, I thought, work as well as anything else. Even though the beginning, this beginning, was arbitrary. It hadn't started with Paige. Nor with Ruby and Opal. Not even with Florence who had been an innocent once, a baby lifting her face into the light with roses in her cheeks, drool on her chin, sunshine in her heart.

'Kat?'

I dragged my thoughts back into the present. Pity lurked there in the past. It wouldn't help.

'Paige came to me to find out something about her past. Florence raised her from a baby, told her that her parents had died in an automobile accident and that her name was Morrell. That was it. That was all she was ever told, all she ever knew. And Florence refused to speak of it.'

'Dear God,' Opal breathed, 'how appalling, and how like Florence.'

'She was raised alone in a loveless home. She had no one.'

The color changed in Opal's eyes, deepened somehow.

'Why?'

It was a large why, a generic not a specific why, and I didn't know. It was the question I had just tried and fumbled.

'Sometimes I wonder what it was in Florence's life that so twisted her, that crippled her capacity to love and feel. She *can't* have *meant* to hurt us, can she? A mother, a grandmother couldn't *mean* that, could she?'

And again I didn't know, though I hoped not.

'Was she beaten as a child? Not given enough food or love? Was her heart trampled on, wrung out and twisted, hung out to dry and laughed at?'

An appalling image of a dripping bloody heart hanging by wooden pegs on a clothesline in the Delta sunshine surfaced in my mind.

'Was she that way to us, to Paige too, because it was all she had experienced? God, it would help so much if I *knew*, if I could understand.'

It would, I agreed, but I thought she would never know. None of us would.

'It would make her a person, not a monster. It would help.'

'Yes.'

'Kat?'

She was asking me, begging me to throw her a

lifeline. I didn't have one to throw. No lifeline; no comfort. Empty words were worthless, were worse than nothing. 'I'm sorry,' I managed at last.

She took a deep raggedy breath and tried to smile. 'Back to Paige then.' I went back to Paige.

'She asked me to find out about her parents. I imagine Florence's death freed her in some way to ask questions.'

'Yes,' Opal agreed. 'It would.'

'I went to Herb Sanderson first. He knew a great deal.'

She smiled, a real smile, and her eyes changed color again, lightened. 'Dear, *dear* Uncle Herb and Aunt Letitia. We loved them so, and they us. After Ruby, that was all I regretted leaving behind me. I wrote two or three times over the years telling them I was all right, thanking them.

'I thought about it on the plane, how sorry I am that I missed Aunt Letitia, how wonderful it will be to see Uncle Herb, dear, loving Uncle Herb.' She thought quietly for a moment. 'And you're right, I think he knew most everything, knew or guessed. Did he tell you?'

'He died before he could tell me.'

The liveliness drained out of her face. 'No! Oh no! How?'

'One evening in his study. It was apparently a heart attack.'

'When?'

'Last week.'

271

She moaned, a low animal sound that sent shivers through me and made goosebumps on my arms.

'There's more, Opal.' I said it gently. 'And it's worse.' I didn't think of the past as pitiful now, but as relentless.

'Tell me,' she whispered.

I had to lean forward to hear her. Her face was drawn in pain. I looked away, not wanting to see that raw, naked look on another's face.

'Florence's will provided for the medical and custodial care of a distant cousin, Garnet Whyte. She was, and had been, in either institutional or home care for the past twenty-some years. Have you ever heard of her?'

'No.' Relief crowded in on her voice and expression. The tension in her face eased, the pain shifted slightly. 'No.' She breathed easily. 'I hadn't, *haven't*,' she corrected.

'She was a relative, but not a distant cousin. Her name wasn't Whyte.'

She looked at me. So? her eyes said. So?

'Her first name wasn't Garnet either. But Garnet was a play on words, a play on her name—'

'No!' she cried out. 'No! No! No!'

I saw it coming, but I wasn't fast enough, was caught too in time, and in her words, emotion, and denial. Her hand struck my mouth, brutally.

'No,' she wailed. 'Take it back! Say that it's not so, say it's not Ruby! Say it!'

I said nothing. My lip felt swollen, bruised, maybe

split. And I felt worse on the inside.

'Say it,' she begged me. Tears filled her eyes, spilled, were as out of control as everything else.

'I can't. I'm sorry.' That again.

She turned away and began pounding her fists methodically on the wooden cabinets behind her. No words, no cries, just a steady rhythmic pounding. It lasted for a long time, a long time and no swan song. Finally she stopped, leaned against the cabinet. When she turned, the young beautiful woman I had known was gone. She looked like Garnet, aged beyond her years.

'Ruby. Where is she? Take me there. Now. Please, *please!*'

'I can't.'

'Why?'

'She's dead.' I tried to say it gently, but there is no way to do that. 'The police think she was murdered.'

'Murdered?' she asked, almost stupidly. It was too much, I think, for her to take in. 'Murdered? Why?'

She walked over to me, reached out and gently touched my lip. When she took her hand away there was blood on her finger. She looked at it in amazement.

'I didn't mean . . . oh, I'm so sorry.' She said it helplessly. 'Ruby.' Her voice begged the world to be a different place.

But it wasn't. Herb was dead. Ruby was dead; worse, her life had been a death, a long, horrible one.

And I had a split lip. I licked it, hating the taste of blood. Blood was coming too easily here, now. I didn't like it and it made me afraid for—

'I thought Ruby was dead. To find out – Oh, God.' She put her head in her hands. 'It changes everything, everything.'

It did, yes.

'I want to see her,' she said finally, looking at me.

'All right.' Only, it wasn't a *her,* it was an it, a body. 'I'll give you the name of the homicide detective in charge.' She winced at the word *homicide.* 'He can help you arrange it.'

'What happened . . . her life, what . . . oh God!' Her mind veered off. It was too much. 'What does she look like? Does she . . . we were identical twins, you know. Do we, did we . . .' Her mind balked again.

'Life was not kind to her.'

'What do you mean?' Opal whispered.

'You are a very beautiful woman; her beauty is gone.'

'Destroyed?'

'Yes.'

The front door slammed. Derek? He was making a lot of noise for a man who generally moved quietly, easily. Footsteps pounded down the hall. Opal moved to the cupboard, hesitated, then opened it, took out a glass and went to the sink for water. A man entered the room.

'You!' He almost spit with disgust. 'What the hell are *you* doing here? Where's Paige?'

It took me a minute to react; I was still in the past.

'Hey!'

'Hi, Paul.'

He cleared his throat and looked again like he wanted to spit. It slammed me into the present. I made a mental note to mention to Paige that it wasn't a great idea to marry a guy without manners. I was sure that was the kind of thing that got worse, not better, with time.

'Where is Paige?' he growled at me. Opal took a last sip of water and set her glass down very carefully in the sink.

'Paul, I'd like you to meet Opal Harnway, Paige's aunt. Maternal aunt,' I added, in case he missed it, but he hadn't. 'Opal, this is Paul, Paige's fiancé.'

Paul's face changed immediately, became quieter, more unreadable. 'Uh.' His speech patterns stayed the same. 'Uh.' He wiped his hand on his jeans and then extended it, walking toward Opal. 'Pleased to meet you, ma' am.'

She took his hand and shook it, then turned back to the sink and filled up her water glass again. Paul did a quick two-step shuffle in place and then looked around helplessly. Opal and her glass of water left, headed apparently for the front room.

'Okay, now—!' Paul spoke in a low and threatening voice. 'Now, tell me what the hell is going on here? What's with the aunt? And where's Paige, huh?' He advanced on me, his right hand slightly raised and lightly balled into a fist.

'You do have a way with words.' I let a note of admiration creep into my voice and tried to keep the sarcasm out, tried and failed. Sometimes I don't try hard enough.

'Why don't I teach him some manners, Kat?' Derek came through the back door and stood behind me, one hand resting lightly and proprietarily on my shoulder. I wondered how much he'd heard of my conversation with Opal. I wondered if he'd been listening. I rather thought so. 'It would be a pleasure. A *real* pleasure.'

I sighed inside. What was it with the men in my life? Why couldn't they stay sidelined when I was dealing with things?

'Uh, look.' Paul's hand dropped to his side. 'No, uh, offense, hey? Look, I was just trying to find Paige, okay?'

'Doesn't sound like an apology to me, Mac,' Derek said pleasantly.

'Uh, uh, sorry. Look, Kat, about Paige—'

'She's out of town for a few days. Why don't you just run along home now, Paul.'

The blood rushed to his face, his fists clenched briefly, then unclenched again. 'Look, do you know where she is, when she'll be back?' His voice stayed polite. His eyes avoided Derek.

'No. Run along now.'

'Please.' It hurt him to say that, or maybe he was just way out of practice. 'Look, it's important I reach her. We had a little disagreement and uh—'

'The lady said good-bye, Mac.'

'Yeah, well, uh, okay.' He stumbled around in his words, then on his feet, then left.

'Derek—'

'I know.' He grinned and threw his hands up in the air. 'You can handle it and you'd rather I didn't interfere. Opal's always telling me the same thing. Kat . . .' His hand brushed my cheek. 'Could we start over?' He leaned over and kissed me gently on the forehead, then on my cheek and finally, tenderly, on the mouth. My split lip was getting puffy now. 'Hello,' he said softly. 'And what happened?'

'Hello,' I returned, and I tried to explain but it got too complicated, so I stopped. My lip was bleeding again; I found a paper towel and started daubing at it with cold water.

'I wish Opal would let me handle things. She's not tough, not like she thinks she is – or wants to be, not like you.'

I tasted blood and didn't feel all that tough.

'Kat.' Opal's voice was soft behind me. I turned. 'Murder? Who could possibly want to hurt Ruby?' Her eyes filled with tears. 'It doesn't sound as though she was capable of bothering anyone.' She brushed the tears away. 'Why?'

'I think you ought to talk to Detective Henley.' To anyone, anyone but me.

'What are you two talking about?' Derek asked. We ignored him. And he knew anyway. I was sure of it.

'You're hiding something. Please don't do that. Let's work together. *Please,*' Opal begged.

I was silent, trying to figure it out. 'Not hiding, necessarily.' I got that far and stopped. I didn't want to do this at all.

'Kat, please.'

'Do you know who inherited when Florence died?' I asked at last.

'Ruby,' Opal said softly. 'Direct linear descent.'

'You both knew?'

'Oh, yes. Always. Florence was very bitter and vocal about it. The estate and income stayed with her for her lifetime but she couldn't, and didn't, inherit. We did. We always spoke of it that way, that we would share. Technically, of course, it went to Ruby, and then to her heirs. You don't think—' She was openmouthed and horrified.

'No, I don't,' I said, but I lied.

'Me? Paige?' Still horrified.

'Cops think like that,' Derek said.

'Yes,' I agreed.

'No.' Opal's hand partially covered her mouth. 'My God, won't it ever end? Why *would* I? Why murder?'

'Somebody killed once to keep the past quiet, hidden. It could happen again.' I spoke, but reluctantly.

'Kat!'

'That's how cops think. They'll consider Derek, too.' I said it, though I didn't believe it.

Opal was now wide-eyed, stunned. 'Have you lost

your mind? Why would *he*?'

'To protect your business, his business. People kill for money.'

He smiled. 'I can be ruthless but I draw the line at murder.' He said it, he smiled, he was charming.

None of us liked the way this conversation was shaping up.

'Or you?' Opal turned to me and I liked it even less. 'Paige was your client. You'd protect her.'

'Wrong job description, Opal. I'm an investigator, not an avenger.' I said it hard, mean. That's how I felt.

'I apologize.' Her voice was contrite. 'It's the shock, and Ruby . . . *oh, Ruby!* . . . I'm sorry, I didn't mean it.'

So I let it go.

'Let's start over,' Derek said. We seemed to be doing that a lot lately. 'And the business. I'm glad that got brought up. Opal, we need to address that, to handle it.'

'Business?' Opal said helplessly. 'I can't talk about that now.'

'We have to. This kind of publicity—' He shook his head. 'A business like ours could go under. We've got to do something about it.'

'What are you talking about, Derek?'

He hesitated so I answered for him. 'A cover-up.'

'No. We can't.' Opal looked horrified.

'We have to.'

'It's not a business decision now, Derek.' I pointed

out the obvious since, apparently, I was the only one thinking clearly. 'It's homicide. And homicide limits your options. Especially when cops are involved.'

Twenty-Four

Almost everyone has dirt under the rug, a skeleton in the closet, a dark secret. Some will lie or pay blackmail to keep it there, to keep it dark. Some will kill.

'I've done enough lying and running away, a lifetime's worth. I'm not doing it anymore, no matter what.' Opal was adamant. I believed her. I didn't think it sounded negotiable either.

'You're upset, I understand, but you're not thinking rationally, not counting the cost.'

That was Derek, of course, not me. In my book, rational behavior, by definition, means cooperating with cops, especially homicide cops.

'I'm through thinking that way, Derek. Nobody counted the cost to Ruby, did they? If I had, or . . .' Her voice ran down. The tears threatened again. She shook them away.

He took her hands. 'I understand your feelings, but don't you see, Harnway Associates is built on the premise of probity, of integrity, of analytical and statistical analysis. If the murder, the deceit, the lies and the cover-up come out, we're through.'

'Maybe not. Everyone has skeletons in their closet. Oh . . .' She shivered and put her hand to her mouth.

'But not in their backyard,' Derek said grimly, brutally. 'I can see the headlines now.'

'Derek, stop!'

I drifted over to the window to let them slug it out. *Dear Charity*, I mused, *Years ago there was a scandal that was hushed up in my family. Keeping it a secret ruined three, maybe four, lives. Now it's started all over again. Keeping it quiet would mean starting the lies and everything all over again too. What should I do?* Signed, *About to be Ruined.*

Dear About, Are you one of the three or four people whose lives were ruined by the scandal and the cover-up the first time? If you weren't, then you will be now. Lies get bigger, not smaller, over time. Charity.

And I thought that was true, about manners and lies both. They don't improve with age. Wine does, and some cheese, friendships if you were lucky, mutual funds if you had any – which I didn't – and were very lucky, and— Opal's voice broke into my reverie.

'I won't, Derek. Even if I could, I wouldn't.' She stated it with finality. Derek stared at her without expression. 'Don't you see? It's starting all over again, this time with Ruby's daughter. Another life is touched, tainted, maybe ruined by it. It's got to stop.'

'We're talking about a murder, Opal, a murder that was buried twenty years ago, not about a traffic ticket.'

'No,' I said. 'Not *a* murder. Murders. And whoever killed Ruby is out there still, walking around still.'

'It's got to stop.' Opal spoke almost to herself. 'When I see what the hate has done, the ugliness . . . to me, to Ruby, to—' she stumbled over the thought, '—to Florence even. Oh, God, how I hate her! Still. I wish I could forgive and I can't. But I can stop, I can do that.' Her hand pushed at her hair. The beauty was back. She no longer looked old, she no longer looked like Garnet. 'I don't know how to love.'

Her voice was sad. The sadness echoed in my mind like words lost in a well because I was afraid I didn't know how to love either. I thought about Hank and our relationship and couldn't bear the idea that I had given up, had run away.

'There's hope still, and it's got to stop.'

I nodded, I agreed. I don't think Derek did. They left for their downtown hotel in his car, Derek unsmiling, Opal with hope in her heart and Henley's number in her purse.

I looked out the kitchen window at the orchard in bloom and the flowers everywhere in the backyard and thought how sad and lonely it was to be buried somewhere in an unmarked grave. Then I thought how much sadder it was to live unloved and imprisoned. And how Ruby was finally free now. Except that dead isn't free. Dead is dead. I heard tires on the gravel driveway and then the slam of a car, or truck door. Now who? Footsteps in the hall. Quiet, paced, slow.

'You been making trouble ever since you got here.'

Nobody was saying 'Hello, how are you?' today. It was that kind of a day.

Wiley held up a strong, thick-fingered, heavily veined hand, then pushed a cap that said *Bob's Feed and Supply* back on his head. 'I'm a worker, not a talker, but I have to talk some now. Have to.' He stood, a stolid unmoving country man, and considered it all for some time without saying anything. I did the same. 'We got to git you to stop making trouble. Got to.'

'I'm not making trouble, Wiley. The trouble was already here. Had been for a long time.'

'Ain't no trouble if you don't stir it up.'

I shrugged. He must be behind the times. He must not know about Ruby's death, or the homicide investigation. And that wasn't going away, not on his say-so, or mine, or anyone else's.

'Paige hired me to do this. It wasn't my idea.'

'But she wouldn't have found out nothing without you. And she'll stop. She's young, she'll learn.' He looked at his hands again. They looked like weapons; it was the way he held them. 'But she ain't gonna stop if'n you don't stop, so I reckon you better stop.' He looked at his hands again and then at me.

I still didn't say anything. I wasn't going to agree with him and I didn't feel like disagreeing, so there wasn't much to say.

The wrinkles in his tanned face were white from constant squinting into the sun, his hair grizzled at the temples, his face wooden. 'You see, miss, I made a promise. It was a long time ago but that don't matter. Them kind of promises never get old and they don't die till you're dead and I ain't dead. It was to old Mr Morrell. I said I'd see to things for the family and I have and I will. It ain't nothing personal.' He looked at me. 'But it's got to stop. You see how it goes, don't you?'

I nodded. I saw how it went.

'That's all right then.' He turned and walked out the way he came. No good-bye either. That kind of day.

I saw how it went, yes; I wasn't going that way but I didn't bother to mention it to him. It didn't seem like the right time, or place. I thought of those hard, thick, heavy hands. And I thought it might never be the right time.

I headed downtown. I didn't call ahead; it was fine with me if I missed Henley. He was in. Too bad. If he was pleased to see me he hid it well.

'So, Kat,' he pointed at a chair, 'sit down, start talking. Turns out you were one of the last people to see Garnet alive.'

'One of the last?'

'Yeah.' He looked almost regretful. Some friend. 'The attendant checked in on her after you left and before she dozed off for the evening. She was fine, sleeping, just like you said.'

'How did she die?'

'Okay.' He leaned forward and looked right at me.

'I'm going to do you a favor and do some talking. Then you're going to do you a favor and do some, a lot of it in fact. This is a new deal now, Kat. This is homicide. Whole new deal.'

'Yes. All right.'

He stared at me, tough-cop shit, then finally nodded. 'She was smothered. The patrol cop who answered the nine-one-one call got suspicious when he saw bruises on her arms and an injection mark. So he called us; right idea, wrong reason. There were a lot more bruises, too, but they didn't show up until later at the autopsy. If it was two guys, one held her down, the other smothered her. If it was one, and I lean to that, he probably straddled her on the bed, pinning her arms down with his knees, and smothered her, maybe with the pillow. There was some lint in her lungs.'

I thought of Ruby and her fear of dark places.

'There were bruises on her face from the pressure. Maybe she fought back and he pressed down. Or she. It could have been a woman, no problem, seeing as the victim was drugged. Homicide, Kat, no question. So start talking.'

I started. 'Here's a copy of the will. I didn't have it with me before. In the will, Garnet is provided for.'

He nodded, slightly bored. 'We've been through this before.'

'Yes, only she's not Garnet Whyte. Her name is – was – Ruby Morrell.' Henley started looking a lot more interested. 'Ruby was Florence's daughter and Paige's mother.' I really had his attention now. He started to interrupt but I held up a hand. 'Wait a minute, I'm getting there. Back to the will. Apparently Ruby inherited, Paige after her. Perhaps she could have contested it though, bypassed her mother, given the condition of the latter. I don't know.'

I thought about it and threw in Paul. With pleasure, enthusiasm even. The thought of homicide cops going at him perked my spirits right up. 'Check out Paige's fiancé. He's got no job, expensive tastes, and Paige is his meal ticket. I don't think he'd like to see that screwed up, or her disinherited.'

'Name? Address?'

'I don't know anything more than Paul. He drives a late-model BMW,' and I gave him the tag. He nodded.

'Ruby had a twin sister, Opal, that Paige didn't know about. I found her in Omaha. She's in town now, with her business partner. She wants to see you.' Okay, I lied. 'And her sister's body. I imagine you can get an ID there and start untangling this mess. She's got your name and number.' I gave him the hotel where they were staying. Then I stopped. This was the second time today that I really hadn't wanted to have a conversation.

'Bill, the grandmother, Florence Morrell, swept a lot of family dirt under the rug.' I winced. When Henley found out that dirt under the rug meant a body buried in the backyard I was in deep shit. 'I've heard several versions now, all conflicting, all secondhand. Why don't you talk to the principals and then, if I can fill in anything, I'd be glad to?'

Henley nodded, bought it. Shoot, I would have too. It sounded reasonable and helpful. It left out the body, that's why. And, now that I had this one pretty much up to speed, it was time to get out of here. If I kept talking I was going to blow it, only a question of time.

'That it? I've got things to do.'

'Yeah. You're not telling me something.'

'What?' I managed to look puzzled, maybe innocent. Maybe not.

He snorted, then grinned like he was letting me get away with something, but only for now. 'Yeah, right.' Of course he knew where to find me. 'Okay, Kat, see you.'

I didn't need to hear it twice. I made tracks.

I went back to my office, answered some messages, made some calls, patched a few things together. That done I called the hotel and asked for Derek or Opal. No answer from either room. I would wait for Derek's call then, and he would call, I knew it. I wouldn't have to wait long. I didn't.

'Kat.'

'Derek.' I heard the relief, the pleasure in my voice. So much for cool.

'Hey, honey.' He heard it too. 'Hang in there. We'll have dinner.'

'Yes, good. Where are you?'

'In Freeport, at Cora Sanderson's. I'd like to leave Opal here for the night. She needs someone to talk to, family especially, someone who understands. And Cora is a nice person.'

It was a good idea. I didn't think Opal should be alone right now either, but for a different reason.

'Can you get away soon, Kat?'

'There's a restaurant in Freeport, Peter B's. I'll meet you there in forty minutes. In the bar.'

I didn't have time to go home so I fancied up at the office. I had stashed a clean blouse and my suede jacket in the closet there and that helped a lot. Same jeans, same gun, though. I made one more call. No answer so I left a long message on Charity's answering machine. Insurance. Then I left. I was on time but Derek had beat me and was sitting at the bar halfway through a Molson.

'Hey,' he said softly as I slid onto the stool next to him. He leaned over and kissed me on the corner of the mouth. 'What would you like?' His eyes smiled at me.

'White wine.' What the hell, I was still on an expense account. 'Chardonnay. With a straw,' I added.

The bartender turned and looked at me. 'Ice?' I shook my head. He looked more closely, saw the split lip and nodded.

I drank. 'It doesn't taste the same with a straw,' I said grumpily.

Derek laughed at me. 'Hungry?'

'Yes.' I was. 'Starved.' I smiled. 'We're going to eat down on the river.'

'Sounds good.' He ordered another round.

I looked at my glass. Wine goes down faster with a straw, I guess. We should be going, but what the hell. It would wait – dinner and whatever else the evening held.

Derek held my hand and played with my fingers as we left. 'Let's take my car and leave yours here. You look tired.'

Good idea, especially since I wasn't driving my car. I had Charity's beat-up '73 Ford pickup. I'd come out of my office an hour before to a switch, and an excuse in a note on the windshield. Time to quit leaving spare keys under the seat, or get some new friends. It didn't take us long to get to the restaurant and it was a nice ride, peaceful and quiet in the early evening. I opened the window and leaned back, relaxing for the first time in a long while.

I love this time of day, when the sun is almost down and the colors soft and serene. The river intensifies everything, making it more beautiful, heightened somehow. In the quiet of the dusk you can hear the birds, their last plaintive cries echoing over the river, insects droning, and the slap of water as boats cruise by. It is a time of day when you pay attention to beauty. I let my hand hang out the window in the wind rush.

There were other sounds. Not good ones. I could

hear the words and questions echoing through the spaces in my head, slapping rudely up against the pilings of my mind. They were sounds I didn't care for.

Warning sounds.

Dr Jonas was right. Americans watched too much TV.

Twenty-Five

Bartenders, cops, medical personnel, cats, and lovers all know about full moons. But not the same things.

We ate at Benny's, a restaurant set up and back slightly from the river. Closed in winter, it's a lively spot in spring and summer. The food was good, the company even better. It should have been a fun, relaxing, even romantic evening, but it wasn't.

'I'm sorry, Derek.' I was watching a small boat putter along on the river and sipping wine through a straw. 'I'm not being good company.' I gave myself a quick mental shake and him a smile.

'No,' he said, 'me either. There's too much going down too fast. I'm worried.'

There was more to come; I waited for it.

'About Opal and our business.' He paused. 'I don't want to sound like a heartless jerk, Kat, and I'm not; I know Opal's going through a really rough time. Still, I am legitimately and reasonably worried about the business.'

He held his hands out, palms up, as if to say: What do I do? 'It's my life and has been for over ten years.

I love it.' His voice was deep, passionate. 'It's Opal's life, too. Maybe we made a mistake, both of us, getting involved in the business so deeply and often to the exclusion of a personal life. Although I think that part of it was a relief to Opal and, after what I've heard of her family, I can understand why.'

'And you?'

He laughed. 'We've all got a story, haven't we? Mine's not as bad as Opal's but it's . . . it's not great. The long hours, the absorbing work, it was okay with me too.' He reached out and put his hand over mine. 'You're kind of an exception in my life now.'

'One that lives sixteen hundred miles away.'

'And that makes it safe?'

'Doesn't it?'

'You're not safe, Kat.'

No, I guess I wasn't. I thought about it for a while and wondered if we were talking about the same thing. Then I thought about how people who are safe don't have to carry guns, and I was; but that was a different kind of safe.

Another boat went by. And a breeze, sweet, fresh, slightly cool. The waitress drifted by as aimlessly as the boat and Derek ordered another round. I finished my glass of wine, making a slightly rude sound with the straw on the last sip.

'Classy.' He winked at me.

I frowned. 'What's the most important thing, Derek?'

'About what?' He leaned back. 'Narrow it down, Kat.'

'To you, and in your life right now?'

'Money, and a life that I've built and like very much.'

'And you're worried about the reputation of Harnway Associates if this comes out?'

'*When*, not if, and very much so.'

'Don't be. No one is going to doubt Opal's business judgment today because of a personal incident, however unfortunate, over twenty years ago, especially in the context of the Morrell family.'

He smiled wryly. 'That's the first time I've heard murder termed "an unfortunate incident."'

I smiled back. 'Not murder, you know that. And the boy was a blackmailer. Public sympathy will overwhelmingly be with the victim, with her family.' I shrugged cynically. 'Perhaps the publicity will even bring you business. Who knows? In any case your professional track record is what you will be judged on. But you know this, Derek.'

He nodded. 'This is not a good time for the business to undergo any kind of scrutiny.'

'Why?'

He flushed. 'I won't bother you with that.' I started to speak and he shook his head. So I shut up.

Our drinks arrived, mine looking slightly rakish with a fresh straw. I drank maybe half of it and then announced that I was ready to go. And I was. I'd had enough fun for the evening, for the day, for the week – maybe even for the month.

We headed back to the parking lot of Peter B's

where we'd left Charity's truck, my transportation. The moon was full, a beautiful spring evening on the Delta. I was full too: with food and wine if not contentment. We drove back in easy silence and I watched the moonlight play and shift on the river. The parking lot was dark and deserted. Derek got out and stood with me as I unlocked the truck.

'I'll call you in the morning. Early, all right?'

'Yes.'

'I need to check in with Opal, of course, help her with whatever needs to be done. We'll plan on breakfast.' He frowned. 'Or lunch.'

'Whatever. It's fine.'

He smiled. 'And dinner. Tomorrow we won't be so tired.' His finger delicately traced my cheekbone and he leaned over to hold me briefly, kiss me. His body felt stiff and hard, his kisses perfunctory. It *had* been a bad week. We said good night and he walked around the truck to his rental. I had just started the pickup when Derek tapped on the passenger window and gestured for me to open the door.

I sighed. Suddenly I wanted the evening to be over. I wanted to be in bed. Asleep. Alone. I wanted all this badly. I sighed again and opened the door.

'Kat.' He got in. 'It doesn't seem right, ending the evening like this. Not after . . .'

'It's all right. There's tomorrow. And the day after, and the day after.' I shivered in the cool of the evening, and decided against turning the heater on yet. The engine was too cold. I touched his knee lightly. 'See you at breakfast.'

'It's a beautiful evening; let's drive down by the river. There's a full moon,' he said smiling at me, 'a Delta moon, a lover's moon.'

God, I thought tiredly. Would men ever get it straight, get the picture? When you wanted them to be romantic they watched football games, drank beer, and belched. When you didn't . . . Phooey.

I shivered and yawned. Right now on a romantic scale of 1–10 I was, tops, a minus 2. I'm not shy; I said so. Because I'm diplomatic, and because it was Derek, I didn't say the first things I thought of. *Can it. Bag it. Get real, Mac.* I was proud of myself for that. Real proud, but it didn't last long. These moments never do.

'Not tonight, Derek, I'm cold and tired.' I shivered again. I didn't mean to, I couldn't help it. 'And I'm not feeling romantic. It's been that kind of a day.'

'Don't make me ask again, Kat.' He had his hands in his jacket pockets and looked like a dejected little kid.

'Tomorrow.'

He shrugged and took his hands out of his pockets. There was a .38 in one of them. It made me feel even less romantic, a lot less, actually.

'Oh,' I said.

He nodded.

'What's going on?' My voice sounded tired and stupid, which made sense, it was how I felt, tired, stupid. 'Derek, what in God's name are—'

'Let's go, Kat.' His voice was as sweet, loving, and gentle as always. Not sarcastic, not mean. The gun made lies out of all that. 'Let's go.' I looked around. 'Nobody. Nothing.' He waved the gun. 'Let's go.'

'Why?'

'I'll shoot you here if I have to.' I glanced at his face and believed him, put the truck in gear and bought time.

'Where's the man I made love with?' I looked at Derek, through him, past him, around him. The clutch was in and the truck idled beneath us. 'Where?' I asked softly.

'Don't be foolish, Kat.'

His voice was hard-edged now, ugly, mean as an unfed pit bull. Was that always there? It must have been. Detectives are no good on their own lives, that's for sure. I promised myself I'd never succumb to a help-me-make-it-through-the-night feeling again. Never. He nudged the gun over in my direction again.

If I had the choice, that is. Catch a clue, Kat. Get a life. I looked down the barrel of the .38. Keep a life.

'Why?' I asked again.

'That was us; this is business, and you got in the way of business.' He frowned. 'I'm not happy that things turned out this way, not at all.'

I looked down the barrel of the gun and swallowed hard. Me either.

'Let's go, Kat, back to the river.'

I put the truck in gear and we drove off. The river it was. I find it hard to resist a cogent argument, or a gun.

'Why?' I asked again. I didn't look at him, I just asked. The road here was tricky; levee roads always are. I thought about it. Driving off the levee didn't sound any worse than getting shot at. Crashing *and* getting shot at did though.

'Why? You already asked me that.' He pinched my knee playfully. I moved my leg and he laughed, resting his hand, the one without the gun, on my shoulder. Stoically I drove.

'Money. Isn't it always money, Kat?'

I thought about the people I loved, the things I held dear. 'No.'

'You're a romantic fool, then.' He squeezed my shoulder. 'I'm not.'

I said nothing, just hated him some more. Even romantic fools can hate.

'Where are we?' he asked.

'Between Freeport and Hood.'

The moon was high, full, and beautiful, and I had never, in my whole life, felt less romantically inclined. I looked sideways, not at Derek, no, but at the gun. It lay across his lap, rested on his thigh. His hand was relaxed. I remembered the way his thigh muscles had rippled, had played against my thighs and my hands.

'All along the river here the towns are four miles apart. They were settled that way, as riverboat stops:

Freeport, Clarksburg, Hood, Courtland, Walnut Grove, Ryde. Everything moved on the river then, not on land. Freeport got its name because—'

'You should have let it be, Kat.' There was regret in his voice, sadness even. 'I didn't want it to come to this. I like you. A lot.' He touched my cheek, rested his hand on my shoulder again. I didn't shudder, didn't shrug it off. It took all I had.

'*Why*, Derek?' I still didn't get it, or didn't want to believe it. 'Not just for the *money*?' I could hear the sorrow in the back of my voice. How could I have slept with him? My mind gave out. More sorrow. '*Money?!* It's *that* important?'

'Midnight Desire, Rambunctious, Black Sox, Omar the Second, Rainy Day Maid, Loverboy, Sweet Nothings, Merrywidow . . .'

I stared at him, uncomprehendingly.

'Horses, babe. I'm a gambler. I sold the business out for the ponies.' He smiled a crooked smile. 'Nice guy, huh?'

'I don't understand.'

'Opal would work out an analysis and make honest recommendations for the client. I implemented those recommendations not on the basis of merit, but on a kickback scheme I'd worked out. The company suffered for it but I couldn't stop, I was in too deep with the horses. And even that wasn't enough, I still needed money.'

I was connecting up the dots now. Finally.

'The ranch, Kat. It's worth a lot, though I had no

idea how much until I got here. It would bail me out, me and Opal and the company.'

'Was Opal in on this?'

'Oh no.' His voice was scornful. 'She's a goody-two-shoes. She didn't even tell me about it. She's a very private person, although I don't think that's what it was, why she didn't tell me. She's obsessed with forgetting the past, pretending it's not there. She doesn't realize you can't put obsessions behind you.'

'Like gambling,' I said.

'Like gambling.' He grinned. 'Or like family.'

'How did you find out then?'

'Sanderson called her. I caught it by chance and listened in on an extension. He laid it all out nice and clear, the niece too, and asked Opal to come back.'

'And?'

'And she said no, said she wanted nothing to do with either the niece or the ranch, then fell apart and hung up. It had promise, this situation, so I decided to check it out. I flew in the next day.'

'Ruby and Paige stood between Opal and the ranch.'

'Yes.' He shrugged. 'And now you.' There was regret in his voice.

I connected up a few more dots and stood back, checking out the picture. Something was missing.

'It wouldn't have worked, Derek. It's not something you could pull off alone.'

He grinned at me.

'Paige.'

It was a statement, not a question. I knew.

I remembered her tears and the floater the first day in the office. And I remembered the cool way she dropped the tears and trembling and asked me to get a copy of the death certificate.

'We met out at the ranch. I pretended to be in real estate and to be looking the property over, seeing if she wanted to sell. We got to talking. We recognized each other, you see, liked what we saw. It didn't take us long to get to know each other. Or to tell the truth.'

I shivered and hated myself; it hadn't taken us long either – in bed at least.

'I didn't have to pretend with her, Kat, like I do, did, with you. She's just like me.' His finger traced my cheekbone and touched my lip. 'Hungry, greedy,' he said softly. He let his hand brush across my breast and made a low sound in the back of his throat.

I broke into that tender moment. 'Who killed Ruby, you or Paige?' My voice shook a little.

He laughed. 'I like that about you, Kat. You're smart, spunky. The night we had dinner and—'

I felt sick inside. He laughed.

'—and spent the evening, Paige broke into your office. We had the address then. She went over to that home care place to do the job but instead spooked the old lady and bungled it. I had a motel room up here. She called in and left a message, so I went out.'

Went out, I thought. I went out to get the mail, walk the dog, pick a flower, pick up a quart of milk. No, I went out to kill someone. It struck me how odd it was that the same simple words could be used with flowers and violent death.

'They made it easy by sedating her. You made it easy by opening the window.'

Made it easy first by finding her, then by telling Paige, *then* by opening the window. Nice job. Thanks, Kat. I thought of Ruby and the beauty there, twisted, thwarted and stunted, but beautiful nonetheless.

There were hot and bitter tears in my eyes. I blinked them back. Thanks, Kat. *Real* nice job. Maybe you'll get a bonus for this one. A body is as good as a death certificate any day. Double bonus, maybe.

'I climbed in and used the pillow. It only took a minute, it was nothing.' He said it easily, dismissing a life. And for him, obviously, it was easy. And he planned to do it again.

Only not a life, any old life, my life. It wasn't going to be easy, not this time.

'But you.' The regret again, heavy and full in his voice. 'You're young, beautiful, and sexy.' His voice dropped. 'I wish—' He looked at me and I shuddered. I couldn't help it, couldn't repress it. God knows I tried.

'Pull over here.'

The regret was gone. He sounded businesslike now. Again. It was a turnout on the side of the road.

For fishermen, lovers, people with car trouble. I had trouble and I'd waited too long. The gun was on me again, readied, leveled, steady.

'Ruby was Opal's twin sister, Derek. That didn't bother you?'

He laughed, a nice laugh, the deep rich laugh that I thought of as his. 'I'm a businessman, Kat. I do what I have to do.'

He sounded philosophical about it, as though he were talking about advertising or bulk rate mailing, not murder.

'You don't always like it, like now, but you do it. Turn the truck off, leave the keys in the ignition. Pop the hood.'

I did and then we sat there, in silence and moonlight, for a minute, both of us reluctant to move into the next phase. Especially me. Oh, especially me.

He opened the door and the interior light went on. His right hand, with the gun, was pointed at me. The left reached up and turned off the light. 'I'm going to get out, Kat. I want you to slide across the seat toward me, slowly and carefully, and get out too.' I did that and then I watched as he held the gun on me, pulled the ignition coil wire, and slammed the hood down.

The levee road here was about thirty feet wide, the turnout another ten or twelve. On the land side the levee sloped down to cultivated fields, alfalfa maybe, I couldn't tell in the dark. On the other side it sloped down to the Sacramento River.

The bank was riprapped there, as it is along great stretches of the river. Sometimes the banks are bare with only occasional trees but there is a lot of vegetation too. The slope was steep. Derek and his .38 herded me down the bank into dense undergrowth and trees.

It looked better, more romantic, at a distance. Even the moonlight couldn't soften the beer cans, an old tire, broken glass, a used condom. The path was worn, beaten in and trailing down the slope at an angle. It wasn't very far to the river. Twelve feet or so down the path you ceased to be visible to anyone on the road. It didn't, unfortunately, take us long to traverse twelve feet. We stopped on a flatish spot. Derek's idea, not mine. I was fresh out of good ideas, which in itself was not a good idea.

'Hold it,' he said, and I did. He still held the aces, the .38 actually. It was getting to be time, past time even, to call his bluff. I turned; we faced each other.

The gun was in his pocket, which made me feel better. But there was murder in his eye, and that kind of canceled it out. Life's like that, up and down. The trick is riding with it, hitting more ups than downs, and ending on an up. For sure.

His hands were on my shoulders. 'I thought about strangling you.' The fingers of one hand caressed my throat, the other rested still on my shoulder. 'It would be too bad though, you have such a pretty face.'

'That's what I like about you, Derek. Your aesthetic sense never deserts you, not even in murder.'

He grinned. Ditto his sense of humor, obviously. 'I'd like to make it look like a sexual crime, like rape, throw them off a bit. That'd be nice, huh?'

I stared back, grim, silent. I guess we meant different things by 'nice.'

'That'd make sense, huh?' His thumb pressed lightly into the hollow of my throat. 'A pretty woman stops to walk along the river and she gets raped and killed. Or maybe she has car trouble, a flat tire, a loose coil wire.' He shook his head. 'That'd be too bad, too *damn* bad.'

It was hard to believe that the hands that had given me so much pleasure were going to kill me. I guess I don't make the business/pleasure distinction as easily as Derek.

His hands tightened again and it got easier to believe, became difficult to believe that I had known this man in any other way than what was before me now. The pressure of his thumb eased and he caressed my neck. I thought of a cat playing with a bird.

'Of course I could do you afterwards, or just jerk off. That would make it look sexual.' His face contorted in distaste. 'Naw. Kinky.'

I thought that one over. Maybe I was missing something, maybe not. 'Jerking off on a dead body is kinky, but murder isn't?'

He looked at me, his eyes flashing with anger in the moonlight. He was perfect for a sexy, romantic lead in a movie. Well, physically perfect.

'No.' He said it hotly. 'It's different.'

'Oh. Okay, kinky's out. How about twisted, warped, sick?' The pressure increased in the hollow of my throat again. I made myself look relaxed. 'How about that?'

'I do it because I have to, because I have no choice. That's reality.' I didn't comment on his concept of reality, but it was tempting. 'Kinky, twisted, is when you get pleasure out of it.'

'You're smiling.'

'You're not.' He smiled.

'Yes. I am.' I was, too. I smiled back at him, broadly, airily, happily. 'There's a guy in a fishing boat not twenty feet from us.' I was grinning away like a relieved, demented version of the Cheshire cat. I couldn't help it. 'And he's listening to every word we say.'

I had his attention.

For sure.

Twenty-Six

The odds of correctly picking 6 winning numbers in the California Lotto are 1 in 22,957,480. The odds of dying by violence are a lot greater than that. Some odds, either way.

'That's the oldest trick in the book, Kat.' The pressure around my neck eased, but only slightly.

It was. Yes. I agreed.

'True,' I said. 'But this time it's for real.' Doubt flickered in his eyes like high beams hitting on, then off. I was still grinning.

'You don't fish this time of night.'

'Yes,' I said, 'you do.' I shook my head sadly. 'You city boys, what do you know? Not jack shit. A lot of fish bite better at night. This time of year he's probably fishing for sturgeon, maybe striper.'

'Striper?' he asked stupidly. His eyes were flicking back and forth nervously like an old maid scared to look under the bed. He couldn't see the river without turning, without taking his eyes off me, so he hadn't. Yet.

309

'Striped bass,' I said kindly. 'Good eating. Sturgeon, too.'

He took the .38 out of his pocket and turned. The pressure of his other hand tightened painfully on my neck. 'There,' I pointed and stepped closer to him. Automatically he relaxed, the pressure eased, the hand slid down my shoulder. I turned my body to his and brought my knee up toward his groin. He blocked it but it caught him off guard. I shoved him as hard as I could down the bank.

I'm in good shape.

It did the trick.

He went over, falling heavily on the riprapped bank. I heard a splashing, plunking sound. Every fiber in my body hoped, begged, for it to be the .38.

'Fuck!'

Derek was sprawled head down toward the water. He'd hit stones with several parts of his body – knees, elbows, maybe head. I'd shoved him hard, real hard. Looking good.

'Fuck!'

Sounding good too.

It was tempting to hang around: point, laugh, get down and dirty about the situation. I resisted the temptation. Still, I wanted, I needed to know about the gun. Derek was on his hands and knees splashing in the water. He leaned over too far and fell in, came up choking and flailing. It was deep there, so the gun was probably gone.

So was I.

I didn't waste any thought on the truck; the ignition coil was still in Derek's pocket. Instead, I took off through the vegetation. I'd put some distance between us, then scramble up the bank to the road. The nearest house? I tried to remember. A quarter to a half mile down the road, I thought.

I was moving as fast as possible. And I wasn't kidding myself. Derek was without a gun, bruised and soaked, but dangerous. Very. He could kill me with his hands. Easily. And it wouldn't even give him nightmares.

I should have killed him, killed him there in the water when I had a clear shot and not much choice. That's why I carry a gun, for life-and-death situations without a choice. But this is my nightmare – I *had* killed a man and I lived with it still, was haunted by it still. I could kill in self-defense, but that was it, that was hard enough. It's not easy to kill; it shouldn't be.

'*Shit*. Goddamn it all to fucking hell!' He was swearing in slow rhythmic tones and scrambling up the bank. His shoes, leather-soled and wet, weren't making it any easier. His temper was getting frayed, I could tell. I heard him slide back, and then I just heard my breathing.

'Goddamn stupid motherfucking—'

Branches whipped at my face and tore at my hands as I pushed them out of the way. There was grass and dirt under my feet now, not the stones of the riprapped bank. I was making good time and started to breathe a little easier, feel a little better.

It was premature.

The blackberry tangle loomed up in front of me and I was no Brer Rabbit. I could hear Derek sliding and swearing behind me. It sounded too close, much too close. Realistically, of course, anything in this county was too close. Blackberry brambles in front of me, Derek behind. I picked the most open spot in the underbrush and plunged in. Beggars can't be choosers. Behind me, Derek had stopped swearing. I found the silence more ominous. It also made it a lot harder to keep track of him, to judge how far away he was.

I kept my suede-jacketed arms (the leather now getting fashionably 'distressed') up and out trying to shelter my face as much as possible. I had been making better time than he, much better. He would close the gap in the blackberries, though; he had me to hack out a trail. And he would catch up if the bramble patch was big enough. I didn't like the way things were going. That was an understatement. A particularly vicious vine whipped against my cheek, bringing tears to my eyes.

'Kids, don't try this at home,' I muttered. 'I'm a professional.'

Ahead of me the brambles opened up, then ended. Life started looking better, started looking like something I might be doing tomorrow. A last vine grabbed my leg and I pulled away from it, stumbled over part of a tire and landed on my hands and knees next to a broken beer bottle. My breath sounded like ragged sobs to me. I didn't think it was my imagination. Derek was right behind me. I *knew* that wasn't my imagination.

I scrambled to my feet and ran, sidestepping trash and junk on the ground. I wished the sound of my breathing weren't so loud; it made it hard to hear Derek, hard to concentrate. It was the way my blood was pounding too. And the adrenaline. I've always hated chase scenes. Always. *Damn.* I don't even like tag. And I *especially* don't like being IT.

Derek sounded closer. He slipped, swore. 'Gonna get you, kid.' He sounded pleasant enough now. There wasn't any doubt in his voice either.

'Hah.' I tried to put a lot of doubt in that word. In my mind, too. I don't think I convinced him. Or me, either. Not entirely.

He laughed. So that answered that question.

Ahead of me I saw a small stand of trees, some of them large, overhanging, beautiful, the way river trees are. I love that about them. I put on a burst of speed, almost my last so I gave it everything I could, picked a large tree up the hill and to one side, and fell in behind it.

Literally.

I picked myself up, leaned on the tree, and freed the .380 from the ankle holster that I usually hated to wear but would love from now on. I'd put it on earlier, before meeting Derek. He would have noticed the gun stuck in my jeans.

I felt a lot better about stuff now. Funny how having a gun in your hand does that, changes your attitude and perception, your perspective on life. The blood was ebbing from my ears back into my body where it belonged. About time. My breathing sounded more like mine and less like a rhino in heat. That was good too. I held the gun loosely in both hands and waited for Derek to come into view and into the small open moonlit patch he would have to cross to reach the trees I was behind.

Time changed and beat oddly in rhythm with my pulse, the lap of the water, and the gleam of moonlight through the trees. I was tired, too tired. I shook myself mentally. The noise and Derek's forward movement had stopped. Now what? Would he backtrack, try to come at me from a different angle? My pulse picked up again. Not good.

The noise started. All right. I could see him now. I knew what was happening now. And where: on the edge of the blackberry brambles, on the edge of the light.

'Kat, let's talk about this.' His voice was soft, seductive. 'We can work it out, I know we can.'

'Can we?'

'Of course.'

' "Rape would be nice," ' I quoted him. ' "I could strangle you, but it would mess up your pretty face." "Jerk off on the body afterwards, make it look like a sex crime." ' I stopped quoting, it was making me sick. I laughed instead, but it sounded hollow, even to me. 'No, I don't think so, Derek. I don't think we have anything left to talk about.'

'Just business, then?' he asked softly.

'Yes, but we have different agendas.'

'There was no one in a boat out there, no one fishing.'

'No.'

'You lied.' He sounded disappointed in me.

'Yes.'

'Kat.' His voice was full of reproach.

'No one's perfect.'

'You lied,' he repeated.

'Sue me.'

He came out of the shadows, started to walk through the moonlight toward the trees, toward me.

'There's something you should know,' I said. He stopped. 'Something I forgot to mention before.' My voice was apologetic.

'What?'

'I've got a gun.'

'No,' he said finally, 'you don't.' But he didn't move. 'I would have felt it if you were carrying.' He started forward again.

'Ankle holster.'

He stopped. 'You're bluffing. I'm coming for you now. When I get you, I'm going to kill you and throw you in the river. After a few days in the water it won't matter that your face was messed up.'

A floater. My fingers tightened on the gun. He started moving again. I stepped out from behind the tree so he could see me. He could see the gun too. He hesitated for a moment, then kept on.

'Stop it right there, Derek.'

He didn't stop. 'I'm going to get you, baby.' His voice was soft, alluring, enticing. A lover's voice.

'I'll shoot.'

'You won't.' He kept coming.

'I'll kill you if I have to. I'm – not – going – to – be – a – floater.'

I said it to myself as much as to him. He was close now. I'd let him get too close. It's hard to kill. I heard myself say it again, about not being a floater. It sounded far away. He didn't say anything, just reached out for me. I heard Hank's words about critical mass: *Shoot for the chest, Kat. If you have to shoot, shoot to kill.*

I squeezed off the trigger.

And stepped back. He was still coming. Maybe momentum. His face was shaded from the moonlight. Maybe not. He was still standing, still coming. I shot again. *Critical mass.*

He fell. I stood there for a long time, the gun in my hand, my arm hanging limply by my side, waiting in the moonlight for him to move.

He didn't.

I bent over him, rolled him over with my hand first, then my foot. I didn't want to get too close. He was alive. The moon glinted off his eyeballs. It made him look evil. I had six shots left.

'I'm sorry, Kat, it shouldn't have ended this way,

should it?' He coughed. 'I didn't want it to, believe me . . .'

I waited for more but there wasn't any. Maybe he was dead, maybe not. I didn't want to get close enough to see. I didn't care.

No, that wasn't true. I did.

I cared, as I had cared about this man. We had been lovers, were learning to be friends. Then he had hunted and trapped me like an animal, brutalized, raped, and killed me in his mind.

I cared a lot.

I hoped he was dead.

Finally I put the gun in my pocket and started climbing up to the road. I didn't look back. There was nothing there I wanted to see.

And a lot I didn't.

Twenty-Seven

Most children are taught that police officers and fire fighters are their friends. This is true, but there are exceptions to every rule.

I was hooking up a spark plug wire to the ignition coil when the patrol cops pulled up. They got out carefully, their hands on their guns.

They looked at me for a long time. I was a looker all right: a split lip, bramble scratches on my face and hands, my clothes ripped, bloody, and dirty. I've never been known for making a fashion statement but this was ridiculous, even for me.

'Help you, miss?' one officer asked warily. I nodded. 'Car trouble?'

I snapped the wire into place and nodded again. 'I'm missing . . .' I stopped. The ignition coil wire was in Derek's pocket and I hadn't been able to face going back after it. 'It's in . . .' I stopped again.

They waited patiently. I took a deep breath and started again. Cops aren't always the easiest people to talk to. 'I killed a man.' I hesitated. Actually, I didn't know if he was dead. 'Shot a man,' I

319

corrected. 'Maybe he's still alive. He's down there.'
I pointed.

'Do you have the gun still, miss?' The officer's voice
was slow, easy, polite.

'Yes.' I started to reach into my pocket.

'Hold it!' His voice was hard, his gun was out,
both of their guns were out. 'Lie down. Put your—'

I was tired and cold. I looked like an escaped
felon, but I didn't feel like being treated like one. I
listened to his spiel without moving, with my hands
away from my sides, away from my pockets and my
gun.

'How about I just take my jacket off and hand it
to you, Officer,' I said wearily. He looked at me. They
both had me covered. 'Then how about you get on to
Detective Bill Henley, Sacramento Sheriff's Department, Homicide. He knows me, he has an interest
in this.'

Mostly, how about someone putting me into a hot
shower, then into jammies and bed. I'd need a large
box of tissues too.

One out of two is a start. They let me take off my
jacket and hand it over. They checked me for more
weapons, went over my ID, went over the truck.
Then one of them disappeared down the hill waving
a flashlight.

'Yeah,' that one said when he got back. 'There's a
guy down there, all right. Dead.' His voice was flat
and hard. They read me my rights.

I hate it when that happens.

I didn't blame them, but it was still a hell of a note. I'd had a hard day and it wasn't getting any better. One of them got on the radio.

'Want to tell me what happened, miss?' the other one asked.

'No.'

I was surly, no doubt about it. I was going to have to repeat it for Henley and God knows who else, so what the hell, why start now? They could wait. We went through the same thing a couple more times; he stayed polite and I stayed surly. They looked at each other, then one of them handcuffed me.

I hate it when that happens, too.

Then they stuck me in the back seat of a patrol car and slammed the door.

Nought for three. I wasn't having a fun night, that was for sure.

There is no way to get comfortable with your hands cuffed behind you. I tried anyway. I hoped Henley would get into gear and move fast. I hoped I wouldn't forever have to think about Derek coming after me, the look in his eyes, the sound of the gun, the blood everywhere.

I hoped I wouldn't start crying.

The back of the patrol car smelled of sweat and fear, dirt and blood, or maybe that was me. I leaned wearily against the door and closed my eyes, listened to the radio squawk, and the voices of the cops in the background.

When I shut my eyes Derek's face floated in front

of me, distorted and bloated, like in a fun house mirror. 'Hey, baby,' he whispered, 'sorry, but I got to do you. It's been fun, baby.'

His face dissolved in blood and then the moonlit water of the Sacramento River played, danced and dappled, splashed gently in the background. I wondered if there was enough water to wash away the blood.

I almost fell out when someone jerked the car door open. I'd been leaning forward and to one side with my hands cuffed behind me. A large hand fastened on my upper arm and hauled me out.

'What the fuck's going on, Colorado? You look like hell, and this story sucks.' That was an understatement; we both knew it.

'Yeah. Take these off, Bill.'

He nodded to the patrol cop, who unlocked the cuffs. The place was crawling with people now, most of them, naturally, cops. A CSI unit had arrived. Henley waved me into his car.

'We got a body down there. I hear you got a story. For your sake,' he said it grimly, 'I hope it's a damn good one. Otherwise, you're going downtown, accommodations compliments of the county, Kat. Free room and board, and lots of friendly company.' He looked at me to see if I was taking it seriously. No problem. I was. 'Start talking, start at the beginning.'

I nodded. I started with Paige because that was a beginning, not the beginning, though. Florence was another beginning, or her parents and how they treated her or ... My mind buckled and collapsed with the enormity of it. I had glimpsed Adam and Eve, and history behind them, and knew that that was a beginning too, but also not the beginning.

So I started with Paige. I wasn't up to the rest of it.

I got to Opal and Derek. And Garnet, who was Ruby. And Florence. And Wiley. Then everyone except Derek twenty years ago. And Jose. And Herb. And Paige and Derek and Ruby. And I wondered briefly whether Paige would have been safe if Derek had lived, and thought not. Greed, after all. And then Derek and me and dinner, and our moonlight ride, and walk, and talk, and shoot-out.

Then I stopped. It seemed like enough to me, more than enough. I was tired.

'Well, haven't you been a fucking busy little bee?'

He was mad; I knew it – he wanted me to know it. I didn't blame him all that much.

'You don't get paid to chase down guys like this. I do. Remember?' I nodded. He was right. Even if he hadn't been, I was too tired to argue. He sighed. 'Tell me again. Take it from the top.'

I told him again. Something in a body bag left and was loaded into the coroner's van. I saw it out of the corner of my eye, but I didn't turn my head, didn't look. Why? My nightmares would be bad enough already. Then we went down the hill and they had me walk through it, point out everything, show them where Derek's gun had gone into the water. I was bone-tired. It was too much, I started to snuffle. They didn't care. I didn't blame them.

Then I told my story again.

And again.

Their idea, not mine. Someone came and spoke with Henley for a long time. I sat in his car where he had put me and dozed, then startled awake when he climbed back in. 'We found the gun, the ignition coil wire was in his pocket, and the rest of your story checks out. So far.' He looked at me warily. 'You can go, but Jesus, Kat, I wish you'd quit pulling this shit.'

Yeah, me, too. I thought that, I didn't say it. 'I suppose you think this is my idea of a fun experience?' I managed a little sarcasm, but not up to my usual standard.

'I don't know what to think. Not yet,' he said wearily. 'Get out. Scram.'

'Can I have my coil wire back?'

'No.'

I got out, tottered over to the truck and climbed in. We sputtered on home, the truck firing on only five cylinders, but beating me. Easy. I ate half a stale candy bar I found in my purse. It was the best candy bar I had ever had. Ever.

When I got home I had a long, hot shower. It washed away the dirt and the sweat – but not the pain, not the blood. I couldn't see it anymore, but it was there, I could feel it.

In my dreams I saw it. Lots of it. Rivers of it. Rivers with riprapped banks. Banks with blood-red stones.

Twenty-Eight

*Every 8 seconds there is a burglary; every
6 seconds a rape; every 23 minutes a
murder. Many of these crimes occur in the
victim's home. A woman's home is not her
castle.*

I woke up tired after a couple of hours so I went
back to sleep. When I woke up again I was still tired
but I couldn't sleep. It was going to get worse before
it got better, I knew that.

I wasn't looking forward to it.

I called Opal who wasn't there, or refused to talk
with me. I left a message with the hotel desk that I
would be at the river house and she should meet me
there. She might, she might not, it was hard for me
to care. I called Paige. No answer. She was,
presumably, still in Tahoe.

I had a third cup of coffee and waited for the
caffeine to kick in. It was looking like a long wait.
When Lindy arrived, I was starting my fourth cup.
As usual she just walked in.

'Oh good, you're here.' She hugged me on her way
to the refrigerator. 'Lately you're never around, Kat.'

I thought about it. Never? Was it that bad? Maybe. 'What's for breakfast?'

I shrugged. 'Whatever you can find.' I didn't have much of an appetite for life, never mind breakfast.

'I'll make something, can I?'

'Yes. Not for me, though.'

She made toast and scrambled eggs and shoved a plate in front of me. 'You'd better eat, Kat, you don't look so hot.' I shook my head but it was there so I ate it after all.

'What happened to you?'

I shook my head again.

'You remember what today is, don't you?'

I didn't, no. I hadn't a clue. 'What?'

'Today's the day I work with you.' I stared at her blankly. 'For my report, remember?' She grinned at me.

I know I don't agree to this kind of stuff so how I ever get in these spots is beyond me.

'Not today, Lindy. I can't,' I added when she began to wail. She was still wailing as I loaded tools into the truck and started to drive off.

'Where are you going?'

'To Paige's. Does Alma know you have her car?' She shrugged so the answer was no. 'Go on home, I'll talk to you later. We'll schedule something soon.'

'Okay.'

That was too easy, she was too compliant; it should have been a warning, but it wasn't, I was too tired. I was on my fifth cup of coffee and still not up to speed.

Not even close. Ditto the truck, but minus the coffee.

I drove to an auto parts store, bought a new ignition coil wire, ignored the sign that said NO REPAIR WORK IN THE PARKING LOT PLEASE!! and installed it. That meant the truck was firing on all 6 cylinders. Too bad I couldn't say the same.

The river house next.

There was no one around. I was hoping Paige would be back. I wanted to see her, would have preferred it that way, but it didn't matter a lot. Wiley was a no-show, too. I didn't see him or his truck. I didn't particularly want to see him but I was spoiling for a fight – too much time with cops will do that to you – and he would have done. Nicely, in fact.

So I was on my own. I got the shovel, the pick, and the wheelbarrow out of the truck. Wiley wouldn't talk; Opal didn't know; I was guessing. Hell of a deal. It sounded like the three stooges. I hoped it would turn out better. I piled the tools in the wheelbarrow and headed for the backyard.

I want to sleep with him under the flowered blanket.

Ruby had said that to me several times.

She watched it all from her bedroom window, crying, screaming, beating on the glass until it broke.

Opal had told me that.

I was guessing, yes, but I had clues, so it was, almost, an educated guess. This is the kind of thing I tell myself when I'm about to do something stupid, or way out of line, or dangerous. It was probably only two out of three today, better than my usual record by thirty-three and one third percent. So I was ahead. This is exactly the kind of reasoning that gets me into trouble.

By eye I picked the center of the flower bed on the edge of the yard and orchard. Then I paced off a rectangle roughly four by six feet. Carefully I dug up the bulbs on that spot and on an access path, and set them aside. I didn't need the pick even as I got deeper. The spring soil was moist but not wet, perfect for digging. I was down about two feet when Wiley showed up.

He had a shotgun.

'What, exactly, do you think you're doing?' His voice was dangerous. Not as dangerous as the shotgun, but close.

I didn't bother to look up again. It would have made me nervous and, let's face it, my nerves were already shot. Talking with cops too long will do that to you. And killing people, ex-lovers for instance. Especially that.

'Digging for gold, Wiley. Shoveling for pay dirt.'

For a long time he was silent. Then: 'You got no right.'

I didn't, no, and I was on such shaky ground with that one that I didn't bother discussing it. I changed the subject.

'Rights aren't the issue anymore, if they ever were. There have been too many deaths now. It started here; so I'm going back to the beginning and then it's going to end.' I said it more confidently than I felt.

The wheelbarrow was full. I put down the shovel, pushed the barrow over to the side and dumped. Wiley didn't took like he was going to spell me so I didn't bother to ask. The shotgun was still tucked under his arm and pointed loosely in my direction. Of course loosely is all it takes with a shotgun at that range so I didn't feel any better about it than I had before.

'I could shoot you, and I jest might do that.'

'And bury me on top of him? The cops know too, Wiley. They're behind me a little but not much.'

I lied with practiced ease. Yeah, right. Sure. If it were true, if I'd been sure, I'd be sitting somewhere with my feet up watching cops dig. I stuck the shovel in the dirt, pulled the sweatshirt over my head, tossed it to the side, picked up the shovel again. Henley was right. I didn't get paid to do this, they did. Maybe not enough, but more than me.

Wiley pumped the shotgun. It's one of the scariest sounds I know. I didn't pee in my pants, but only just. I stopped shoveling and let my breath out slowly.

'It's too late, Wiley, it's out, the party's over.' Some party anyway.

'Hi, guys.'

We both jumped. The shotgun swung around and covered Lindy. She stared wide-eyed and white-faced at it. Shotguns do that to me; I had no idea they would do it to Lindy. As far as I knew she was still in her stupid and fearless teenager stage. I found her reaction promising. Maybe she was growing up after all.

'I just said hi,' she bleated.

Wiley dropped the gun slightly. 'I'm going to call the cops. This is private property. You've no right.'

'That sounds like a hell of an idea to me.' The best he'd had so far, hands down. 'I'll be right here.' He stared at me long enough to make my skin crawl, then turned and left. I started to breathe again. And dig. It felt good.

'What are you doing, Kat?'

'It's a long story, Lindy, and I better save my breath to shovel. Besides, you're leaving. Now. Pronto. Scram. Adios.'

'I'll help.'

I was tired. It was, in spite of my better instincts, tempting. I got over it. I loved Lindy and all I could think of was shotguns and rivers of blood. And what I hoped I was going to find. And dreaded finding.

'No, you won't.' I went back to shoveling. 'You're out of here.'

'Yes.'

'No.'

I still hadn't gotten rid of Lindy by the time Opal arrived. I had dug quite a bit deeper, though, so I guess I was making progress. I have a hard time telling sometimes.

She was still perfect, unwrinkled, and in her black outfit of yesterday.

'What's going on?'

I looked at her for quite a while before I answered. 'I'm surprised you have to ask.' She flushed. 'There's another shovel in the truck. Get it. Help me. The past isn't past anymore, it's present, and there's nothing to do but dig it up. Then it can be buried again.'

Maybe, I thought. Maybe not. Probably not. I thought some more. 'And call Wiley off, too.'

Opal stared at me, then off into the distance. Lindy bounced off with alacrity and enthusiasm. She wasn't leaving, of course. Fat chance. She was getting the shovel, I'd put money on it.

'Derek.' Opal breathed it out finally, on a sigh and a sob. 'The police told me that you . . . you . . .' She stopped and looked at me.

I was too tired to be diplomatic, to pull punches. So I didn't. 'I killed him, shot him. He killed Ruby and tried to kill me.'

'No! Not Derek.'

I looked at her for a little while, marveling at the power we give denial, then went back to digging. That, at least, was going to get me somewhere.

'Kat, you have to understand.'

I did, I thought, I did. But maybe you had to have been there. I jabbed viciously at the soil with the shovel. Dirt was flying. Lindy had come back with the other shovel and was standing at the edge of the pit staring at me openmouthed. Opal didn't even notice.

'He had a hard life, that's why he is, was' – her voice filled with tears – 'the way he was. You have to forgive him.'

I shook my head and thought maybe I would have to puke if I heard that excuse one more time, especially about a murderer, rapist, or child molester. My shovel was flying, dirt was flying. No, I sure as hell didn't have to forgive. Not him, or Eichmann, or Nixon, or drug dealers, or the dog down my street who dumped in my yard. I didn't, and I wasn't.

'Please.'

I was down about five feet now in spots, and making time, making progress.

'Kat?'

'He murdered your twin.' I looked at her finally, stopped shoveling finally. 'And you're asking me to forgive?'

'Yes.' She said it on one whispered, sobbing sigh.

'He sold out your business too. He was a gambler.'

She sobbed some more, in shock, I thought, and not really taking it in.

'No one ever forgave me, but I wish—' She broke off. 'We *have* to forgive!' She said it desperately, and I wondered what she needed to be forgiven for.

'It's a cop-out, Opal, and I don't buy it. Maybe you need to so that you can understand and accept the fact that your partner killed your sister, planned to kill me, and sold out your business. That's your choice. Me? I'd rather mourn Ruby and Herb, maybe even the Derek I thought I knew, but the Derek who died? No, he was a killer.'

Her eyes filled with tears. 'You're so harsh.'

I shrugged. 'There are a lot of things to forgive in this world. And forget. I won't forget Ruby or Herb. I don't want to. I won't forgive Derek. I don't want to do that either.' I wished I could forget though, wished it badly, very badly.

'Please,' she whispered, and I wondered what the issue was here, and who needed forgiveness. Not Derek. Opal? 'Please forgive him.'

I went back to shoveling. 'I can't. To me, he's lower than dog meat.' I remembered the lover's hands and kisses, the killer's hands and words. 'I can't forgive. I can't even understand. Don't ask it of me again.'

I looked up at her. She was ready to ask it of me. Again.

'If you do, I'll tell you how it was, what he said to me, how he meant to kill me.' Her face went chalky and white. Lindy gasped. Damn. Damn! I'd forgotten she was here. 'Asking that of me is like me asking you to understand and forgive Florence.'

Her face was still and set, white and immobile, like a plaster cast without a sense of humor. 'Oh,' she said at last.

'Yes.' I went back to digging, five and a half feet now, I thought. Was I wrong? My heart sank. Then what? But I didn't know: I had no more guesses, was out of hunches, out of luck, and out to lunch.

'Kat.' Lindy's voice was tentative and scared.

My shovel chipped on something. A rock? I bent down to see. It didn't look like a rock, and it was whitish.

'Kat?'

Not Lindy's voice this time. Paige's. Where the hell had she come from? I kept on digging, but carefully now. She had sounded puzzled, not mad, even though she had a right to be; I was digging up her cherished flower bed. I was on my hands and knees, brushing dirt off what looked like a human pelvis.

'Kat!' Paige was almost yelling, almost crying.

But I didn't know what to say: Paige, meet your father? No. Instead I pushed dirt back over the white thing, climbed out of the hole and called the cops. It seemed like the best plan, unenthusiastic as I was about seeing homicide cops again so soon.

Twenty-Nine

Life, liberty, and the pursuit of happiness:
inalienable but not guaranteed rights.

'I've changed my mind, Kat.' Lindy was crying. 'I
don't want to be a PI after all.' I hugged her, trying
to comfort her and looking around frantically for
Paige. The place was starting to fill up with cops,
cops and people from the coroner's office.

'Getting shot at, killing people, a dead body. Not
even a body,' she hiccoughed, 'a skeleton, an *ugly*,
nasty skeleton.' I thought skeletons were preferable
to bodies, decomposing floaters, for instance, but I
let it go. 'That's no kind of a job, no kind of a life.'
She had a point there, a couple of them actually,
and good ones; I didn't argue it. The sobs subsided
finally into sniffles.

'Honey, I need to talk to Paige. Do you think you
can go on home, talk things over with Alma?' She
looked at me with large, betrayed eyes, then
squeezed a tear out. Damn! I will never have
children. 'It's even worse for Paige,' I explained.

'Why?'

'Because that,' I waved vaguely toward the pit,

tried for tact, and failed, 'could be what's left of her father.'

Her eyes got even wider, her hand flew to her mouth. She looked sick. 'Oh!'

I nodded. 'Exactly.' So that was how I got Lindy packed up and out of there. Paige was next.

'I thought we were in agreement that you'd stay out of this kind of shit.'

I was wrong; Paige wasn't next. Henley was wrong too; we weren't in agreement on that.

'Hi, Bill.' I said it with resignation.

'Funny how in three *goddamn* hours last night you never mentioned digging up a *goddamned* body.' Details I thought, but his temper sounded a little frayed, so I didn't say it. I felt a little frayed, too.

'I figured it out later.' It was feeble but it was the best I could do. He snorted. I shrugged. 'Bill, what would you have done if I'd come to you and said: Ruby spoke of wanting to sleep with her lover under a flowered blanket, so let's dig up the flower bed? Would you have? No way. You would have laughed in my face and called me nuts. Even if you bought it, which you wouldn't have, you couldn't have gotten a warrant, and Paige was out of town.'

I was right and he knew it, but that didn't help any. There were shouts and new noises in the background. 'As soon as I knew I called you.' He looked pissed, real pissed. 'Any way of getting an ID on him?'

'Him?'

I glared at Henley. What was it, an it?

'Detective.' Henley turned toward a guy in jeans wearing a jacket that said POLICE. 'We found this on the body. There's an inscription.' He was holding a gold crucifix on a delicate chain.

Henley reached out a hand for it and read, then grinned.

'What?' I asked, holding out my hand.

'See you, Kat.' And he walked, the bastard.

It was my turn to be pissed, and I was. Big-time. Okay, now Paige. She was next. I looked around.

'Kat.' Opal was white, shaking, and standing in front of me. 'What do I do now?'

'What do you mean?'

'The police. Everything.'

'Tell the truth.' We were walking away from the house and toward the orchard. It wasn't my idea; I was following her.

'Everything?'

'You said you were tired of lying and hiding and wouldn't do it anymore.'

She turned her hands up and out, helplessly, impotently. It was, somehow, an innocent and touching gesture.

'I said that, I know, but it's so easy to say, Kat. No, that's not what I mean. I said it, and I meant it, and it's what I want to do.' She gripped my wrist. 'I just didn't realize it would be so hard, so *damned* hard.'

Her fingers tightened on my wrist. She could have

taken my pulse, but she didn't. There were tears in her eyes. Maybe. I thought about how I was getting cynical. I thought about love and life and lies, all L's. I thought about Derek, about Lindy and Paige. And about Hank, though I wasn't sure how he got in there. Not L's; love maybe.

'The thing is, you get so used to living a lie it becomes the truth. You start to believe it because you have to, because you couldn't stand living with yourself and the lies otherwise. You forget the rest. And to change it, you have to admit that you've been lying all that time and oh, God, Kat, it gets so hard and so complicated.'

I nodded. I could see that, and it was, yes, but what was there for me to say?

'And if the lies are the truth, and they are in a way, why go back to the other "truth" and confuse and muddle up things? Why?'

I didn't have an answer, so I didn't say anything. There were things I thought but didn't say. That's unusual for me; it was because here I knew they wouldn't help. It doesn't help to say: There's only one truth; because there's not. Or: The truth is simple; because it rarely is. Or: The truth will set you free; because sometimes it does, and sometimes it doesn't, and mostly there's no telling. Or it gets rained out.

'Kat?'

I looked at her finally. 'You have to decide what you can live with.' I started to call her by name, to say Opal, but then I didn't. 'And who you are, and who you want to be.'

'What do you mean?' Her eyes were wide and frightened.

'You know.'

'Say it.'

I didn't say anything. I didn't want to. I didn't want it in words.

'Say it!' She screamed at me. And again.

So I said it. 'You're not Opal.'

She sat down, not as though she had thought about it and decided she was tired, but as though her legs had given out and just plopped her down into the orchard dirt next to a pear tree. I sat down on the dirt with her. It was fitting somehow.

She didn't speak for a long time and that was fine with me. It was fine with me if I never heard any more Morrell secrets, or confessions, or illegal and illicit plans. It was fine with me, but I didn't think it would work out that way.

And it didn't.

'Very few could tell us apart. We had different clothes and things, and sometimes did our hair in different ways, but we traded. Always. It was a game with us. Uncle Herb, Aunt Letitia, and Florence were the only ones who could always tell. Sometimes even we couldn't tell.' She smiled wryly. 'How could you guess?'

'Garnet—' I broke off and moved my hands helplessly. What to do about names now?

'Never mind,' Opal-who-was-Ruby said.

'All right. Garnet told me that that wasn't her name. Then I called her Ruby. She looked displeased and asked if I wouldn't, couldn't, get her name right. It started me thinking.'

Opal was mashing dirt clods between her fingers.

'Nothing is ever the same as anything else. Not exactly. No one is ever the same as anyone else. Physically you were very alike, but emotionally you were as different as night and day.'

'Not that much.'

'Morning and evening?'

'All right.' She started to smile.

'Taking Opal's name maybe helped you take on some of her characteristics, her strengths. As Opal you started your own business and ran it well, efficiently. But emotionally you were still,' I didn't want to say 'weak' though that's what it seemed, 'vulnerable. Opal would never have needed, or allowed, someone like Derek in her life.'

She stopped looking at me then and concentrated on busting up dirt clods, as though something depended on it, but nothing did. Opal would have met my eyes, I thought. 'But you, Ruby, would, did, need someone to lean on, depend on. You wouldn't mind, as Opal would have, that Derek was assertive, domineering; you needed that, wanted that.'

And, I thought, she had no way of knowing he would take it so far, would play the ponies, gamble away the business, would murder.

'Yes,' she agreed with me finally, finally looked

at me. 'And yet I think of myself as Opal now. Odd, isn't it?'

I shook my head. I didn't find it odd. I thought it might have happened to Ruby-who-was-Opal too. Time, drugs, horror, and confusion had blurred reality for her. The identity she assumed became hers more and more. I remembered how she had spoken of sleeping under the flowered blanket. Had Jose come to seem like her lover instead of her sister's? Better a fantasy than nothing at all? I found it immeasurably sad.

'Over the years the truth has slipped around a lot and now, now I'm not even sure.'

It was my turn to listen so I squashed dirt clods and then busted up a twig and watched a ladybug that landed on my arm.

'All that I told you?' I looked up. 'About us and Florence and Jose and Wiley and the past? It was true, all of it. Almost.' Her eyes dropped again. I nodded to no one who was watching.

'Almost, only I was Ruby and she was Opal. I still have scars on my arm where I got cut on the window glass that night.' She held her arm out, the creamy white flesh touched with long-ago jagged, roughly healed scars. We sat in silence for a while. I listened to the birds, the insects, and the wind slipping through new spring leaves.

'My sister did all the planning. You have to understand how much, how very much, we loved each other.'

343

Her eyes filled with tears. I looked at the ladybug on my arm.

Ladybird, ladybird, fly away home!
Your house is on fire, your children all gone.

'It happened so fast. Opal figured things out, she always did. The next night, or the next but one, Florence told Opal to pack, that she was leaving to go to school in the East the very next morning. Opal packed and then she said that we would trade, that I was to go in her place.' She was silent. I didn't break the silence. I couldn't.

'We both knew, you see. Florence had always disliked everything about the idea of having children, had tolerated us at best. Now, after this horrible thing that had happened, she would hate us, and especially me. She would not let the pictures and the death come out. It would have ruined her, destroyed the life she knew. So it was not to be allowed. Simple. Instead, Opal was to go away and I—'

'And you?' I asked finally.

'We didn't know. We couldn't imagine anything as horrible as what, in fact, she did.' Her eyes filled with tears. 'But we knew that she would do something to silence me. I could not be trusted to keep a secret. And I could not have, not as Ruby, although as Opal I did.

'We never spoke of this, you know,' she interrupted herself. 'It was too horrifying to know that your own mother didn't love you, would wipe you out, erase you if she could. Did Hansel and Gretel speak of their father's betrayal?' She shook her head. 'I'm sure not. No, it is too difficult, too frightful for a child to face. We never spoke of it either, but we knew. After she announced that Opal was to go away to school she never saw or spoke to us again. Can you imagine?'

I couldn't, no.

'Florence must have had Wiley drive Opal away, as he did me. She never said goodbye.'

Ladybird, ladybird, fly away home!

'Opal said that I was to go to the eastern school in her place, that I could not stay alone with Florence, that she would, that she was strong and would get away. And she was. We both believed it, believed that it would work that way.'

Your house is on fire . . .

'But she didn't get away. She was to get a post office box so that we could write, plan. I sent her letters, several of them, but I never got an answer. Then Florence wrote and said that she had died. Oh, dear God.' Her voice broke. 'I should never have let her talk me into it. Never. *Never!* It wasn't fair, not to her.' She stopped until she could control her voice again. 'Still, I don't understand. How could it happen? How did it? How could Florence have kept Opal away somewhere?'

Peter, Peter, pumpkin-eater,
Had a wife and couldn't keep her.

'And for so many years? Opal would not have

345

allowed it. I know, I *know*!'

So he put her in a pumpkin shell,
And there he kept her very well.

'She was placed in an institution. They used drugs at first, for a long time perhaps, and then it wasn't necessary anymore. They broke her.' And I thought of a horse I had seen, beaten and broken, spiritless, head bowed and eyes dead.

Opal trembled. 'I should never have done it.'

Ladybird, ladybird . . . your children all gone.

'She loved you. She did it out of love.'

'Yes.' Tears spilled down her cheeks.

'Life isn't fair.'

'No, but still—' She stopped. Life isn't fair and there is no answer to that. 'The baby? Was it Opal's?'

'Oh yes, I think there's no doubt of that. I'll turn up the birth certificate sooner or later.'

'And the father? It's not Jose. I *didn't* get pregnant by him and she *couldn't* have.'

I shrugged and shook my head.

'We'll never know?' she asked.

'I don't think so, not unless she named him on the birth certificate, but that seems unlikely.' I considered telling her what I had been told: the rapes, the cold, dark place. And I decided not to. It couldn't help; it would hurt too much.

'Oh, God, it's my fault. Why did I let it happen?'

I touched her hand gently, briefly. 'Why do victimized children blame themselves when horrible things like this happen? It is not the fault of the children, but of the adults.' And I wanted to say her name but I didn't know what to call her. And I knew, too, that she wasn't a small child when it happened. And that made a difference.

'This is what I have to live with.'

'Yes.' I was glad I didn't.

'How?'

'I don't know.'

And I thought about the time that she had screamed at me that I shouldn't play God. And how she was right. I didn't know the answer to her question and I couldn't, wouldn't guess.

'What should I call you?' I asked instead.

'I don't know.' Her eyes were deep and empty, and where they weren't empty they were sad.

'There's more to it, you know?'

Yes, I knew. There's always more. Always.

'If I tell the truth, the first truth, I inherit the ranch. I don't want it. From what you've told me, the child, Opal's child, should have it but she won't, not unless we go through a messy and public legal process.'

I listened to the breeze in the pear trees, the songs of the insects and the birds, and thought how peaceful it seemed, wondered then how many other skeletons there were waiting to be uncovered. In backyards and closets and—

'But if I go on like this, live the other truth, the truth now . . .' Her voice drifted off, then back again. 'Then it's okay. And maybe, through Paige, I can start to pay Opal back.' She was silent for a bit. 'I couldn't have pulled it off before.'

I raised an eyebrow in a question.

'Uncle Herb would have known who I was, and Aunt Letitia. Florence, of course. It's why I never came back. Wiley won't know, he never did. Florence had him take me to the airport that day and he didn't notice. Florence would have known, would have seen, but he didn't. And Cora won't know. No one but you, just you, Kat.'

'Who?' I asked.

She looked puzzled. 'Don't you see? I'm asking you—'

I said nothing.

'Oh?'

'What should I call you?' I asked gently.

She smiled. 'Opal? Opal Harnway?' There was fear in her eyes. 'You won't tell? Ever?'

'No,' I said. 'Never. Cross my heart and hope to die.' I meant it, too.

Cross my heart and hope to die, stick a needle in my eye. I meant it.

She smiled again.

The ladybug flew away.

It was too late for the children.

Thirty

Is there a morality or code of ethics that supersedes our legal system? People don't agree on that, yet almost everyone agrees that sometimes it is necessary to take the law into your own hands.

I couldn't find Paige. Nobody could. Henley was mad about it. I wasn't mad, I was worried. I left messages with anyone who would listen and went to my office. A kid with a boom box sat on the steps of my building warping his brain and reducing his hearing capacity with rap music. *Pump it up / let's do it / do it / do it.* I shooed him off.

Mr A. was tinkering with something as I walked by his office. 'Hiya, doll face, did you know that—'

I waved and kept moving. I wasn't in the mood for his statistics, I had my own. I wasn't in the mood for them either, but I was stuck with them: ninety-eight percent of bodies left in the ground for twenty years are nothing but bone, boot leather, and a crucifix with an inscription I don't get to read; seven percent of identical twins make a permanent or semipermanent switch at some point in their lives;

two percent of men try to kill their dinner dates; one percent succeed. Great statistics. Fun stuff. I got to my office and looked at the open door, turned, looked at Mr A.

'You have a visitor, that's what I was trying to tell you.'

'Oh.' Good. Great. Fantastic. I was really in the mood for that. It would have to be something special to take my mind off things.

It was and it wasn't. That's life for you.

'Hi.' She said the one word with difficulty and as though it took a great deal of effort and determination.

'Everyone's looking for you.'

'Who?'

'Me. Detective Henley. Your Aunt Opal,' I stumbled over the name but only slightly. 'Paul.'

'Why?'

I looked at her, walked over to my desk, picked up four quarters from a carnival glass bowl there. 'Do you want a Pepsi?'

She shook her head. 'Yes.'

Okay. I went with the word and came back with a Pepsi for her and a diet Pepsi for me. We roughed it and drank right out of the cans.

'Are you okay, Paige?'

She shook her head and said, 'Yes.' It didn't feel like we were getting anywhere very fast, or not anywhere I recognized or understood.

'What's going on, Kat? Tell me. I saw all those

people, cops too, at the ranch and I got scared. I— I ran. It was dumb, I guess, but—' Her eyes were wide and frightened, her hands clutched nervously.

'Why should you be scared?'

'I don't know. I . . . What were they digging up? You too? My flowers, my pretty flowers—' She reached for the Pepsi and almost spilled it, her hand trembling, fragile and translucent-looking, the blue veins standing out in sharp contrast.

My heart went out to her; I almost believed her. I couldn't help it, she did it so well.

Tremulously she smiled at me as her eyes filled with tears, big, splashy, sparkly beautiful ones. How did she do that?

'Oh, Kat, I'm *so* glad you're on my side.'

My heart hardened.

A tear splashed down her cheek and she wiped it away with the back of her hand. 'The flower bed? What in the world—?' There was a tremble in her voice now too.

'Twenty years ago a young man was killed.' Her already wide eyes widened further. 'He had come to the ranch to blackmail Florence with pictures of your mother.'

'What kind of pictures?'

'Intimate ones. The boy was the son of a local farm worker. Florence was enraged at the blackmail, at the presumption, at the boy.'

Paige's mouth was open. Slowly she shut it. 'Yes, she would be,' she agreed at last.

351

'Florence struck him. He hit his head against the cabinet and died. Then they buried him in the back yard.'

'Oh.' Her hand flew to her mouth.

'Opal was sent away to school; your mother, Ruby, was placed in an institution. A year or so later, after your birth, Florence brought you here.'

'She's a fiend,' Paige hissed. 'A fiend! I'm glad I—'

She stopped, thank goodness. I felt like I was drowning in Morrell confessions. There seemed no end to them. We sat in a long silence which I hoped Paige wouldn't break.

She did.

'I killed Florence.'

The sigh that filled the room was long and sad and heavy. I couldn't tell if it was mine, hers, or ours.

'I hated her so much, but that wasn't it, that wasn't why. I had to, had to.' Her eyes and voice implored me to understand; her hands were clasped almost as in prayer. 'I had to before she destroyed me inside. Not killed me like that boy, but – oh, do you understand? You do, don't you?'

I nodded. I did. Perhaps I wouldn't have if I hadn't known Ruby who was Opal, but I had, had seen what Florence was capable of.

'How?' I was in it now. I might as well know.

Paige stared blankly at me. 'She had a heart condition, had medicine for it. That night she called for me because she couldn't reach her pills. I started to get them, but then I didn't, I couldn't. Instead I sat down in the chair near her bed. She begged me. I made her beg over and over and I made her call me Paige instead of Pearl and still I didn't give her her medicine.'

She looked at me. I had trouble meeting her eyes. I don't get paid for this, Henley's right.

'I laughed in her face and then I watched her die. I rejoiced in it. I sat there until she turned gray and ugly, like the Wicked Witch of the West, and then I turned out the light and went to my room. I didn't sleep. I lay there in the dark all night and tried to feel bad, or sorry, for what I had done, but I wasn't. I'm not. In the morning I got up and made my bed and ate breakfast and called the doctor. He was very kind and helped me with everything.'

A siren sounded and came closer, then stopped. Tires squealed going around a corner. I heard a child call out and cry and then her mother's voice, calm, soothing, loving. The crying stopped.

'Did I murder her, Kat?'

'Legally? No. You withheld medical attention, but that is not a crime, not unless you were her medical caretaker.'

'But ethically, morally?'

'I don't know.'

The simple answer was yes, but there was no simple answer, not with a Morrell. And was it murder, or self-defense, or equitable retribution or— I didn't know, I didn't want to know.

'Kat, I *had* to do it, I had to! Florence was evil, she turned people into floaters, she would have done it to me.'

I saw white, bloated, ugly bodies in clear, clean water. I nodded. Yes, she would have, but it was still a hard thing to live with. I was glad I didn't have to; it was the second time today I had felt that.

I was hanging out with the wrong crowd again. Definitely.

'Kat, I *had* to!'

Ladybird, ladybird, fly away home!

'A floater,' she sobbed. 'A *floater*! I couldn't bear that, couldn't allow it. And so I didn't.'

Your house is on fire, your children all gone.

'Kat.' Paige's eyes begged me for help.

I wasn't going to give it. I couldn't.

'Was it easier the next time?' I asked, genuinely curious. I wasn't on her side any more.

'The next time? I don't understand. Kat, please help me. *Please*.' The tears started again.

'Ruby was your mother. You couldn't inherit if she were still alive, so she had to die. You didn't know that your Aunt Opal,' I took a deep breath and lied, 'was the oldest twin. You let Florence die, you killed Ruby, and you did it for nothing. You don't inherit. Opal does.'

'No,' she screamed. 'No, no, no!'

She kicked my desk, swept the papers off the top with her hands, then began pulling books from the bookcase and flinging them about. Derek's flowers hit the deck (that was okay), the just-repaired window smashed again as a book tore through it (that wasn't), loose paper flew merrily about. I leapt up, grabbed her by the shoulders, slam-dunked her into a chair, and slapped her. Hard.

The silence was instant and unbroken, then her body convulsed in dry heaves. I waited it out. She looked at me finally with dry dead eyes. The slap mark was red on her cheek.

'I don't know what you're talking about.' Her voice was dead too.

I laughed. 'It's a little late in the day for that, don't you think?' Worth a try though, I thought sadly. It had worked before.

She made her eyes lighter and wide again, sweet. Now the slap mark didn't fit. 'I *don't* know, Kat. *Really*.' She tried to smile but it slipped off her face. 'I don't. I'm stressed. I just overreacted.' She tried the smile again.

I laughed. It was hollow and forced and probably the last laugh I had in me for a while. 'Derek talked, Paige. He was planning to kill me, had nothing to lose by telling the truth. Now—' I stopped.

'Now?'

'He's dead.'

She swallowed hard. She was tough as nails – no tears, no questions.

'Okay.' She smiled winningly at me as though we were cohorts in crime. And maybe we were. I'd set up Ruby so nicely, so neatly for them. 'I'll explain. I didn't *like* it, you can't think that. But it wasn't as though Ruby was a person, a real person.'

I stared at her.

'No, Kat, she *wasn't*. She was a shell, a nothing, a—' she stumbled over the words, '—a floater. So it didn't *matter*.'

'You mattered but she didn't?' I asked, keeping my voice level.

'Yes, that's it, exactly it,' she said eagerly. 'I knew you would understand. Thank you. And it's better this way, I'm sure, much better. She's happier. That was no life.'

'She's happier dead?' She had said that about her grandfather too, I remembered now.

'Yes.' She nodded eagerly. 'Yes.'

'And Herb?' I was still keeping my voice level. It was getting harder.

'Herb. Oh, that *was* a problem. You see, he knew who Ruby really was. Or wasn't – she wasn't Garnet. He didn't actually tell me. I found out when I read the files. He *told* me that he wanted me to inherit and that we would advertise for six months and then I would but—' She shrugged. 'I couldn't really take that risk, could I? It would have been a silly thing to do. *Too* silly.' She shook her head and smiled.

Silly? I thought it over but couldn't make sense of it. 'What happened?'

'Well, nothing then. The night he died we went out to his house, Paul and me. Paul yelled at him. God, he's dumb. I got *so* tired of it. I broke up with him, you know.' I raised my eyebrows. 'Well, you don't think I *loved* him, for crying out loud? He was just,' she searched for a word, 'convenient.'

'Happier dead,' 'silly,' 'convenient': It was adding up.

'Herb?' I asked.

'Well, Paul was yelling and Herb got really angry. He let Paul have it,' she said, a note of grudging admiration in her voice. 'He was a tough old bird, I'll give him that.'

'Did Paul hurt Herb?'

'Oh no. Herb was at his desk, then he got up and told us to leave, and then, then he just kind of toppled over.'

'And?'

'Paul left.'

'Without helping?' I asked sadly, knowing the answer.

'Yes.'

'You didn't either?'

'Oh no, I didn't either. It worked out perfectly, Kat, it did. *So* convenient. I really didn't want to have that meeting the next day with him and you. You see, now I had the files, I *knew*, and there was no need for you to know, to figure out—'

She stopped. 'It was just *really* convenient, for me *and* for him. He wanted to be with Letitia and now he is.' She looked pleased with herself.

'And don't you see, Kat, I didn't *do* anything, not *really*. Nothing bad. Not *bad* bad, anyway.'

357

She smiled again, got up, and hugged me. I didn't hug back.

'Didn't I do a nice job making things come out right? Didn't I?! And Opal doesn't want anything to do with the ranch, Derek said so, so it will be mine. *All mine*.' She did a little dance in place. 'It's neat, isn't it?'

I thought of all the bodies: Florence, Herb, Ruby, Derek. It didn't seem very neat to me.

'*Mine, all mine!*' She pirouetted on her toes with her arms above her head like a ballet dancer. 'Mine!'

The phone rang.

Thirty-One

Blood tells; the camera doesn't lie; in tequila, veritas. No. Truth is as elusive as a shadow on a cloudy day.

I didn't answer it; I was stunned, shocked and frozen by Paige's words. She pirouetted by me toward the phone.

'Kat?' Her voice was impatient. 'Kat!'

She pirouetted again, curtsied to an imaginary audience, picked up the phone and spoke. I watched impassively as she conversed, then giggled, smirked. She hung up on a half pirouette.

'That was Rafe. He says it's Alma's birthday today and did you forget?' I put my head in my hands. I had, yes. 'The party's at Alma's. Right now. He invited me too and I want to go.'

I got up.

'Rafe *sounds* very good looking. And sexy. Is he?'

I nodded.

'Single?'

I nodded again. She smiled and whistled softly to herself. I went to the bathroom, threw up my diet Pepsi, and brushed my teeth.

'Where is it? I'll follow you, okay?' I agreed, beyond protest or alternative. 'Kat.' Paige sounded concerned and sweet. 'What is it, what's the matter?'

I looked at her without flinching. There were, I realized, holes in her head as well as holes in her heart. She had watched her grandmother die, left an uncle to die, planned her mother's death, and heard of the death of her lover/partner without missing a beat. Now she was excited about a party and asking me what was wrong.

Big-time holes. *Real* big-time. Swiss cheese.

I called Lottie and asked her to please find Opal and bring her over to Alma's right away. Maybe I was playing God again. Then I set the phone to call forwarding and headed out the door, Paige tagging along and babbling happily.

'Ranch . . . Rafe . . . party . . . so excited . . .'

I needed to talk to Opal. Badly.

On the way over I tried to get into a party mood. No dice.

The house was jumping. I walked in glumly, Paige dancing behind me.

Lindy ambushed me affectionately; Rafe handed me a beer.

'I can't decide, Kat,' Lindy said.

'What?'

I slugged down half a beer and waited hopefully, impatiently, for the alcohol to kill off some brain cells: the ones that remembered Ruby, and Derek's hands around my throat, and the blood; the ones that knew about the twin switch and the circumstances of Florence's death and Ruby's and Herb's and—

'Now that I'm not going to be a PI, should I be an advice columnist and spend a day with Charity . . .'

Charity drifted over in time to hear that and blanched. She knows Lindy well, knows how long a day with her can be. Al was with Charity so we all did the: Hey,-how-are-you? routine. Paige had found Rafe.

'Or . . .' Lindy thought for a bit. Rafe walked by, Paige tagging along, saw the crumpled beer can in my hands and traded me for a full one. What a guy.

'Or?' I asked.

'Or be a cop. Maybe I could hang out with Al for a day and check it out?'

She looked in Al's direction and he nodded and smiled. Of course he doesn't know Lindy at all, never mind like Charity and I do. He would though. A day would do it. Charity and I stared at Lindy. A year ago she'd been a scared and angry hooker I'd pulled off the streets. And she'd known a lot of cops: *Fucking cops!* is how she put it. Now she wanted to be one? Charity and I were speechless.

'Sure, that'd be fine, Lindy. Let me know.' Al smiled, then walked over to talk to Rafe as though nothing had happened.

I stared at Charity. 'I take it all back. He's obviously in love.' She primped and preened. Lindy got bored and left. 'But should we allow it? The poor guy has no idea what he's getting into.'

'Are you mad?' she hissed at me. 'Better him than us.' True, she had a point there. 'Besides, he's tough,' she said proudly. 'And he has handcuffs, guns, tear gas, that kind of stuff.' I looked at her sharply. 'Just kidding, Kat.' She smiled her innocent Madonna smile.

Alma's front door opened and Lottie marched in. She had a triumphant look on her face and was herding Opal along. There was untapped potential there, I thought, sheep handler or crowd control agent. Lottie cut a path across the room, shooed Opal over, and delivered her to me. Paige drifted in our direction.

Opal gasped.

'Dear God, you look so much like your mother, like me, at your age.' She started to hold out her hand, then opened her arms instead. Paige walked right into them. 'Only prettier,' Opal said. They both started crying. I watched for a moment, then walked away.

Happy birthday to you

Alma was beaming, laughing, and waving a cake slicer in time to the music.

Happy birthday to yo-o-u

Paige was holding Opal's hand and smiling enticingly through half-lowered tear-frosted lids at Rafe who was lazily grinning back.

Happy birthday de-e-ar A l-l-ma

Charity and Al were kissing.

Happy birthday to yo-o-ou.

There were tears in my eyes, but not because of a birthday, or love, or—

The phone rang. It was for me, which was not surprising but not a rush either.

'Yeah,' I snarled. The ugly sound of my voice pleased me. Not good.

'Henley,' Bill snarled back. Phooey. I tossed in the towel. Your average cop can outsnarl your average citizen any day.

'Hey, Bill.'

'You got any information on Jose Mendez's family?'

'Yes, why?'

There was a long silence, the ominous kind, so I quit being cute and gave it to him. I like Bill and he's a good cop. I didn't know why I was being a jerk, this investigation I guess.

'Have you identified the skeletal remains as Jose's?' Silence. 'Have a heart, Bill.' I appealed to his better nature, which is actually a good chunk of him. He growled, sort of. 'The inscription?' I asked and waited out the silence.

' "Jose, from Mother." In Spanish.' Henley growled again, but just a teddy bear growl, and hung up.

I thought about Mrs Mendez, her beauty, her cake, her grandchild, her lost child who was now found, and her prayers. I thought that I would go and see her again, but not right away, and that I would take her a present, cookies or flowers or something. And I wondered if prayers worked. I hoped so even though I hadn't seen it happen much.

Behind me Charity and Rafe started arguing about the meaning of life. I tried to stay out of it, naturally, but Rafe snagged me. 'It's bullshit. Listen: *Dear Charity,*' he said in a sarcastic voice, holding firmly onto my arm, '*I lost my job, my significant other left me, the dog is sick, and I just drank my last beer. Life is pretty bad. What shall I do?* Signed, *Grim Tale.* Now, here's the bullshit part. *Dear Grim—*'

'Oh, shut up,' Charity said crossly. 'Do.'

'*Dear Grim,*' Rafe continued inexorably. Getting him to shut up is a formidable task. I wasn't up to it right then and Charity never is. '*Keep trying and look on the bright side. There are good vets, jobs, and new people to love.*'

'Don't forget the beer,' Charity snipped at him.

He grinned. 'You're right. Don't *ever* forget the beer.' He toasted us grandly with an empty beer bottle. 'It's not only simplistic bullshit, Charity, it's sappy.' That's Rafe, tactful and subtle.

'It is not,' she said hotly.

'Is too.'

'Is not.'

'Kat?' They both turned to me. Damn. I hate it when that happens. I squirmed a little and tried to get away. Not a chance.

'It's simplistic,' I said and Rafe looked triumphant, Charity looked pissed, 'but not sappy.' They traded: Charity looked triumphant and Rafe looked pissed.

'Cake!' Alma hollered. 'Eat up, there's ice cream too.' Everyone headed for the dessert.

Sappy? I thought about it and didn't think that to hope, love, and try your best was sappy, just hard. *Very* hard.

'Thirty-eight percent of Americans eat pizza once a week,' Mr A. announced at my elbow, 'nine percent eat cake, and seventy-nine percent have hamburger.'

'You won't be one of that nine percent unless you move fast,' I said, watching Rafe, Lindy, Charity, and Paige pack it in. Al wasn't doing too badly either but he wasn't in their league. Obviously love had not blunted anyone's appetite. Mr A. scampered over to the cake and heaved a large slab onto a paper plate.

I had cake and ice cream too, and more beer – even though beer and cake and ice cream are not the best combination.

Later, when everyone had left, I walked into the kitchen. Alma and Lottie had said they were going to clean up.

They lied.

They were salting the triangle between the thumb and the first finger on the back of their hands, licking it, biting limes, and shooting shots of gold. And giggling.

'Have a snort.' Alma held out the bottle to me.

'Have two,' Lottie said and held out salt and limes. They giggled again.

I shook my head. 'I'm driving. And I hate tequila.'

'Me, too.' Lottie snickered.

'Driving?' I asked, alarmed.

'Certainly not!' Alma said with dignity, but slurring her words. 'She's' (it sounded like sheeez) 'staying the night. Pass the salt please' (pleeez). They salted up, bit limes, slugged shots, and giggled.

I left.

Before they got sick, before it got ugly.

Paige was waiting for me outside on the porch. I wasn't surprised. I wouldn't get away from ugly tonight after all. I wasn't surprised again. She was crying. I still wasn't surprised.

I was a natural for the detective business, no question.

'Opal ... Ruby ... Kat ... I – I had no idea. I didn't see that—'

She broke off and sobbed quietly. I stared at her stoically. She'd cried too often; I'd fallen for it too often.

'Opal is *beautiful*, Kat.'

'Yes, she is.'

'And intelligent, successful, kind.'

I nodded.

'She and Ruby, my m-mother, were identical twins. Ruby didn't look like that, or seem like that, but maybe ... ? Oh, God, Kat, what have I done? I helped kill her and maybe ... It was wrong, wasn't it?' Her voice begged me to disagree with her but I didn't.

'Yes.'

'I couldn't help it, it's not my fault.'

Her voice was childish and petulant and she scuffed her feet. She plopped down on the porch steps pulling on my sleeve so I would sit with her.

'Oh my.' She sighed loudly and looked at me sideways through half-lowered lids. 'Don't you feel sorry for me, Kat?'

I thought of Herb and Ruby, even Florence and Derek, and shook my head.

'Not even a little?' She tried to tuck her hand in mine but I wouldn't let her.

'No.'

She sighed. 'Have you ever been in love, Kat?'

I nodded.

'What's it like?' Her voice was wistful, sad. 'Nobody ever loved me.' She was matter-of-fact.

'You and Derek were lovers.'

'Lovers, yes, but love?' She laughed. 'I haven't a clue, but I know I didn't love him. I don't think either of us knew what love was. I loved being with him because I didn't have to pretend. Paul—'

She made a face.

'Ugh – I always had to pretend: to love him, to want him, to think he was great in bed.' She snorted. 'Paul is a bad joke. Derek and I knew each other and we didn't pretend, not ever. It was simple: money and sex and we were greedy for both. Two of a kind.'

She smiled sweetly. A new mood for every sentiment, I thought to myself.

'I hated you for sleeping with him though.' Her eyes got narrow and dark. 'You used him, but he used you too. He liked you and he told me about it. He told me everything.' She spit on the porch.

'It's why, partly, I made him kill you, well, try. I wouldn't have though if I'd known he would fuck it up.' She spit again. 'You made me jealous and I didn't like that. I didn't want to feel anything.' She smiled. 'Florence taught me that.'

'Paige—'

'Pearl,' she corrected me.

I stared at her.

'You see, don't you?'

And I did. Finally.

'Say it.' I hesitated. 'Yes. Please,' she begged me.

'Pearls are created out of dirt and muck.'

'There is more,' she said. 'Some – very few – are beautiful, but most are misshapen, deformed, ugly.'

Yes. Beauty is not born of filth. Love is not born of hate. Can a child raised by a monster escape somehow? No.

'Misshapen, deformed, and ugly.' She smiled at me, her eyes wide and beautiful, innocent. 'Florence taught me well. Only sometimes, just sometimes, I am sorry that I am this way, and I wish I weren't.' She tipped her head toward me, her hair falling over her eyes.

'Paige – Pearl—' I stammered over the words. For I had lied earlier; I was sorry for her.

'Don't start,' she smiled wryly. 'What's to say?'

'You think it's settled and over, but it's not.'

'No, I saw that tonight after being with Opal. It couldn't just be, could it?' she asked wistfully, hopefully.

I shook my head.

'You'd tell, even go to the cops?'

'Yes.' That's where I would start in fact.

She stood up. 'Will I go to jail?'

'I don't know.'

'But I'll lose the ranch?'

'Yes, probably.'

Her face went white. Then she smiled again and crouched down, looking me in the eye. 'Evil makes you old, Kat. I'm older than you are. You believe the best of things but I don't.' She shrugged. 'That cop? Henley? I'll turn myself in.' She stood up. I stood with her. She shook her head.

'No. Please. Leave me with some dignity; let me do it on my own.' Our eyes held for a long time. 'Thanks for trying.' Her eyes were clear and cold. She nodded. 'See ya, Kat.' And she smiled.

I was afraid, but I let her go.

It was the wrong call.

They pulled her out of the slough two days later. A floater, her worst nightmare. She paid the only way she knew how. I cried for both of us. She never had, and now never would.

Then I slept.

Thirty-Two

*Hopes and dreams, nightmares and fears,
reality: it gets tangled up. That's how life
is.*

I slept for hours, days maybe. No dreams. No hands
reaching out to strangle me, no blood, no twins torn
apart and crying, no skeletons in the dirt, no murder
and mayhem, no shots of gold with limes and salt.
No floaters.

Hell of a deal.

For breakfast I had corn flakes and philosophy. I
would have preferred my corn flakes with milk and
a banana but I was out of both.

The philosophy I couldn't help. It played, like a
broken record, over and over again in my mind. So I
thought about Opal and hoped she had learned and
would not now be prey to the Dereks of the world.
Or to the Florences. I thought about hate, and about
money and greed, about the abuse of the helpless
and sick, the sacrifice of things that matter for things
that don't.

I thought about how Paige, Opal, and Ruby had
looked for, and longed for, parents who would love

them, and how I have done that too, only I have never admitted it. And I thought about how when you've been hurt that badly you are too afraid, and either you pick the wrong people, Derek and Paul, or you run from the right one, Hank.

And I had done both.

I thought how much easier corn flakes were to digest than philosophy. And how much more palatable and nourishing.

Then I stopped thinking.

I packed only the basics, the essentials: toothbrush, bathing suit, underwear, shorts, tops, Ranger, Kitty. I stopped for gas twice, in Fresno and then in Barstow. It's a sixteen-hour drive but I made it in less; I was speeding. I lost track of it all – time, miles, and thoughts – after a while.

I stopped on the edge of town at a minimart with a phone. He answered on the second ring.

'Do you want to go out to dinner?' I asked it calmly, coolly, even though the butterflies in my stomach and the eighteen-wheelers whooshing by were a distraction.

'This weekend?' He sounded puzzled.

'Tonight.'

'Sweetheart, it's two-thirty in the morning.'

'Oh.' I considered that. 'Breakfast then?'

'Where are you?' A truck, air brakes belching and tires whining, growled by catching us in a noise warp. 'Kat?'

'Here. Vegas.'

There was a silence, a long one. The butterflies in my stomach started to turn to lead and crash. Me, too.

He laughed. 'See you in a few minutes then.'

'All right.'

I hung up. My stomach hurt, damn stupid butterflies. I broke some more speed limits but nobody in Nevada ever seems to care. I didn't either. The door opened as I walked up to the house. Mars came barreling out and he and Ranger tangled up. Hank stood barefoot, shirtless, and in jeans, at the front door. I got halfway there before my legs gave out and I just stood stupidly. The kitten mewed.

'Hi, Hank.' My mouth worked; too bad my legs didn't.

'Hey, Katy.' He said it softly.

'I'd be moving faster but I'm standing on my shoelaces.' He grinned and walked out to me. 'I missed you.'

'Yes.' He leaned down and kissed me. 'Let's go inside.'

I shook my head. 'Not yet. I have to tell you about stuff. Explain,' I said lamely. He laughed and picked me up.

So that was that, and it was fine.

'I love you,' I told him later, 'but I'm afraid.' Terrified was more like it. Petrified, out-of-control panicked, that kind of thing.

'You can't let anything make you afraid to love, Katy.'

'I know,' I agreed. 'You're right. But it has, they do, I am.'

'Shall we try again?'

'Yes.'

I wondered what percent of people get what they want, or even know what that is. Hank ran his hand up and down my side. His back was warm and strong under my hands. I shivered. He kissed me. I was going to get what I wanted.

The phone rang.

'*Damn*! Don't answer it.'

'I have to, sweetheart, I'm on call.'

He spoke for a while, not in his cop voice, and laughed. Then he handed the phone to me, reached for his beeper and turned it on. To say that I took the phone reluctantly, and without enthusiasm, would be a gross understatement, a lie even.

'Yes?'

'Katy?'

The phone connection was terrible. I could hardly hear, hardly understand.

'Alma?'

'Can you send money, dearest? We just got here but somehow . . .' The silence was long. 'Hangovers are frightful, aren't they, dear? Anyway, somehow we lost our traveler's checks and—'

'We?' I asked.

'Lottie and me.'

'Traveler's checks?'

'Of course, dear,' she said patiently. 'We wouldn't

dream of traveling abroad without sufficient funds but—'

'Abroad?'

There was a scuffling sound, or static, or both. Then a new voice.

'Kat?'

'Lottie?'

'We're in China. Oh, and it's *wonderful*, so colorful and exotic, I can't tell you. It's a dream come true! I am *so* excited!'

I sighed. Old ladies shouldn't be allowed to drink tequila. Not at all, not ever.

'Kat?' That was Alma again. 'A thousand should do it. If you just—' A thousand?! A thousand what: pesos, yen, marks, francs, *dollars*? Hank's hand played along my thigh and distracted me. Mmmm. Kisses? The kitten mewed. I have to name him, I thought, so he won't be a floater.

'—so thanks, dearest. American Express, all right? And right away!' The connection was broken.

Hank took the phone off the hook.

The sun was coming up. It was a new day.

A selection of bestsellers from Headline

APPOINTED TO DIE	Kate Charles	£4.99 ☐
SIX FOOT UNDER	Katherine John	£4.99 ☐
TAKEOUT DOUBLE	Susan Moody	£4.99 ☐
POISON FOR THE PRINCE	Elizabeth Eyre	£4.99 ☐
THE HORSE YOU CAME IN ON	Martina Grimes	£5.99 ☐
DEADLY ADMIRER	Christine Green	£4.99 ☐
A SUDDEN FEARFUL DEATH	Anne Perry	£5.99 ☐
THE ASSASSIN IN THE GREENWOOD	P C Doherty	£4.99 ☐
KATWALK	Karen Kijewski	£4.50 ☐
THE ENVY OF THE STRANGER	Caroline Graham	£4.99 ☐
WHERE OLD BONES LIE	Ann Granger	£4.99 ☐
BONE IDLE	Staynes & Storey	£4.99 ☐
MISSING PERSON	Frances Ferguson	£4.99 ☐

All Headline books are available at your local bookshop or newsagent, or can be ordered direct from the publisher. Just tick the titles you want and fill in the form below. Prices and availability subject to change without notice.

Headline Book Publishing, Cash Sales Department, Bookpoint, 39 Milton Park, Abingdon, OXON, OX14 4TD, UK. If you have a credit card you may order by telephone – 01235 400400.

Please enclose a cheque or postal order made payable to Bookpoint Ltd to the value of the cover price and allow the following for postage and packing:

UK & BFPO: £1.00 for the first book, 50p for the second book and 30p for each additional book ordered up to a maximum charge of £3.00.

OVERSEAS & EIRE: £2.00 for the first book, £1.00 for the second book and 50p for each additional book.

Name ....

Address ....

....

....

If you would prefer to pay by credit card, please complete:
Please debit my Visa/Access/Diner's Card/American Express (delete as applicable) card no:

Signature .... Expiry Date ....